the
SWEETHEART
DEAL

the
SWEETHEART
DEAL

MIRANDA
LIASSON

Entangled Publishing, LLC
10940 S Parker Road
Suite 327
Parker, CO 80134
Visit our website at www.entangledpublishing.com.

Amara is an imprint of Entangled Publishing, LLC.

Edited by Liz Pelletier and Lydia Sharp
Cover design by Elizabeth Turner Stokes
Image of kitten © Dioniya/Shutterstock
Image of town © ff25/Shutterstock
Image of porch © Yashkinn Ilya
Interior design by Toni Kerr

Print ISBN 978-1-64937-027-3
ebook ISBN 978-1-64937-040-2

Manufactured in the United States of America

First Edition February 2022

AMARA

ALSO BY MIRANDA LIASSON

BLOSSOM GLEN

The Sweetheart Deal

SEASHELL HARBOR

Coming Home to Seashell Harbor

ANGEL FALLS

Then There was You
The Way You Love Me
All I Want for Christmas

THE KINGSTON FAMILY

Heart and Sole
A Man of Honor
The Baby Project

For Ed

CHAPTER ONE

The moon brings the man. That's what Grandma Sophie would say.

Tessa Montgomery shook her head at the thought. If the moon was supposed to bring her a man, he must have gotten lost along the way.

She wheeled the giant rack full of warm baguettes up next to the scarred wooden front counter of Bonjour! Breads. It was only six p.m. in the middle of May, but the moon was already visible, huge, hanging over Main Street like it was peeking into the windows of her family's hundred-year-old boulangerie. A *romantic* moon.

But for Tessa, there was no romance in sight, and there hadn't been in quite a while. Not since last summer, when her fiancé left her for someone else.

While Tessa didn't believe the moon-man connection, she had to admit that the big round *boule* in the sky sure was beautiful. Although, she thought wistfully, it *was* a shame not to have someone to share it with.

The bell above the door tinkled, and she put on her usual customer-friendly smile. Which was sometimes difficult when she had to endure a lot of sad headshaking and endless questions about being dumped. Yes, still, even after almost a year.

That was the thing about a small town—the first thing you did in your life that was gossip-worthy became the defining trait of your existence.

She breathed a sigh of relief, though, as her favorite customer walked into the empty bakery. "Good evening, Arthur," she said to the older gentleman who came in every Tuesday like clockwork. At least *he* was a man she could count on.

Tessa leaned over the countertop to address the little Yorkie that had strolled in with him. "Hello to you, too, Millie."

The dog put her paws up on the glass of the display case and wagged her tail.

"I have just the thing for you." Tessa handed Arthur the freshly made latte and egg-and-cheese croissant she'd already bagged, his usual Tuesday dinner, and grabbed a dog biscuit for Millie. As Tessa walked around the counter and stooped down, Millie daintily plucked the treat from her palm.

Tessa patted her head. "She's such a lady."

"So are you, Tessa," Arthur said, beaming.

She glanced up at him. "Aw, thanks. Where are all the nice guys when you need them?"

Not in Blossom Glen, Indiana, that was for sure, where the biggest attraction was the new scents reveal from the famous candle factory across the street. Although, to be fair, visiting with her regular customers was one of the things she loved the most about their little town. And the rows of crab apple trees that lined Main Street, now in glorious bloom with rich pink flowers, that gave their town its name.

"I don't believe for one second that stuff they're saying about you."

She held up her hands in mock protest. "I swear I only

spent five years in prison," she said jokingly. "An honest mistake." But inside, her heart sank. Because she already knew what everyone said behind her back. Phrases like *such a shame*, and even *spinster*, now that she was thirty-two and single. And stuck in Blossom Glen, Indiana, baking bread twenty-four seven.

"You're not an Ice Queen," he said. "You just need someone who understands you."

Ice Queen. She hadn't heard that one yet. Well, could she help that the few guys in town who were her age were immature and foolish and she didn't hesitate to let them know that?

Or, a little voice deep inside her seemed to say, was it because shooting one-liners at people was her best defense against being an object of pity?

"If only I were forty years younger," Arthur said with a wink.

"Eighty *is* the new sixty," she said with forced cheer. It wasn't his fault she was stuck. Or that the only happily ever afters she'd be seeing were in romance novels or Hallmark movies.

He left his usual bill with a big tip, which she fought him on every time to no avail. "Okay, doll," he said with a wink. "See you tomorrow."

"Hey, Arthur, one more thing," Tessa called just as he reached the door. She grabbed a flyer off the counter and ran it over to him. "The library's having a botanical lecture this week about perennials. I was thinking it might be a fun place to meet someone who loves gardening as much as you do."

"Thanks, honey," he said. "The last woman I met online

was nice, but she just wanted companionship."

Tessa frowned. "What's wrong with that?"

He grinned. "I may be eighty, but"—he dropped his voice—"my parts are still in working order."

Okaayyy. That was TMI. "Have a nice night." She shook her head as he left. "Great," she said to herself when she was alone. "Even the eighty-year-olds around here have a better sex life than I do."

Her stomach rumbled, reminding her that she'd arrived at the bakery at four thirty this morning and had been so busy she'd forgotten to eat lunch. She snuck a chocolate croissant from the case, the one sweet thing her mother would allow in the bakery because it was still bread.

The bell tinkling again caught her mid-chew. Wow, two customers in a row—the busiest they'd been in ages.

Turned out her excitement was unfounded as she looked up to see Sam Donovan, her ex-fiancé, stroll in.

He still wore his shirt and tie, no doubt just finishing his day at the candle factory. He looked a little tired, his thick hair tousled, as if he'd been raking his fingers through it during a stressful day in the accounting department.

In the past, she would have asked him how his day was. And if he was hungry. Listened to him discuss complicated problems in the accounting department as he got them off his chest. And his rumpled overworked-executive look would have made her heart flutter a little.

But not anymore.

"Hey, Tessa." He flashed what she read as a guilty smile and pushed up his glasses. "How're you doing?"

"Great," she said with a forced smile. Could he not see he was the only customer in the shop? Even after a year, she still had to curb the urge to hit him on the head with a stale baguette. But she knew in her heart that even *that* wouldn't install any sense.

"It's still busy as ever over there." He hitched a thumb over his shoulder to indicate the candle factory across the street. "I have at least another hour of work. Mr. Brighton's cracking down, dumping all kinds of extra projects on me. It really sucks. Can I get a ham and cheese?"

She didn't know why he came in here multiple times a week, clearly expecting her to soothe his worries, give him reassurance, and sympathize with his grievances. And pretend that they were still friends.

As she assembled the ingredients for his sandwich, she practiced calming breathing. It was easier to serve him and get him out of the bakery as soon as possible, because their town wasn't big enough for her to handle more than one massive feud.

She'd grown up with her family giving the cold shoulder to the Castorinis next door, and that had been uncomfortable and awkward for as long as she could remember. She'd vowed never to let that happen with anyone in her own life.

"I was wondering if I could ask you something," he said as she put his perfectly made sandwich in a bag. "Um, do you remember the name of that Italian restaurant in downtown Indy?"

"Which one?" She narrowed her eyes.

"I wanted to take Marcy to that rooftop one, but I couldn't think of the name."

"The one where you proposed to me?" She fought to keep her voice even.

Sam had the decency to blush. He should blush, because

who would forget the name of the place where you proposed?

Forget about hitting him in the head with the baguette. She was now tempted to shove it somewhere dark and deep. Maybe that would keep him away. Because it was bad enough having to see your ex practically every day in their small town, but having to interact like this…the worst. "Google might know it," she said, refusing to be hurt.

"Or should I take her to that other place—you know, that one that overlooks the river. With the great sunsets."

The one where they'd celebrated her thirtieth birthday. "Sam, I think it's kind of creepy to ask me for that kind of advice when you're in a new relationship."

"Well, we were friends for a long time, Tessa. And you always give such good advice." He looked at her a little sheepishly. "I'm terrible at making these kinds of decisions."

Tessa reached into the register and pulled out a quarter. "See this?"

"It's a quarter."

"Correct." She reached out her hand and dropped it into his palm.

"How's this going to help me?"

"You're going to go home and flip it. That will help you decide." She handed over his bagged loaf, even though she still felt like clubbing him with it. "Bye, Sam."

"Thanks, Tessa." His eyes darted around, indicating he was nervous.

She should've paid more attention to that shifty-eyed habit, because it probably would've let her know far earlier that he'd cheated on her.

Not to mention he'd been vocal about his dissatisfaction.

He'd told her she wasn't passionate. That she was hard to please, in bed and out. And he'd used those as excuses for his cheating. Which, a year later, still left her angry and hurt.

"Anything else?"

He took the sandwich and the coffee and left her the exact price, down to the fifty-three cents. Not that she wanted his tip, but his precise nitpickiness extended to… well, everything. "Thanks, Tessa. You make the best sandwiches."

She fought not to roll her eyes. *Please leave now*, she thought but didn't say. Instead she smiled.

"Seriously," he said. "I mean it. I would never pretend with you."

"Bye." She opened the door and saw him out. "That's funny, Sam," she said to herself, finally letting out her anger as she leaned against the door. "Because I sure got good at faking it with you."

As she headed to close out the register, she heard a faint chuckle. So faint she thought she'd imagined it. But then a chair scraped on the wood-planked floor as someone rose from the corner table, hidden from view by the bread rack beside the counter.

Oh no…

A man stepped into view, his back to her, but she could see he was tall and well built, jeans wrapping around muscular legs.

How long had he been there? How much had he heard? Surely *everything*. The early evening sun hit his wavy dark hair, making it shimmer with gold highlights until his big shoulders blocked it out.

And then her breath caught. Because as he turned and moved toward her, she recognized his stride, his athletic grace, and his big, warm eyes, the color of a fine espresso. The nose that would seem a little too big on another man but somehow fit his too-handsome face perfectly. And the defiant jaw that the men in his family couldn't seem to avoid inheriting, right along with their stubborn natures.

Leo Castorini.

The son of the family who ran the Italian restaurant next door. For a flash, she was back in high school, watching him walk down the hall, his easygoing demeanor and good looks drawing her—and every girl—like a magnet.

And he wore that same smirk, like he was laughing at her. *Still.*

She'd had a terrible crush on him. He'd actually asked her out, even though they'd been in neck-and-neck competition for the candle factory scholarship. But stuff had happened, and she'd ended up learning that he'd never really liked her at all. He'd just been fake-pretending to be friendly with the competition, she guessed. And he'd laughed at her. Which had hurt more than losing the scholarship to him.

She could see herself as she was in school—the braces, the flyaway hair, the unruly brows, the ten pounds she wished she could shed. But all that had changed…contacts, a good haircut, the miracle of waxing, and the right clothing to complement her shape, thanks to input from her two sisters.

Leo sauntered up to the counter, which for some reason made her a lot more anxious than when Sam had done it.

"Hi, Tessa. Busy evening?" The deep tone of his voice

vibrated clear through her in a way that put her even more on edge. Also, the years had been too kind to him. Little crinkles had formed around his eyes, making it seem like he laughed often, and he had a maturity in his physique that made him even more appealing.

But the place was empty besides the two of them. "You're hilarious," she said, deadpan.

Which wasn't funny. But for some reason, he full-out grinned.

That feeling in her gut was *not* butterflies. She was just getting queasy from him pointing out their obvious lack of customers.

"Did someone die?" she asked.

His wide, big smile faltered a bit. "That's a bit morbid, even for you."

She crossed her arms. "Well, I'm sure your dad didn't send you over for a cup of sugar." Not when their families had been giving each other the cold shoulder since before she and Leo were born.

"No one died," he said. That damn smile was back. Did he ever stop smiling? "I was just wondering if we could talk."

She raised a brow. The last time they'd *talked*, it had been about the fact that their high school GPAs were .0004 points apart—but his was higher. After that, she'd spent the whole night kneading and baking away her frustration. She'd made more brioche than the entire town could have eaten in a year.

Technically, she would have beaten him for the top spot in their class.

But that *technically* was a whole other story. A secret she mostly wanted to forget.

Except it reminded her of his true character. Leo was like an éclair. Pretty and charming on the outside, but with a core that was all fluff and no substance.

As if sensing her apprehension, he threw his hands up, palms out. "Just talk."

"Talk about what?"

"Business," he said. "A business proposition."

Well, this was interesting. But it was absolutely, positively not going to happen. Everyone in Blossom Glen was aware that the Montgomerys and Castorinis did *not* do business together, and Tessa and Leo knew that better than anyone. "Did you have a wine-tasting at your restaurant today? Are you drunk?"

"Sober as a preacher." He lowered his voice and leaned forward a little. "This can benefit both our businesses. I think it's worthwhile for you to hear me out."

What was he up to? He'd made a fortune in New York, or so everyone said. And he'd been in town for a couple months now, helping his dad in their restaurant and managing a local apartment complex. Wasn't he busy enough? And what did he want with her?

She couldn't help but notice that he smelled really good. Whatever clovey-spicy shampoo he used to wash those jet-black locks was...practically edible. Though truthfully, she was easily impressed these days. She hadn't been this close to a man who didn't smell like yeast in quite a while.

Plus, she reminded herself, women had been falling at his feet for as long as she could remember. Which was why his friends used to call him Leo the Legend.

"Can I get you something?" She waved her hand over the bakery case. To be polite. Because she *was* on the clock.

"I'll have whatever you just had," he said.

She frowned. Was he playing games? "How do you know what I just had?"

He tapped the corner of his mouth. "Because you've got a tiny little speck of chocolate right there."

She quickly swiped at both sides of her own mouth, her cheeks lighting on fire. How was it that he could make her feel like an awkward sixteen-year-old again? "Fine. Sit down. I'll get you something chocolate." But it wouldn't be the chocolate croissant she'd had. Because it was amazing, and he didn't deserve it.

She gestured for Leo to sit down and walked into the back room. Thank goodness her mom usually took Tuesday afternoons off. If she knew Tessa had just invited Leo to stay and sully their bakery with his Castorini DNA, gorgeous though it was, she would fumigate the entire place.

Tessa walked over to a baking tray and decided to change her tactic. She selected a perfectly formed chocolate croissant to put on a plate. Despite the fact that she'd only stayed in this tiny town to help her mother and grandmother in the bakery after her dad died, while Leo left to attend the best schools on the planet, she wouldn't let that bitter pill ruin her reputation as a quality baker. Life might have waylaid her dream of becoming a real pastry chef, but it hadn't killed it. Until she could actually realize it, she'd studied tirelessly and taught herself as much about baking as she could. And so she was going to hand him the best one of the entire bunch.

Just let him try to find fault with it.

"Aren't you living in New York?" she asked as she walked over to a table by the window where he sat scrolling through his phone. She set the plate in front of him and stepped back.

"Not anymore." He gestured for her to sit down, like they were old friends, not frenemies. "Got my MBA, and now I'm back," he said, eyeing the croissant. "To help my dad."

Between his dad and her mom, it was a complete toss-up who was more obstinate. And she knew for a fact that in Leo's case, the apple didn't fall far from the tree. Whatever brought him here to actually speak to her had to be important.

She looked out the window and scanned the street nervously. "If anyone sees us in here together…"

He casually crossed his arms, which showcased biceps as nicely rounded and perfect as one of her *petits pains*. "Isn't it time for that silly feud to end?"

She tilted her head. "Tell our parents that." She wasn't going to let her guard down with him, no matter how friendly he seemed. Those moony brown eyes might make other women melt, but not her, *no siree*.

"So, about business." He took a bite of the croissant.

"Business," she repeated. *Talking business with a Castorini.* What a weird day this was turning out to be.

"It's no secret that…" His voice suddenly trailed off.

"What is it?" she asked as he went quiet. Was he choking on her croissant? She'd never performed the Heimlich on anyone. What if she did it wrong? How would she explain his dead body when they weren't even supposed to be talking?

He didn't seem to be in distress, though. Now he was holding up the croissant and examining it closely. "You made this yourself?"

"Yes…" she said carefully. If he dared to insult her baking, she was tossing him out. Of course, he would probably just bounce on the sidewalk with that perfectly tight behind.

He devoured another bite and licked his fingers. Which was just the tiniest bit sensual—enough to bring those non-butterflies back. "It's phenomenal," he said.

There went her cheeks again. Pretty soon she'd need a fire extinguisher. "Oh. Thanks," she said as nonchalantly as possible, considering her face was probably the color of the chair covers.

"It's no secret that neither of our businesses is doing that great," he said.

That caught her attention. Because today they'd just lost their contract with an organic grocery store chain that had been bought out. "I've been telling my mom we need to diversify our inventory," she admitted, finally taking a seat. "But she keeps insisting we're a boulangerie, and that means bread only."

He nodded. "My dad won't accept any menu changes, either. Let alone farm-to-table, organic, new takeout options, or…anything. But he's going to have to agree to do *something*, or our restaurant isn't going to make it." He took the last bite and made a noise in his throat that could only be interpreted as him *really* liking it, which left her strangely pleased. "I was thinking we could contract with you to use your bread. And maybe other things, too. Do you make desserts?"

He'd just said her magic word.

And he'd hit a nerve. "My mother would never go against tradition. It would change the whole business."

But maybe that's what they needed.

Leo's shoulders slumped. "That's a no, then?"

"Not…necessarily…"

The gears in her head churned. She'd page through her many recipe books. Watch some online tutorials. Study the market. And figure out what she could bake that would go with their cuisine—something other than the basic tiramisu every other Italian restaurant in the country served.

It would have to be French to feel unique; that's all there was to it. Because who would expect a French pastry in an Italian restaurant? Would they even care if they weren't told it was French? All the customers would know was that they were getting something they'd never had there before. Let people assume what they wanted, if it kept her mother from struggling.

And if her mother were no longer struggling, then Tessa could seek out her own dreams without worry.

Her head whirled with the possibilities.

"We could really use a contract," she said. They were past desperate for business, and doing a dessert or two would be…so much fun.

Fun. A word she hadn't used for a long time. *Excited*, that was another one. Maybe her life hadn't turned out as she'd expected, but she was hungry to try something new. *Starving* for it, honestly.

"Okay, great," Leo said. "So, you'll present the idea to her?"

Tessa hesitated. In her desperation, she'd been about to trust the enemy. "Wait a minute," she said. "What's in it for you?"

"The couple who bakes for us just retired. But to be honest, their bread is just so-so. And we have to pay transportation costs from Evanston. That and the fact that my dad's been serving only crème brûlée and tiramisu for thirty years. Plus, the old theater remodel is done, and people will be wanting later dinners, so that's an opportunity to give both of us more business, even though it'll be after hours for you. Maybe it's time for our businesses to combine forces so they can both survive."

He'd clearly thought it out carefully. Still, it seemed too good to be true.

"You've been successful in New York," she said. "At least, that's what everyone says. Why don't you just use your money to reinvigorate the restaurant?"

"My dad refuses to accept my help. Plus, pouring all the money in the world into it won't help if there are no customers. The menu is outdated, and there's nothing fresh to appeal to younger people as well as keep the older regulars. It needs rebranding, and I have great ideas. But I need to come up with some way for my dad to trust me enough to use them."

As if sensing her doubt, he said, "Our parents wouldn't even have to get near each other. I could be the go-between. Something to help both businesses survive."

"This insanity is a long shot," she said. But it was intriguing; she'd give him that.

His dark brows knit down. "How much of a long shot?"

"Um, as unlikely as a snowball in hell. Or when pigs fly." She waved her hands in the air to emphasize the point. "Castorinis and Montgomerys don't even talk, let alone do business together."

He leaned in, looking way too sexy. "*We're* talking."

"No," she said. "You're talking to me. I'm just…answering."

"At least you're not *fake* answering," he said pointedly.

She blushed—again—which showed him he'd gotten to her. And reminded her that he'd overheard her entire conversation with Sam. Even worse, he'd somehow managed to wipe all the snappy retorts out of her, which almost no one was capable of doing. For a second, she was thrown. "Fine," she conceded. "I'll mention it, but don't expect much."

"My dad doesn't know I'm doing this," he said. "Maybe I'll wait to hear how your mom responds first."

She laughed. "You're assuming that my mom is less set in her ways than your dad."

"I really hope so." He stood. "Thanks for the croissant."

She watched him scan the bakery cases—taking in the baguettes, the ancient industrial espresso machine, the faded Impressionist-like panels on the walls her mom had painted years ago to look like Monet's water lilies. "Things haven't changed much around here," he said.

"Yeah," she agreed. This time her blush belied embarrassment at the shabby surroundings. "Bet you can't wait to get back to the city." She suddenly saw herself as he must see her, in the middle of this run-down old bakery, well on her way to becoming the town spinster—minus her cat, Cosette, whose tiny head in the window of her apartment greeted her without fail every afternoon as she pulled up. And with chocolate blobs on her face to boot.

"No, I—" He swung his gaze to hers, brows furrowed. "I meant it in a nice way, Tessa. There's some comfort in the familiar."

That threw her. That and the way he'd said her name, low and soft.

"Tessa?"

Her blood froze, because this *Tessa* did not originate from the body of a male with a rich, gravelly baritone. It was the distinct voice of her mother, who almost never showed up on her afternoon off, calling from the back room. Had she somehow known Leo was here?

"My mom," she whispered, like she was sneaking around in high school, then scrambled out of her chair. "You've got to go." She herded him toward the door. At least she tried to, but his arm was solid steel, and all that muscle mass did *not* move easily. "You should leave."

He looked about as alarmed as a squirrel who'd just stuffed himself full of nuts, in no rush to scurry away.

"I'm glad to be back in Blossom Glen," he said, as if he had an hour to stop and chat. "The croissants are better here."

Better than in New York City? He had to be teasing.

Then he gave her a little wink and left.

A *wink*.

What was up with that? Was it friendly, condescending, or flirty? Or all three? Good thing she didn't have time to think on it too long.

"Honey, is that you?" her mom called a moment later, entering the room.

Tessa clutched her chest, swearing she was having a heart attack. How could she explain why she was standing by the door? *I was just waiting for the paramedics, Mom.* "Just me," she said cheerily, then took a long, calming breath.

Her mom walked over and scanned up and down their familiar Main Street. The few outdoor tables. The banner draped across the ever-popular Blossom Glen candle factory across the street that read: *We light up your life.* "I thought I heard voices," she said. "And the door."

"Yes, I was out…looking at the moon." She peered through the window. There it was again, big and round, looking down on all her secrets. "Have you seen it?"

"It's going to be a lovers' moon tonight," her mom said, looking up. She gave Tessa a squeeze. "That's what your dad would've called it. One that sees but never tells."

Let's certainly hope so.

"What are you doing here?" Tessa asked.

"Just restless. I wanted to go over the numbers again. And I see you've been baking."

Her mom was looking at the chocolate croissants she'd left out. She loved all of Tessa's pastries—she just wouldn't sell them. Still, she hated to see her mother stressed. "Don't worry, Mom. I'm working on some new ideas for us that might bring in more business." She thought about mentioning Leo's proposition but chickened out. "Um… have a croissant," she said. "They're fresh."

"Those do look really good."

That simple compliment gave Tessa the boost of confidence she needed. "They *are* really good," she said. "I think people would—"

Her mother started to turn around, talking over her. "Maybe I'll make us some coffee to go with— Oh, look at that. Someone left their phone."

Tessa's stomach dropped. Not just someone. *Leo*.

She scurried over and slipped the phone into her apron pocket. "There were a couple of teenagers sitting there earlier," she said. "I'll keep this safe until they come back for it."

Thankfully, her mother shrugged and went to the coffee

machine. Tessa let out a long sigh. She was going to get struck dead by lightning for lying.

But despite the fear, something inside her felt different. Like a part of her that had been loaded with dust had suddenly been shaken—a part that had been preventing her from taking risks for a long time.

Because she knew that if she didn't take any soon, she'd be stuck in this bread shop forever.

CHAPTER TWO

"Hey, Mr. MBA, where you been?" Marco Castorini looked up from the old, scarred table in the back room of Castorini's Family Restaurant the next morning. His thick gray hair was combed straight back from a widow's peak, making him look somewhat formidable. "This place won't run itself."

Leo's father was clipping bright red flyers containing tonight's special into the center of each menu. His Aunt Loretta and Uncle Cosmo were manning the kitchen, and a local teenager named Andrew was waiting tables. His eighteen-year-old sister, Gia, worked there, too, but today she must be at track practice or one of her many extracurriculars.

A quick glance outside revealed only three cars in the lot, and from what Leo had seen on his way in, all the customers were white-haired couples enjoying early bird specials. So judging by the number of menus his dad was preparing, he was a diehard optimist.

His dad finished and straightened the pile. "What's up with you? You look like the cat who just ate the canary."

Leo hadn't realized he was smiling, but of course he was. Because yesterday he'd had the satisfaction of stopping Tessa Montgomery's sharp tongue, which was still just as cutting as ever, and he'd been thinking about it ever since.

He'd expected the zippy one-liners and her disbelief at seeing him. But he hadn't expected his own shock when those pretty blue eyes stared at him. Or the thick, dark hair piled atop her head in a messy bun. The soft curves. The tell-tale speck of chocolate near her full lips. Tessa Montgomery had grown up from that shy, awkward teenager he once knew.

And she was a knockout.

Whoa there. What was he thinking? Tessa had made it clear long ago she'd wanted nothing to do with him. In high school, after their one and only date, he'd found her kissing someone else. Sam, actually. And it was clear the same feeling held now. *Crystal* clear.

Plus, if his dad got a whiff that he'd been talking with her—with any of the Montgomerys, for that matter—he'd never hear the end of it.

Unless he could arrange a deal his dad simply could not refuse.

Sitting down at his laptop, Leo pinched the bridge of his nose and got down to business. The grim numbers in front of him were red-alerting *Danger! Danger!*

"So, what's the bottom line?" his dad asked.

Leo's stomach pitched. His MBA brain knew what the problem was, but generations of stubborn Italian blood pumping through his veins told him his dad was not going to take it well.

Tradition was important. It was what drove him to come back home to help his father, to save the family's livelihood. Sometimes new traditions had to be created, though, to keep the old ones from dying. He looked at his dad, working to keep his voice level. "We have to try something different to get our numbers up."

"Different, shhmifferent." His dad waved his hands. "This is a family restaurant with family values. It's been that way for a hundred years."

"We've been serving the same classic dishes for a long time, Leo," Aunt Loretta called from the kitchen. The same ones that his mom had helped create many years ago.

Uncle Cosmo pitched in. "People love them."

Leo believed that was true of their regulars, but it wasn't enough. The restaurant needed a big sales driver — something to make people line up on the street, like in the days when his mom was alive. "We have to give people a reason to eat here and not drive into Bloomington or Indianapolis for a chain-restaurant experience." *And* to attract people under the age of sixty.

"It's just a little downturn right now." His dad gathered the menus and tapped them definitively on the table.

The downturn was more like a circling-the-toilet-bowl-and-plunging-into-the-abyss kind of situation, but Leo held his tongue.

His dad, sitting across from him in the old red leather booth, crossed his muscular arms and set his jaw. He used to laugh a lot more when his mom was around. But she'd been gone for nearly seventeen years now.

They still used the same menu design his mom had created, reprinting them when they became too worn to read anymore. The giant fresco in the dining room of a balustrade patio overlooking the Mediterranean had been there forever, as had the made-to-look-ancient vases and the small-scale Michelangelo's *Pietà* right next to the cash register.

All these things gave him a pang in the chest. Yes, his mom was still everywhere. Like she was going to come bursting in from the kitchen at any moment, full of sunshine and laughter. *I swear, Mom, I'll do my best*, he vowed. *But it's not going to be easy.*

"Have you thought about my idea for the farm-to-table options with full takeout service?" And delivery, too, but he didn't dare mention that. Not right away. Saying the word "delivery" was as bad as dropping an f-bomb at the kitchen table.

"Takeout?" His dad said it with disgust, as if Leo had said *pestilence* or *locusts* or *the plague*. "Eating in a restaurant is a social thing," he went on, talking expressively with his hands as usual. "People get dressed up a little, they bring their friends, they sit out on the patio and drink wine and look at the pretty flowers and celebrate occasions. Food bonds people."

Leo couldn't argue with that. But his father was missing the point.

"Yeah but, Dad," Leo said, "maybe it's okay for a family to order takeout one night when they're too exhausted and stressed to leave the house. And maybe it comes as a full-course dinner with all fresh, locally sourced ingredients and homemade pasta. Wine, too. Same food, but with a different spin. I think there's a market for that. It would attract younger customers—"

For a moment, his attention was pulled away. In front of the restaurant, an old van with faded lettering that read ABC Bakery Supply pulled up to the curb. The door slowly opened, the driver turning around in his seat, then gingerly placing a cane on the ground.

"Delivery is even worse than takeout," his dad was saying. "At least takeout brings people by to say hello." A lecture was coming. One Leo knew too well. "Don't you want the restaurant to succeed?"

"Of course I do, Dad."

Outside, the driver had just lowered himself to the ground. He was a frail man, Leo would guess around eighty, with a wisp of white hair on the top of his head that blew in the wind. When the man finally managed to walk, he was hunched over, leaning hard on the cane. He'd only taken a few steps when Tessa, her mom, and her grandmother, all in their aprons, walked out of the bakery and met him on the sidewalk.

"I'll tell you how to do it." His dad, oblivious to what was going on outside, leaned across the table and dropped his voice. "Become a family man. No one will trust Mr. Fancy-Pants-Bachelor-MBA. You need to get married and settle down. In fact, Vito Rosalini just told me his daughter Annette is back in town."

"Annette?" Reflexively, he shuddered, remembering the one date they'd gone on in high school. She'd grown up with five rough-and-tumble brothers. Leo told her a joke, and she'd punched his arm—in jest—but with such enthusiasm that he had a bruise the next day. At sixteen, he'd been too insecure to go on another date with a girl who was stronger than him. But now, as an adult, maybe he should give her another chance?

"She's a nice girl, and she's from a good family. Her father said you could come over for dinner one night."

"I'll consider it." Then, just to try and curb the matchmaking, he added, "I can find my own dates, though. I'm thirty-two years old."

"Yes, but are you married? No. Your mother and I were married at twenty. By the time you finally have kids, I'll be dead in my coffin."

Outside, the old man opened the van door to reveal the entire back loaded with boxes. That was all it took to get Leo up and walking to the entrance.

"What do you think you're doing?" his dad asked.

"Going to help." He nodded toward the door. "I'll be right back."

He'd almost reached it when his dad said in a foreboding tone, "Do not go out there."

Leo felt like he was twelve again. "You're kidding, right?"

"They do what they do, and we do what we do." His dad had turned away from the windows and was now at the cash register, opening the till. "That's how it is, and that's how it will always be. They don't need your help, anyway."

"Isn't it time for this nonsense to end?" Leo should have controlled the edge in his voice. And he shouldn't have used that word because his dad had picked right up on it.

"Nonsense?" he exclaimed. "That family has been trouble ever since their ancestor tried to stiff your great-great-grandfather for money. Fortunately, Guido got away from those crafty, scheming Montgomerys before it was too late."

"You can't judge the whole family on one ancestor." Besides, his mom had told him once that maybe Guido wasn't the angel he was made out to be.

"Oh, yes I can." His dad waggled a finger. "My grandfather vowed never to speak with them and it would be sacrilege not to respect his wishes."

"Almost a hundred years later?" Leo fisted his hands as he watched the three women unloading the boxes, which probably contained flour and sugar and other heavy baking supplies. He held back only because it soon became clear that the women could handle the load without him—that they'd been hauling baking supplies for generations. And out of respect for his father.

But still, he vowed, this feud was going to end. It was ridiculous.

Outside the window, Tessa was chattering, carrying three boxes at a time, while her grandmother and mother, each carrying one, laughed at something she was saying. The old driver sat down on a bench between the two shops and lit a cigarette.

Nothing much here had changed. And his dad was just as stubborn as ever. Maybe coming back home was a terrible idea. Maybe Leo was wrong to think he could not only save this business but, together with his dad, make it something… wonderful.

Then he thought of his mom. She was sweet yet smart, and she could keep his dad in line. Often with a smile. "I just got back to town, Dad," Leo said, approaching his father. "You've got to give me some time. To trust me a little." The things he could do with this place if only his father would loosen the reins…

But his dad shook his head. "You're going to make all these changes and then go back to your fancy-schmancy corporation."

Leo's job as a financial analyst in New York had been eighteen-hours-a-day grueling for the past ten years, and he was ready for a change. He'd taken a leave and come home because his dad was in trouble, but he had to admit, the idea of injecting new life into this musty old place appealed. So did learning how to prepare the traditional dishes he had so many great memories of. And if he could pull this whole thing off, he would ensure a good retirement for his dad. And rejuvenate the place. Make it something special. Continue its legacy. That's what he really wanted.

"I'm staying for as long as it takes to get this place going strong again," Leo said. And maybe longer, if he could get through to his dad and have him try some of his ideas. "I have the 'fancy' education and a decade of experience. Now let me use them."

"I don't know why you had to go away so far. You're going to stay for a while, and then off you'll go again, back to the big city." He made big gestures with his hands, like he was scattering chicken feed, then headed through the kitchen.

Leo followed. "I'm serious about staying." He'd been missing something in New York. Fresh air and open spaces. Family. *Home.*

"You want to show me you're serious?" His dad stopped near the back door and turned, his thick brows rising. "Settle down. Get a wife. *Then* I'll let you put your ideas into the restaurant."

Leo sighed. He wasn't a romantic, and he had no great urge to settle down. Maybe because he'd never met any woman he wanted to settle down *with*. Plus, he'd had a lot of fun keeping his dating life light. A wife, kids…someday, maybe. But certainly not just to please his dad. He had way too much to accomplish before then. And besides all that, his father's idea that he needed to have a family to boost their sales was just ludicrous.

Deep down, Leo knew his father was pushing this because he wanted grandchildren. It had nothing to do with the restaurant—or at least, it wasn't *only* about that. Starting a family was much more serious than changing items on a menu, but his dad didn't see it that way, mostly because that's not how it had happened for his parents. They met. They fell in love. They got married. They never questioned it.

For Leo, it wasn't that simple.

"Don't go putting ideas in Gia's head about leaving, either," his dad continued. "There's a great college right down the street." He hitched a thumb toward Bloomington, about sixty miles west. "Why go away?"

It was good he was home, to protect his baby sister from his dad's rigid thinking. "Getting away lets you see the world, and it makes you learn what you want. And you never know—sometimes kids come back." He swept his hands wide, demonstrating that he was, after all, home.

His dad wagged a finger. "Sometimes what you want is right here in front of your nose."

"Maybe." Leo was glad he'd gotten away. Gia, who was eighteen, didn't seem to have that same desire to leave. With his dad talking like that, why would she?

His dad set down the menus and looked at Leo. "You're a good boy, Leo, to come back and help us." He patted his cheek like he was a kid again. "But find a wife, okay?"

"Dad, enough with the wife thing."

"It's the only solution."

Leo tossed up his hands, his patience cracking. "Fine, why don't I just marry the next woman who walks in here? That would solve everything."

"Don't get smart with me, Leonides," his father said, shaking his finger. "If you're really serious, you've got to plan for the future. No *maybes*. No *try it for a year and see what happens*. People have a certain faith in the restaurant. They want a family man with family values, not a Romeo who's going to hit on their daughters and make them feel uncomfortable."

Leo bit his tongue. "I would never hit on their—"

There was a quiet rap on the big back window, then a face appeared. A pretty face with sparkling blue eyes. A ponytail full of thick, black hair. And a white apron with smears of chocolate on it…an apron that gave just a hint of the curves hidden underneath.

Tessa.

His dad got up and opened the door.

What? He was letting in "the enemy"? After giving seven reasons why Leo couldn't go help them a few minutes ago?

"Here you go, Mr. Castorini," Tessa said brightly, handing him a white bakery box wrapped with a brown-string bow. "There's plenty, so give one to Gia, too, okay?"

"Thanks," his dad said very softly, immediately setting the box down on the table and fidgeting his hands. He looked… busted. How long had he been letting Tessa in? And accepting secret gifts of pastries from her? This was bizarre.

"Nothing for me?" Leo teased.

When she looked over and saw him, her cheeks colored a little. "There's enough for everyone. Even you." She barely gave him a glance; then she was back to his dad.

Smiling sweetly. Had he *ever* seen her do that? Usually if she smiled at him, it had a grenade attached in the form of a whopping one-liner.

She approached the table, facing Leo now, with her back to his father, discreetly pulling something out of her apron pocket and handing it off to him. His cell phone. He'd been so focused on the croissant that he'd left it on the table. For a beat, he met Tessa's smarty-pants cornflower-blue eyes.

She dropped her voice and said, "I couldn't help noticing that someone named Svana has called, like, twenty times. Just wanted you to know in case it's…important." She said that smugly, her words dripping with disdain. But why would he care about that? She glanced toward the front windows. "I like the new sign."

"Thanks. I had the old one cleaned up and re-fabbed." Leo pocketed his phone. As far as Svana…seeing her was fun but he just wasn't interested in anything serious.

"I don't like anything too new," his dad said.

"Oh no," Tessa countered. "It looks just right. The neon spaghetti and meatballs is very, um, eye-catching. Especially with the new flashing meatball." She brushed some flour from her cheek. "Well, I gotta go."

Then she turned and left him staring after her.

The door clicking shut behind her shook him from his thoughts, and his dad was biting into—wait, was that a cannoli? A chocolate-chip one.

"Ooh, cannoli!" Uncle Cosmo had walked back from the kitchen and helped himself to one. "Wow, this is *good*. Who made these?"

Leo opened his mouth to answer, but his father silenced him with a look. Right. No mentioning the Montgomerys. "Amazon made them," he said. "They were just delivered. I must have accidentally used my business address instead of my home one." Now he was resorting to lies. This feud would be the death of all of them.

"What a delicious mistake," Aunt Loretta said with a laugh. She took a bite and made an *mmm* sound in her throat.

Leo took out a perfectly formed tube of flaky crust wrapped tightly around fluffy chocolate-chip crème filling and sank his teeth into it.

His chewing instinctively slowed, keeping the flavor on his tongue just a little longer before swallowing.

Even better than her chocolate-filled croissant from yesterday. She needed to be baking this stuff and selling it to people, not giving it away to whoever would take it, because this was… *Amazing* wasn't a strong enough word, but his cannoli-drugged brain couldn't think of anything else to describe it.

CHAPTER THREE

The next day, Tessa glanced out the bakery window and sucked in a big breath for courage. It was another beautiful, sunshine-filled May morning, the breeze full of the sweet scent of pink crab apple blossoms from the trees that lined Main Street. A perfect day to do just about anything, except what she had to do, which was round up her mother and grandmother and ask them about Leo's proposition.

She approached both of them as they worked behind the counter, stacking bread onto a cart. "Mom, would you come and sit down for a minute? You, too, Gram."

Her grandmother shot her a look of startled concern. Tessa could usually count on her for moral support and to put in a good word to her mom, but Gram's expression told her she was expecting the worst.

"I'll make us a coffee." Gram wiped her hands matter-of-factly on her apron. "Give me five minutes."

A coffee. That was her family's solution to any difficulty. The French kind, strong and bitter, capable of making you shake in ten seconds or less.

Tessa's mom turned to her. "You're not pregnant, are you?"

That was the first conclusion she'd jumped to? "From what? Immaculate conception?"

Her mom blew out a relieved breath. "Sorry, it's just that you *never* ask to talk. My mind just went there."

At that moment the bell tinkled, and Beatrice Hawkins, a

senior who lived in the same apartment building as Arthur, walked through the door. "Hi, Bea," Tessa said in her usual friendly manner. "How are you?" She hated to ask because the answer was usually ten minutes long. And today, every second she put off talking to her family was another second of anxiety-fueled torture.

"I heard that Castorini boy has got some wicked plans up his sleeve," the elderly woman said.

Tessa took a quick look around, making sure her mom and grandmother had gone into the back. "Leo?"

"Yes, Leo," she said, adjusting the beads around her neck. "Since he's been back in town, he's been dating my friend Marie's daughter from Bloomington. A beautiful girl. The size of a model and a lawyer to boot."

"Is her name Svana?" slipped out of Tessa's mouth.

"How did you know?" Bea exclaimed. "She's a sweet girl. But apparently Leo is only interested in one thing."

"One thing?" Tessa asked

"*You know*." She waggled her brows so hard that her cat-eyed glasses nearly fell off. "Also, I heard he's evicting tenants from our complex."

Tessa didn't care about Leo's love life. But evicting tenants? It was hard to believe he was that cold-blooded, but who knew? "I'm not sure he'd—"

Bea wagged her finger, which held several large jeweled rings. "He's a ruthless one, just like the rest of the Castorinis. I'm entirely on your mother's side. You can't trust that family as far as you can throw them."

"All right." Tessa sighed but kept her smile in place. She was *not* going to ask. But then curiosity got the better of her, and she caved. "Why is he evicting tenants from your facility?"

"Well, he took over the management, and people are saying he's remodeling, but he's really getting rid of old people so he can rent out their units to younger people with more money."

"That's terrible." She grabbed a baking tissue and handed her a croissant. A buttery, flaky croissant always helped any kind of distress, right? "These are fresh from the oven."

"*Somebody* told me he was over here last night," she said as she took the offering.

Tessa sucked in a breath so hard, it made a squeaking sound, just as her mom walked out from the back.

"Tessa hasn't seen Leo in a long time, Bea," Tessa's mom said. "And I'm sure that if something's going on with the tenants, your board will sort it out, so don't worry. Want some bread?"

Her mom somehow managed to assuage Bea, get her to buy bread, and see her out the door in under a minute.

"Mom, how do you do that?"

"I'm not as kind as you." Her mom gave her a squeeze and looked her over in her usual assessing way.

The door opened again, bringing Sam in. Oh, they were never going to get to that talk.

"Hey, Tessa," Sam said, "can I have some of that delicious country loaf? I think Marcy and I are going to drizzle oil and cheese on it and call it a meal." He suddenly seemed to notice Tessa's mother standing there. The fact that she wasn't smiling didn't stop him. "Oh, hey, Mrs. M. How are you?"

Her mom glanced at Tessa and cut right to business. "I think I have one in the back. Give me a minute and I'll bring it out."

Sam leaned on the glass case. "We're house hunting," he

said to Tessa. "Would you go for cute and charming, or sleek and modern?"

House hunting. So he and Marcy were moving in together. Nice. Before she could even think of a way to answer, he went on. "We saw this one place that's got a lot of charm. It's a few houses down from Lilac's." He chuckled. "That should tell you everything."

Okay, if he was going to insult her best friend, she was going to sprinkle arsenic on his rustic loaf. Lilac was one of a kind, and she wasn't afraid to show it. And it was what Tessa loved the best about her. "I don't understand."

"Oh, you know, those house are unique. But they come with hefty price tags. Not to mention needing tons of renovation work. They're all around a hundred years old."

Yes, the Blossom District was unique. Tessa loved it. Sometimes Tessa rode her bike up and down the streets just to admire all the cute houses.

"We found a place that's got arched doorways and crown molding and built-in bookshelves in the living room. And a brick patio. But Marcy said the houses in that neighborhood are too close together. She doesn't like having neighbors. And she'd like to blow all the walls out and make the whole first floor open concept. That sounds costly. What do you think of that?"

"About buying an old house? Well, I think first of all that you should like old houses. Maybe Marcy would prefer a more modern one." If she was going to essentially gut it, wouldn't that be easier?

"Well, she likes the convenience to downtown." Marcy worked in marketing at the candle factory, where Sam worked in accounting. While Tessa was slaving away in the bakery, he was apparently trying to have his cake and eat it, too. Or burning his candle at both ends, if she stuck with the candle-factory analogy. Ugh. Where was that rustic loaf?

"Well, good luck with that," she said.

"Here you go, Sam." Her mom walked out of the back, handing over the loaf, as polite as ever.

"Thanks, Mrs. M.," Sam said with a little salute. "You ladies have a good day."

As soon as the door closed, Tessa's grandmother appeared. "He's got some nerve, coming in here like that," she said. "If he had any insight at all, he'd be ashamed to show his face."

"I have to agree," her mother, who rarely said an unkind word about anyone, added. "I don't understand why you tolerate him."

"I just want to keep things cordial between us." The truth was, she didn't know the best way to handle Sam. And she didn't know how to tell him to stop coming into the bakery.

So she changed the subject. "We should sit before anyone else stops by."

Her mother gave her a concerned look and smoothed some hair back from Tessa's face. "How are you doing with everything, anyway? He's moving in with that girl?"

So much for trying to change the subject. "Everything" was code for her post-Sam life. "I'm doing okay. Lilac and I are having lunch this week." Her eccentric best friend, who was a children's librarian, kept her supplied with books and humor. And of course her two sisters, Juliet and Vivienne, were always in her corner. Tessa also had her YouTube ladies who always watched her baking videos that she uploaded a few nights a week and left kind comments. They were her cheering squad that helped her keep her dream alive of one day becoming a pâtissier.

Gram returned, carrying a little tray holding three coffees. Two were bitter black espressos. Tessa's was topped with steamed milk and a lot of foam. And any one of these was capable of keeping a person up for a double shift.

"Be sure to say hi to Lilac for me," her mom said, talking as Gram took a seat with them at one of the tables. "I'm glad we get a rare moment to sit down together, but I must admit you've got my nerves up."

Tessa took a sip of Gram's wonderful coffee, licking the foam off her lips and gearing up for what she had to say. She had a sinking feeling that any sentence she'd utter with the word *Castorini* in it was destined to create a volcanic eruption. But she plunged in anyway. "So..." she began, "I've been trying to get us new accounts to replace the GoodFoods chain pulling out."

"Yes," her mom said. "I have, too. I had a couple of leads as far as Illinois and Michigan, if we could hire the transport so the bread arrives fresh."

"Well, that might not be necessary. I found a potential local customer." *Really* local. "No transport required."

"Is it a chain?" her grandmother asked. "We'll need more than one store."

"Not a chain." Tessa had to remind herself to breathe. Dread prickled the back of her neck. "It's a family-owned restaurant. The son is planning to go into business with his father, and he wants to use our bread. They...would like some desserts, too, which I'm happy to work evenings to make." She took another deep breath. "And...I'd like to do a shelf of pastries here. Just a tiny shelf, to see if they'd be popular. If they are, well—maybe we could sell those, too. Diversify our inventory. And maybe start selling them to our other accounts?"

There. She'd said it. All of it.

Her mother gave her a shrewd look. "Which restaurant?"

Well, okay, *almost* all of it.

"It's very well established, and—"

"Tessa, *who*?"

She waved her hand toward next door. "Our, um…neighbors."

"Out of the question," her mother said, bringing her hand down hard on the table. "We are a *boulangerie*. Not a patisserie. I've been telling you that for a *long time*. We're not having this discussion again."

Tessa bit the insides of her cheeks to keep from saying something she'd regret. It was the same spiel she'd heard dozens of times before, and it was usually amended with, "But that doesn't mean you can't go out and become a patisserie chef somewhere else."

But this time her mother added, "And we do *not* supply Italian restaurants—especially not *that* family's Italian restaurant—with our *French* bread. That's just absurd."

Again, Tessa caught her grandmother's eye. Gram knew that Tessa was too faithful to ever leave her family during a time of need, because family loyalty was baked into her DNA.

"You know, Joanna," Gram said, "these are desperate times. Maybe we need to change our way of thinking."

Her mother shook her head. "There's a difference between changing our ways and changing our *principles* and *values*."

That was just the thing, though. Her mother was not

budging on the definition of *tradition*. She'd rather lose the business than tweak it a little in a different direction.

Tessa looked out the window, where the sun shone brightly on the little shops lining the street. Someone from the candle shop was planting urns with bright red flowers near the main entrance. People were walking by, talking to each other, chatting on their phones.

A sense of pure, utter longing enveloped her and nearly brought her to tears. A ridiculous image appeared in her head, of her running down the street, arms outstretched like Julie Andrews in *The Sound of Music*.

Free.

What did *free* feel like?

Everyone here had a place. A job. A life.

Well, she had a life, too, but it wasn't the one she wanted. Her die had been cast as the steady sister, the one who kept everyone on track. And while her mother might talk like Tessa was free to leave, she'd also made it nearly impossible for her to go.

• • •

"Why are you hiding in here on such a beautiful night?" Tessa's grandmother asked that evening as she entered the back room of the bakery. Gram took a seat at the big wooden counter, right at home amid the bread racks, electric ovens, and stacks of bagged breads, watching Tessa ice an opera cake that had taken her about three hours to make. It was a masterpiece, with carefully cut layers of almond sponge cake, coffee-flavored buttercream, and ganache.

"I'm not hiding," Tessa said as she smoothed out the

chocolate glaze until it was flawless. "What are you up to?"

Her grandmother held out a hardcover book. She was dressed in a pretty floral blouse and capris, her nearly white hair cut in a stylish bob. "On the way to book club."

"Oh, how fun." Tessa silently read the title, *Women on Top*, and raised a brow. "Gram! What on earth are you reading?"

Her grandmother slid her hand down the front, uncovering the rest of the title. *Succeeding as a Female Entrepreneur*.

Much more in character. "That's an interesting selection."

"I suggested it," Gram said. "I was hoping I'd learn something to help us."

"I'm working on that." Tessa hated that her grandmother was worried about the business at her age. Gram felt obligated to pitch in, but Tessa and her mom didn't give her more than three half shifts a week. Still, Tessa wanted her to enjoy a real retirement that she'd earned after so many years of hard work.

"What's all this stuff?" her grandmother asked, pointing to a light ring Tessa had set up. Her phone was suspended on a stack of books next to her cake.

"I just made a baking video and posted it to my YouTube channel."

Her grandmother sighed. Then she sat down—always a bad omen.

"I know what you're going to say," Tessa said.

"Okay, if you're so smart, what is it?"

"You're sorry my mother won't take the baking deal. Or let me bake what I want."

"Not exactly," she said. "I was about to say that you don't have to make every decision for the family. We'll be okay if you leave."

Tessa bit down on her lip. How on earth could she, though? Also, she didn't want her grandmother to have to choose sides. "You really should be sleeping in and sitting by a pool somewhere, drinking pastel-colored cocktails instead of working three days a week."

"You're young," she said, undeterred. "You can't keep deferring the start of your own life because the family business is in trouble."

She didn't know what to say to that, so she started cleaning up the mess she'd made during the cake project. But she must have been silent too long.

"Knock, knock," her grandmother teased. "Where are you?"

Tessa shook her head. She needed to change the topic—fast. "Just thinking about my love life. Or rather…my lack of one."

Gram raised a fine brow, encouraging her to continue. They had the kind of relationship where Tessa could be honest about things like that with her and not be humiliated. Or at least, not *too* much.

Tessa shrugged. "I don't know. Maybe I'm just afraid to take a chance again."

Her grandmother tapped the battered wood surface that they kneaded dough on each morning. "Don't worry. You have the Montgomery curse," she said matter-of-factly.

Tessa dumped her measuring spoons and mixing bowls into the sink, then turned to face her. "The *what*?"

"The Montgomery curse. We're hopeless romantics, all of us."

"Is that a good thing or a bad thing?"

"Well, if you don't settle, it's a good thing." She tipped her head toward the Castorinis' place. "But it's also what started the feud with our neighbors to begin with. In 1937, to be exact."

"I know, I know." Tessa rolled her eyes. "One of our ancestors fell in love with a Castorini, and he left her at the altar, in front of the whole town. Shamed our family."

Gram nodded. "A wolf can be a wolf, or he can be a sheep. That particular Castorini, Guido, was a charming, handsome man who had everyone fooled."

"Did the poor woman ever get over it?"

"She joined a convent and started rescuing stray cats."

Tessa groaned. She'd never become a nun, but she might as well rescue a couple more cats and settle in, because no decent man was *ever* going to find her in this town.

"My darling," her grandmother said, squeezing her shoulder. "You don't need a man to be happy. But if you meet the right one, your heart will know. You won't be able to help yourself from falling."

It wasn't that she didn't believe that was true. It was more she was afraid to trust it.

After Gram went on her way, Tessa sat down next to her finished cake and decided to make another. Baking was the one thing she did where all her troubles fell away. Lilac thought she was good enough to make a go of it on her own, but she wanted to learn proper techniques from the best teachers. She wanted to learn how to set up her own business. And she wanted to understand everything about pastries. That's why, one night after a little too much wine, she actually hit send on her application to pastry school.

It wasn't the right time, she knew. Not with the business floundering. So if by chance she got in, which would be a miracle, she'd have to say no. But she couldn't help wondering if she'd get in. For so many years, she'd dreamed of getting *that letter*.

By nine thirty, Tessa's stress baking was still not relieving her stress. Now she was visualizing her application to the Chicago School of French Pastry sitting in a pile on a famous chef's desk. She'd be French, of course, and would murmur approvingly at Tessa's experience in her family's multigenerational bakery.

But then…she'd see the bread on the résumé. Only bread, bread, and more bread. *Where is the pastry experience?* she'd ask. And just like that, Tessa would get tossed from the *maybe* pile to the *no way* pile.

Tessa sat in the silent bakery, noticing the light from the big, bright, pizza-pie moon flooding in through the window. The lovers' moon was still there. She might carry a romantic gene and a curse on the women in her family that doomed them to fall head over heels, but her sensible side knew that some fairy-tale moon wasn't going to save her. Nothing short of getting out of this town for good would do that.

Wine. That's what she needed.

She checked the fridge in the back and all the storage cabinets. *Nada.* And she knew she didn't have any at home in her apartment. She even rummaged through her deep desk drawers in the very back room, but the spreadsheets were still open on her computer, reminding her of their troubles. And that made her even more determined to find a bottle somewhere.

A glance at her phone told her it was almost ten o'clock. The grocery store was closed, and a trip to the next town and back would take an hour.

Then she had a ridiculous idea. The restaurant next door might still be open…in the old days when there were more people dining in, they'd stayed open till ten. They wouldn't turn down a paying customer, would they? Even if she was a Montgomery.

Mr. Castorini didn't let that stop him from taking her desserts. Of course, that was only if she delivered them to the back door and never let anyone but him see her.

Leo had seen her the other day, though. His father's taboo indulgence wasn't a complete secret anymore. Maybe that was enough that she could start using the front door now.

She untied her apron, tossed it into the dirty apron bin, and walked out into the quiet street. The little brick shops were shadowed, their windows warmly lit in the fragrant spring evening.

At first glance, the Castorinis' place was dark, but then she noticed a very faint glow. As her eyes adjusted to the darkness, she could see Leo hunched over a laptop, a small lamp burning at his table.

Call it the moon, call it desperation, call it whatever you wanted, but something made her rap on the glass.

Leo jerked his head up. His brows lifted in surprise, and he gave her the hold-on-a-sec sign.

Her stomach tumbled. *What have I just done?*

"Hey," he said as he pulled the door open. His usually perfect hair was a little disheveled, like he'd been raking his hands through it. Dark, dangerous stubble shadowed his face. His discerning gaze skirted quickly over her from head to toe, like he was trying to find some visible reason she'd be here.

This had been an awful idea.

On closer examination, she noticed he had circles under his eyes, and his button-up shirt was halfway untucked. Could it be that he was feeling the same stress that she was?

"Did you need something?" he asked.

"Yes?"

He smiled a little, then stepped aside to let her pass. "Come on in. It's safe. I'm the only one here." His voice was low and gravelly, in a way that reminded her of a sexy model in a cologne commercial as he awakened in a breezy-curtained villa, throwing back the silk sheets and walking naked to his balcony overlooking the Adriatic Sea.

Okay, stress was making her imagination go wild. And also, *safe* felt like a real misnomer.

She followed Leo back to the table where he'd been working and ran her hand along her carelessly swooped-up bun, thinking she must look a mess after working all day and into the night. But why should she care? She wasn't here to impress.

As she sat down across from him, he asked, "Do you have good news for me?" He gave her a hopeful look that made her want to lie. That made her think that maybe they weren't so different. They both loved their families. They both wanted their hard work to bring success.

But this was business, so she straightened her spine. "No deal with the bread. My mom won't have it. She'd rather be bankrupt than have us bake for your restaurant. I'm sorry."

He sighed heavily, and for the first time ever, he didn't seem to be shrugging things off with a smile.

"Any luck on your end?" she asked. "I mean, about selling your ideas to your dad?"

He sat back, tossing his pen over the many scattered papers. "No," he said simply. Just one word, jam-packed with frustration.

She should just go home. What was the point of continuing a conversation? Yet she recognized a look in his eyes—the same desperate desire to do *something* to stop these ships from sinking. And…and she was now past want. She *needed* that wine.

"I—" She felt her voice giving out. "I actually was wondering if you had any wine. I mean, I'd pay you for it."

He looked her over in what she was coming to learn was a thoroughly assessing way of his, a mixture of curiosity and something more intense that made her feel stripped down to the bone. "What are you doing downtown at this hour?"

She hitched a thumb toward the bakery. "I was just sneak baking." She mentally head slapped herself. Why had she confessed that? It was private. To most people, anyway.

He frowned. "What's *sneak baking*?"

"Oh. Sometimes I go in after hours and bake whatever I want. It's…a way of unwinding, I guess. Being creative. Forgetting about everything else."

"I might have to try it. Because all I do after hours is pore over the numbers. And then I can't sleep."

"I hear you," she said.

"You probably shouldn't be downtown alone at night."

In Blossom Glen? Tessa waved a hand dismissively. "Like you?" He smiled a little at that. "I've been doing it for years. It's my therapy."

His lips cracked a slight smile. "Wine sounds like a great idea." That warmth in his eyes was back, and it was directed at her. Only briefly, though, and then he got up and went to the back room.

She was hungry—yearning, even—for what was *really* at stake here: her dreams, her life, a way *out*—and her imagination was in overdrive lately. But while she was way too smart to make the same mistake that she made when she was eighteen, to think that Leo had actually *liked* her, she knew what it meant when a man looked at her a certain way.

Heat and desire from her nemesis. Now *that* was a real recipe for disaster.

While she waited, something caught her eye. Not the faded old mural of the sea, or the creepy philosopher busts, or the checkerboarded tablecloths. In a standing cabinet near the cash register was a sizable trophy. And she knew exactly what it was for.

She snuck over to get a closer look. There, safe behind glass, among a bunch of restaurant awards, was a big gold statue of a woman with wings, standing triumphantly on the top of a dark wooden base. At the bottom, the plaque read Leonides Leonardo Castorini, Valedictorian.

Ouch.

After all these years. Still *ouch*.

0.0004. That's how close she'd come to having a different life.

She sat back down at the table just as Leo returned with two wineglasses and a bottle of white that he opened smoothly and expertly poured.

"*Salute,*" he said, lifting his glass. He was all polished grace, as if he should be drinking on a patio overlooking the cliffs of Lake Cuomo instead of in a tiny Indiana town, in an old Italian restaurant with vinyl tablecloths and a marble bust of some guy with no pupils staring at them from the shelf.

"*À ta santé*," she returned.

He lifted a thick, well-groomed brow as they clinked glasses.

Tessa swirled her glass and inhaled the rich essence before she took a sip. It was smooth and went down easy, definitely not something you'd buy at a drug store for a late-night college run. "It's sweet," she said.

He sat back, his tall, lean body relaxing into the booth. "It's a dessert wine. Moscato. One of my dad's favorites, and tonight, it's on the house."

"Oh, you don't have to—"

"I need this just as much as you do," he said, his exhaustion and frustration clearly weighing down every word.

"All right, um. Thank you." She took another sip and then sighed, setting her glass down. "The upscale grocery chain that buys our bread is changing ownership, and they've dropped our account."

He nodded in sympathy. "I'm sorry about that. The restaurant is barely breaking even, yet my dad refuses to try anything new. It's like he's stuck in the nineties."

She let the fizzy, fruity taste of the wine dance on her tongue. It was delicious, but she doubted it was strong enough to take the edge off her nerves, which were practically galloping at this point.

Suddenly, she felt vibrations emanating from the floor. Like when you're in church and the little kid behind you keeps kicking the pew.

She peeked under the table to find Leo's leg bouncing rapidly. Mr. Fair, Sunny, and Easygoing was as nervous as she was.

He's human.

Across from her, Leo slumped. His quick glance up at her exposed the worry etched in his face. The tiny candle highlighted the outline of his granite jaw and the shiny black of his hair. "My dad thinks the solution is getting married."

Tessa choked on her wine. Hitting her chest and sitting up, she finally managed, "What?"

"Right? That's what I said." His tie was askew, and his five-o'clock shadow somehow made him look roguish and vulnerable at the same time.

"How would *that* solve any problems?"

He refilled their glasses. "My dad says this is a family restaurant and he needs someone in charge who's a family man. He believes success is all about image."

She considered that; in a small town like theirs, there was some truth to it, but it certainly wasn't the only factor. "To me, success is all about the bottom line. And if I can't find some way to improve our bakery's bottom line, my mom's going to have to sell it."

He folded his muscled arms in a way that looked casual, but she could sense the tension rolling off him. "Is that such a bad thing? Selling?"

She nodded adamantly. "The bakery is over a hundred years old. It would break my family's heart. And selling wouldn't even give my mom enough money to live on for very long. I can't imagine her getting a job doing something else…" She twirled her glass. "What will you do if the restaurant folds? I'm sure there are similar opportunities for you to turn businesses around in New York. Why do it here, where people are so set in their ways?"

He leaned forward, conviction lacing his voice. "Tradition

and family mean something to me, too. I came back here not only to help my father but to work with him. I just need to convince him to implement my ideas. *Those* are what are going to save the restaurant."

He sounded...superbly confident. But then, he always had been. "Well, nothing short of a miracle is going to save our bakery. It needs new accounts and more business. And I have big plans for my life that actually involve leaving town. But I can't when everything is in the mess it is now."

He reclined back again. "And where might you be going, Tessa Montgomery?"

With his wolfish grin, that sounded like there should be a sinister, toothy *My Dear* tacked on at the end.

And somehow, that made her smile.

Or maybe it was the wine.

She wasn't going to get into the details of her life plans with *him*, but why lie? "I've applied to pastry school."

"A rebel at heart." He raised his glass.

Her face heated with a flush. He had no idea how against-the-tide it was going to be to get herself to pastry school. But she *would* do it. She *had* to.

"Sounds like we're birds of a feather," he said.

No. No, they really weren't.

"I'd love to help you," Tessa said and meant it, "but even if you used our bread or even some pastries, I don't see that helping either of us all that much."

"You're right," he said, pointing a finger at her. "We need more than that. We need a *partnership*. Birds of a feather flock together."

"A partnership?" Her head was buzzing, and not just from the wine. What was he suggesting? She'd already told him her mother would never get on board.

"Exactly." He drummed his fingers on the table as he thought out loud. "Something to make my dad *have* to listen to my ideas."

She snorted. "While you're at it, come up with something that would convince my mother of the same thing."

"If we had a partnership, we'd have more power together than we do individually. Then both of our families would listen."

"We could make them an offer they can't refuse," she said in her best Godfather voice. Then she chuckled, because her best impersonation was probably the worst she'd ever heard.

He chuckled, too. Maybe they'd *both* had a little too much wine.

"Oh! Tessa, that's it." He smacked his hand down definitively on the tabletop, making her jump. "I've got it."

"*What* have you got?" She laughed again. "What's *it*?"

He looked at her with a laser-sharp gleam of confidence in his eye. "We need to get married."

CHAPTER FOUR

Tessa sat across the table from Leo, unmoving, her startled blue eyes big and round. She appeared to be waiting for him to say something. Maybe like, *Ha-ha, just kidding*.

Except he *wasn't* kidding. He was dead serious.

When she had a couple glasses of wine in her, even this light stuff, she was fun, and she had this way of crinkling up her nose that was kind of…cute. But he had a feeling that if she'd been completely sober, she'd be way too uptight, too by-the-book to even consider something this far out of the ballpark.

She clearly wasn't a risk-taker. If she was, she wouldn't still be trapped in a job she disliked.

And he hadn't been planning on proposing to her, either, but as soon as the idea hit him, he knew it was perfect.

"I might be a little tipsy," she said, taking another sip, "but that's never gonna happen."

She was adorable, with her messy bun and a streak of flour on her cheek. And the same determination to help her family as he felt.

But he couldn't trust her. She'd proven her insincerity by messing with his feelings back in high school. He reminded himself that she was still a Montgomery. He could not afford to allow his hormones to get involved in what he was proposing—even though what he was proposing was marriage.

Ideas were rapid-firing through his brain, a combination of desperation and the genius driven by a truly excellent vintage. Either he was incoherent and didn't know it, or he'd actually hit upon the answer to both their problems.

"It's the only way." He looked her directly in the eye. "The *only way* for both of us to get what we want."

"But I don't even like you," she said. "Even if you're hot." She put a hand to her mouth. "Oops, didn't mean to say that."

Leo cracked a smile despite himself. She might be a little mellowed out and fun now, but it was just a matter of time before her sharp, cutting tongue returned.

"This isn't about *like* or any other emotions," he said in his most practical tone. "It's a business partnership. Nothing else." Frankly, he didn't *do* anything else. All his past relationships were strictly for fun—if you could even call them relationships.

"Business," she echoed, staring at her wine. He couldn't tell if she was starting to lean toward agreeing to this or contemplating how to change the subject. Or murder him.

"Trust me," he said, "marriage isn't my style."

He liked to be positive, upbeat, and to see the best in a situation…in honor of his mother. She'd made him promise to do that. It had taken a lot of effort and discipline, but after years of practice, it had become part of him.

Tessa finally looked up at him. "You're serious."

"As a heart attack." He set down his glass with a *clink*.

"You're giving *me* a heart attack. A marriage and a business partnership are two entirely different things."

He leaned back in the booth, the soft leather squeaking at the shift in his weight. "They can be the same thing. Think about it. In both, people compromise; they work together; they get things done. Simple."

She shook her head adamantly. "This type of arrange-ment only works in romance novels. *Historical* romance novels," she added. "It's archaic. When I marry, it will be for love."

He scoffed. "Good luck finding Prince Charming in this town."

"Hey." She looked offended. "I'm not ashamed to say I want a family one day just because the road there might be difficult." She paused. "Don't you? Want a family?"

He shrugged. "I've been too busy building my career to think about that." And having fun. His friends didn't call him Keep-it-Light Leo for nothing.

"Well, don't think too long, or you'll be running after your kids with a cane in one hand."

"I'm still young," he said. "I have plenty of time."

She rolled her eyes. "Not that young. Don't forget we're from the same graduating class."

He dramatically grabbed his chest. "You wound me."

"All thirty-two years of you." She snorted.

That familiar spark hit his chest, urging him to keep sparring with her. It had gotten him into trouble when they were younger, but he couldn't remember right now why he needed to avoid that. "There's more to me than just my age, Tessa. And you're welcome to see it for yourself."

She went still, leaving those words hanging between them. Had he really just—

"Geesh," she said. "Do these terrible lines actually work on women?"

He leaned over as if he were about to tell her a secret. "*Yes*," he said simply. "They do."

She laughed. *Laughed.* Now he really was a little hurt.

"Anyway," she continued, "I'm not leaving my future to fate. I'm going out to get it myself."

His eyes narrowed at her. "You're really leaving Blossom Glen? How soon?"

Her turn to shrug. "The Chicago French Pastry School has rolling admission. Classes start in July and January. I could get in at any moment. Well, okay, it's already May, but you never know. They could call me any day. But…I can't leave my mom in a lurch."

"Yet another reason why my plan is perfect. We'd work hard *together* to get both businesses profitable. Then your life would be yours." She had a conviction about her that he hadn't given her credit for prior to this moment. Maybe she had more ambition than he thought. She'd been competitive in high school—he knew that better than anyone—but until now, he'd assumed she'd been driven more by stubbornness than a will to succeed.

"You're asking me to do something ridiculous—not to mention legally binding—for an idea that might not even work."

He sat up, his eyes drilling into hers, but she straightened her spine and stared right back. And, he was shocked to find, he was drawn to her defiant expression. Her full lips. She was *challenging* him.

Then something buzzed and crackled in the air between them.

Tension. *Sexual* tension.

He shook it away and chalked it up to the fact that he hadn't dated anyone since Svana. He really needed to get back out there. So he wouldn't be tempted by troublesome women like Tessa. "Oh, it would work."

"You're so cocky," she said, stabbing at the air. "And too arrogant."

He shot her a smug look. "Those words mean practically the same thing."

"Still the same know-it-all from high school. Just like all those years ago when you thought you were going to win that scholarship."

"I *did* win that scholarship," he reminded her. "But you were right behind me. It was practically a tie."

She rolled her eyes.

"Come on, Tessa. You can't hold that petty grudge against me forever." He was being obnoxious, he knew. But he had to protect himself from getting pushed around. And from the current that was snapping to life between them.

"I don't hold grudges, Leo," she said sweetly. "But I remember them. And it reminds me never to get involved with you again."

This woman was…unbelievable. As his fake wife, she wouldn't respect him; she'd harass and poke fun at him. She'd compete with him and argue with him at every turn. And she would annoy the hell out of him. Did he really need all that to save his family's business?

Yeah. He did. And she needed it, too.

So he went back to sales mode. "My idea is innovative. And yes, a little risky. But it can have a huge payoff. For *both* of us."

"How would I explain this to my family? They'd be… heartbroken. Or, more likely, they'd never believe it in the first place."

A sly grin spread across his face. "Sure they would. It's classic."

"Classic hatred?" she quipped.

His turn to eye roll. "Classic Romeo and Juliet. We're the Montagues and Capulets. Except with a happy ending."

"You consider *divorce* a happy ending? Unless you mean we'd kill each other first. Because we can't stay fake married forever. I'd like a real husband at some point, and I can't look for him with a ring on my finger. I mean, I guess I *could*, but I won't. Because I won't cheat, even if this is all pretend."

He hadn't thought of that, and he was impressed by the depth of her loyalty, but he wasn't about to admit it. "Anything's happier than death."

She gave him an incredulous look, then dropped it. "Actually, you're right about that one. I hate when you're right. But you're not right about this…this…fake marriage. No one will buy it. They know us too well."

"What's that supposed to mean?"

"Well, we don't…like each other, for one. How are we going to coexist when we have to pretend we do?"

"Tolerating each other for a few months—let's say six—is a small sacrifice."

"Says you."

"Hey, I'm tidy. I cook. And I don't snore."

"I will *never* be close enough to where you sleep to know that."

Despite himself, he chuckled. "That's not important." Somehow they'd gotten off track. And it was making him imagine an entirely different kind of sparring. He forced himself to focus. "*This* is what's important. When the partnership saves both our businesses and you get on your way to…wherever it is you're planning on going, *that's* the happy ending." Then he added, "And we have a chance to finally end that ridiculous family feud. No more Montagues and Capulets or Montgomerys and Castorinis. Everybody wins."

There. He'd laid it all on the line. Given her his best defense. All she had to do was say *yes*.

She swallowed her last sip of wine, then stood. "I'm sorry. I couldn't possibly take part in this scheme."

He stood with her. "Give me one reason why."

"It's…sneaky."

She had him there. "I would do anything for my family," he said, desperation taking over. "Including *this*. But I guess I was wrong to think you'd make the same sacrifice for yours."

"Don't worry," she said, looking offended now. "I'd never make you endure marriage to me. That kind of…*sacrifice* would be far too cruel."

His wasp-tongued frenemy made for the door, surprisingly walking in a straight line. She wasn't drunk, then; only a little buzzed, like he was. He could still try to reason with her.

He rushed past her and got to the door first, scrambling for some way to keep her from walking through it.

He hated to press his agenda, but he was out of options. Down to fumes in the gas tank. "Your association fee is due."

She stopped mid-step, tripping a little before she planted her feet and glared at him.

"Actually," he said, "Bonjour! Breads didn't pay last month's, either."

The Montgomerys owned the bakery space, but the Castorinis owned the strip of shops that contained it, so they owed a fee of several hundred dollars every month for grounds maintenance, parking-lot upkeep, water and sewage, outdoor lighting—all of that.

"What are you getting at?" Her tone was horrified. She looked at him like he was a reptile that had just crawled out of the sewer. Something despicable. Which he really couldn't argue with right now.

"Tomorrow is the first of the month."

"You wouldn't dare evict us." She paused, worrying her lip. "Would you?"

"Of course not," he said, and she let out a breath. "But I *would* charge interest for every day you don't make that payment. And you're already a month behind. That could pile up fast."

Her eyes flashed with anger. "You know what, Leo Castorini?"

"What, Tessa Montgomery?" Whatever insult she was about to throw would cut him to the bone, but it wasn't because he had a fragile ego. It was because he knew he'd lost.

She poked him in the chest, then swung her ax. "I hope someone strings you up by the balls and leaves you for vultures to feast on."

She moved past him, threw open the door, and left.

"So is that a yes?" he asked and finished his wine.

CHAPTER FIVE

The next morning, Tessa went to work with a massive, hammering headache. Last night, the wine had been too good, and the company...well, it had been fine until Leo suggested they get *married*.

Leo Castorini had unique ideas—that was for sure.

He was an innovator, just as he'd been in high school. Like the time he'd used real bakeries for the senior class bake sale fundraiser, ran a social-media campaign, and ended up raising ten thousand dollars for Riley Children's Hospital in Indianapolis.

But *this* idea was...outrageous.

On top of her throbbing head, she remembered the extra upkeep money she did not have. She'd believed him when he said he wouldn't kick them out of the bakery. But charge interest? Of course he would, and he'd do it with a smile on his gorgeous, infuriating face. She resolved to call twenty-five more places to sell their bread as soon as this headache was gone.

Marry him. Ridiculous! There *had* to be a better way.

Suddenly the bell above the door tinkled. Her younger sister, Juliet, whose long red hair was pulled up in a ponytail, practically bounced as she burst excitedly in.

"I think Jax is going to pop the question," she said excitedly, stretching out her arm and wiggling her bare fingers. "As soon as I'm done with work, I'm getting a test manicure so I can pick the best ring-ready color. Tessa, want to come?"

Juliet didn't seem to notice her startled expression. "Is that coffee?"

Juliet's off-again, on-again relationship with Jax had taken one too many runs through the roller coaster, in Tessa's opinion. Tessa didn't get how she could be a tough, kick-butt marriage counselor yet put up with Jax. Case in point: What kind of boyfriend made you take your shoes off before you get into his 1970 Firebird, which he probably spent more time with than her?

"We had a little spat, but we talked that through, and things are *amazing* now."

Was this what being a parent was like? Like endlessly banging your head against a wall? Also, two weeks of not talking and many shed tears on Juliet's part did seem to merit a stronger word than *spat*.

Plus, her sister deserved the best. She was full of love and life, always sweeping them away to museums, local festivals, concerts—always up for anything. She'd somehow convinced Tessa to run a 5K for the library last year, something Tessa swore she'd never repeat. And enter a cake in the Blossom Glen cake-off for the mental health center (she won). Juliet never said no to an adventure…or to a marriage proposal, apparently, because she'd also been briefly engaged to her college sweetheart a few years ago, and that had ended in disaster a few days before the wedding.

"Aren't you happy for me?" Juliet looked a little offended.

Tessa had learned to usually say yes to this question.

"Of course I am." She went to hug her.

Juliet scanned Tessa's face. "Are you going to lecture me?"

"No. Of course not." Tessa didn't miss the little dig.

Somehow, over the years, her relationship with her sisters had devolved into more of advice-giving and being a surrogate parent than a sister—and she wasn't quite sure how to change that.

"Good. Because this time it's for real. We've navigated all our differences, we've matured, and…and I love him. He's *the one*." She stood there as if she'd just confessed a huge revelation.

Yes, *the one* to cause endless heartache, Tessa truly believed. "What makes you think that he's planning on popping the question?"

"He asked me to go for a hike in a few weeks in the same park where his parents got engaged. Then he made dinner reservations at that new winery where everyone eats overlooking the lake. And he said we have something important to discuss."

"Just please be careful. I'd hate to see you hurt again."

"Don't ruin this for me, okay?" From that almost-an-eye-roll look her sister just cast her, Tessa could tell she was holding back. Vivienne had never given her lip like this. "Please try to resist playing mom."

Tessa bit back her tongue. She'd *had* to play mom after their father died, when their mother had been overloaded with stress and grief. Someone had had to step up and mother her sisters. And somehow, even after her mom had recovered from the shock of their father's death, Tessa had kept the role. All of them had sensed that their mother could take only so much overload, and Tessa had always picked up the slack. She held up her hands. "Okay, no more warnings. I hope he *is* the one."

Then Tessa's phone rang, and the image of her youngest

sister, Vivienne, lit up the screen.

She picked up the phone and held it so Juliet could see too. "Hi, Viv!"

"Hi, Tessa! Hey, Juliet!" Vivienne called. "I miss you!" She was smiling widely, but maybe a little too widely. Tessa heard a slight tinge of sadness in her voice. Probably just homesickness, as Viv hadn't been home since last Christmas.

"You called at the perfect time," Tessa said. "It's just the two of us."

"I think there's going to be an engagement in the family soon," Juliet said in a sing-song voice.

"Tessa met someone?" Vivienne asked.

"No, Viv," Juliet said a little indignantly. "I'm talking about Jax and me!"

Oh dear. This wasn't going well. But on a positive note, at least one of Tessa's sisters still held out hope for her to find love, too.

"Oh, I'm sorry, Jules," Viv said. "I thought you two broke up."

"We've resolved our issues," Juliet reported. "And things are going really well."

"That's great," Vivienne said. "Congratulations."

"How's your art internship?" Tessa asked, changing the subject.

"Awesome." She rushed on to say, "The d'Orsay is quite a place. I'm learning so much. And every day I walk by the Monets and I can't believe how much more stunning they look in person than on postcards and umbrellas. Tonight we have a dinner to recognize up-and-coming artists."

The d'Orsay. Monet. Viv was living her dream. Tessa was really happy for her baby sister. And, she hated to admit, a little sad for herself.

"Is your photography going to be on display at that gallery you talked about?" Juliet asked.

"Not yet. But maybe someday! Hey Tessa, I thought of you. Because I actually ate in that patisserie in the Marais you used to have a photo of in your room, remember? I took all kinds of pics for you. I'll send them."

Tessa felt a tiny stab in her gut that she quickly shooed away. Never mind that she'd longed to do every single one of the things portrayed in the many photos Viv sent to them: visit the Eiffel Tower, eat macarons from Ladurée on the Champs-Élysées, stroll the markets for fresh cheeses and bread, and walk the cobblestoned streets of the Marais in search of a wonderful café to have a croissant and a coffee as she watched Paris stroll by.

And the patisserie in the photo… It was her absolute dream pastry shop. With a black and white tile floor and a pink glass chandelier and a killer view of the famous Pont des Arts over the Seine. *One day*, she'd told herself, she'd have a little shop just like that. Minus the Seine, but hey, you can't have everything, right?

"Oh, Viv, that's wonderful," Tessa said. She loved her baby sister, and she was thrilled that she was in Paris and living her dream of working in the art world.

Even though it had really been Tessa's dream, if you substituted *pastry* for *art*. Instead, Tessa had baked and decorated cakes at night, Juliet had taken on tutoring in addition to her bakery shifts, and the whole family had scraped together enough for Viv's study-abroad experience. Since then, Vivienne had managed to support herself, and Tessa was proud of her.

All Tessa wanted now was the opportunity to find her own dream, instead of helping everyone else's come true.

But *when*? When would it be her turn?

A thought formed in her still-throbbing head. *Leo. His strange plan could make that happen.*

She pushed the rogue thought aside. That "plan" would create havoc among both their families. Plus it was… marriage, fake or not. Something not to be taken lightly.

"How's everything going in the bakery?" Viv asked. "Are things better? You can tell me since Mom's not around."

Tessa and Juliet exchanged a tacit glance off-camera. Vivienne didn't need to know the whole truth, because she was too far away to do anything to help. Why ruin all her plans by making her rush back when it probably wouldn't even matter?

Besides, Vivienne hated working in the bakery. Part of the reason was that she had gluten sensitivity—and that precluded her from eating anything they made there, which was a special torment for her.

"Business is…better," Tessa lied. It might be if she and Leo joined forces. But surely there was a better way.

No lightning bolt suddenly struck her with a better idea, that was for sure.

If she agreed, she could use Leo's resources to get more accounts for the bakery. Plus she could bake her desserts for real, showing her mom she was serious. Their parents would have to soften to each other, because they'd be family. And Leo's father would be inclined to listen to his ideas.

She had to admit, as outrageous as Leo's idea was, it could actually work. For both of them.

Then she would be free to pursue *her* dream.

"How's Mikhail?" Juliet was asking.

"Mikhail is amazing," Vivienne said in an overly bubbly voice. "He's just started his surgery residency, so he's pretty busy. But I am, too. So are the crab apple trees blooming? Could you use the phone to let me see?"

Tessa grabbed the phone and walked outside to show her the trees bursting with pink blooms along both sides of Main Street that gave their town its name.

Every year, they bloomed anew. A symbol of hope and promise.

"Oh, look," Viv said excitedly. "They're beautiful!"

"Yes," Tessa said. "But they probably can't compare to the trees along the Champs-Élysées, right?"

Viv was too busy exclaiming about the familiar sights to hear that. "Oh, look, I see the candle factory. They're planting flowers! And the dance studio. And the ice-cream shop. And the Castorinis' place! Oh, Tessa, I miss home so much." Her voice cracked a little.

Tessa pressed the flip button so her sister could see her face. "Vivienne, are you okay?" Her sister was always upbeat, talked a mile a minute, and grabbed life by the horns. She was also terrible at faking anything.

There was a pause as Vivienne sucked in a breath. But then her beautiful smile returned, as bright as ever. "Yeah. I'm…great. I feel so lucky to be here, Tessa, and I want you to know that if it weren't for you, I never could have had this experience. I won't ever forget that."

"I know that, honey. You've done us proud. But are you sure nothing's wrong?"

Viv smiled brightly. "Of course I'm sure. I couldn't be better. How—how about you?"

"Everything's the same." Tessa thought about telling her about Leo. About *everything*. But that wasn't the kind of relationship she had with either of her sisters.

"Tessa, I've got to go. We'll talk soon, okay?"

"Okay, honey," Tessa said. "You know you can call me anytime, right?"

"Yes, of course. *Au revoir!* Love you." Then she hung up.

Suddenly Tessa realized something. Everything really would stay the same if she kept on her usual path.

She sucked in a breath of warm spring air and pocketed her phone. She loved her sisters dearly, but she was so done watching them live out their lives the way they chose, rotating around her like she was the sun and they were planets. In that they moved and she…stayed stagnant.

When Tess popped back into the bakery, Juliet was on the phone with her mom, telling her about her big announcement. Soon Tessa was swept up in looking at photos of engagement rings on Juliet's phone, listening to her talk excitedly about Jax, her upcoming date, and all her plans and dreams.

Her sisters were moving on with their lives, come what may.

Tessa knew what it was like to fail. Her broken engagement had made that very public, but she'd somehow survived.

Staying here doing nothing wouldn't give her family financial stability. And it wouldn't get her one inch closer to fulfilling her dreams. So maybe it would be better to fail spectacularly than to keep on a pathway that promised absolutely nothing.

• • •

Leo brought out a plate of fresh cannelloni and placed it in front of his sister, Gia. Aunt Loretta had taught him how to make the ricotta-and-spinach stuffing, and his dad had showed him how to stuff each tube and present it properly on a plate, drizzled with homemade sauce and sprinkled with parmesan.

He'd taken great satisfaction in doing something with his hands. Something that his parents and grandparents and, many years ago, in a small village in the north part of Sicily, his ancestors had done as well. He was excited to continue those traditions. To continue the family pride in these recipes. To put down roots.

Which was why he'd decided to look for a house. Just a small one, nothing flashy, to settle into the community. And, he was hoping, one that might entice Tessa to get on board with his plan. Maybe it was his need to *do something*, but he'd scheduled a few showings with a realtor this afternoon.

The more he thought about a merger between Tessa and him, the more he knew in his heart it was an unstoppable plan. Together they could turn both these businesses around.

All he needed was for her to say yes.

And the best thing was, she was planning to leave. They'd dissolve their marriage as soon as they could and go their separate ways, no awkwardness or hard feelings. Mission accomplished.

Gia clapped a little on seeing the heaping plate of steaming cannelloni and said something about just coming from Mathletes. Not that he really knew exactly what that was—just that she was a smarty-pants and headed for great things, and that was good enough for him.

Except maybe she was a little *too* good. He couldn't believe he was actually thinking that. Gia was sweet natured, laid-back...and did not rock the boat. She didn't break curfew, she hung out with two super-nice friends, and, as far as he could tell, there were no boys in the picture. And his dad made it sound like she'd already decided on her college choice—a great school, IU, about an hour away.

His dad had never understood why Leo had left Blossom Glen for New York City—so he certainly was never going to encourage Gia to look a little further. And yes, money was tight, but Leo had the means to make it happen.

But his sister didn't want it. At least, that's what she said.

"So, what are Mathletes, anyway?" he asked as he set his own plate on the table and they both dug in. The kitchen was quiet, with his dad, Aunt Loretta, and Uncle Cosmo taking their customary lunch break before returning to hit it hard before dinner.

They sat by the window, where they could look out over the gorgeous day and people strolling the walkways in front of the shops under the pink crab apple blossoms.

Gia sat across from him dressed in her track outfit, her dark hair swept up in a ponytail. And she was scarfing down his dad's famous dish like nobody's business.

She shrugged. "It's where you do stuff with numbers. Then I had track practice. I'm *starving*."

It was spring of her junior year, and time was ticking on her college decisions. Leo just wanted to make sure that she knew the world was her oyster, regardless of his dad's deep desire to keep her close. "I was thinking we could make a few college road trips together this summer. What do you say? You've never been to New York, and—"

She stared at him like he was speaking another language. "I'm staying here, Leo. IU has a great biomedical engineering program. I think I can get in."

"That's great. Have you looked at Purdue, too? They've got an fantastic engineering school." One of his two best friends, Jack Monroe, the mayor, had graduated from the architecture school there.

"I want to go to IU," she said. "I'm studying for the SAT."

"You'd live there? In Bloomington?"

"Probably not." She was still shoveling in the pasta, and he was still trying to figure her out. At her age, he couldn't wait to get away, see the world, cut loose.

He got that not everyone was made that way. But he wanted to make sure that staying local was *her* choice, not his dad's.

Her phone buzzed with a text. "My friends want me to go somewhere tonight, but I have to work a shift."

"Look, I'm home now," Leo said. "You don't have to worry about taking care of Dad."

"I still have to work." She smiled at him in a way that made him feel like *she* was the older sibling. He knew that his leaving had made her the center of his dad's attention. The apple of his eye. But maybe it had also made her into the kind of kid who worried too much for her age and felt too responsible. "If I get a scholarship, I'll get free tuition."

"I don't want you to worry about money."

"Thank you, Leo," she said between bites. "But I want to score as high as I can on the SAT and get as much money for school as I can."

"Those are great goals, but—"

"I don't want to go to college parties and fool around. I want to get my engineering degree and go to med school."

Okay. Were they really related? Because he'd be the first to admit that when he got to college, he'd looked for where the parties were before he'd looked for the library. That wasn't to say he hadn't kicked butt to keep his grades up and land an investment banking job in New York that he'd kept for almost ten years.

He'd made some money. But the super-long hours meant he missed fresh air and rolling hills and…his family. He was all about working hard, but he liked playing hard, too. And he enjoyed creating things. Creating food.

Gia knew what she wanted; that was for sure. But how much of this was worry over leaving their father alone? Or maybe she was simply the most mature seventeen-year-old on the planet. "Are Emma and Wen going away to school?" Surely her two best friends were headed somewhere other than Blossom Glen?

"Yes, but their majors aren't as demanding as BME, and everybody says that if you want to go to med school, you can't screw up your GPA. I want to stay here where it's quiet so I can study."

He wanted to ask her about her dating life, but he didn't know how to bring it up. He'd heard his dad tell her, half jokingly (or maybe not), that there was no dating until she was eighteen. Actually, Leo would probably prefer to make that thirty or so. But he decided to table that discussion for another time.

Instead he smiled, squeezed her hand, and said, "I'm really proud of you. You know that, right?"

"Yeah, yeah," she said, finally smiling.

He got up and brought over the bakery box from yesterday. "Tessa brought these over. She said to be sure to save you some."

She tore into the box immediately. "Chocolate chip. These are the best." She pulled a perfectly shaped cannoli out and took a giant bite.

Leo cleared his throat. "Did you—do you talk to Tessa?" Because it was odd that Tessa seemed to be crossing the invisible line they'd never crossed once in all these years. With baked goods as her bait.

Clever.

She *was* clever. In the most annoying, challenging, headstrong ways. He felt completely rattled. How could he get her to change her mind and say yes?

Gia shrugged. "Sometimes she's in the bakery at night and I say hi when Dad's not around. She lets me taste test her pastries. She's really sweet."

Another person describing her as sweet? And Tessa had clearly made an impression on his sister. Hmmm. More interesting facts.

Gia shoved the rest of the cannoli into her mouth and began to gather up her things. "I've got a calc test and a track meet tomorrow, and I'm *exhausted*."

He got up to see her out the door. "Hey. I'm—I'm glad to be back home. I—missed you."

"I'm glad you're back, too." She kissed him on the cheek.

"Hey, would you do me a favor? Go with your friends tonight. I'll cover your shift." He handed her a twenty. "Pizza's on me."

She looked at him and then at the bill. "Really?"

"Really."

"Well, if you put it that way, I won't say no." Then she smiled, snatched the bill, and was gone, taking her plate into the kitchen on the way.

That left him with a little bit of hope that she was still seventeen and liked having fun. But where was that mischievous little sister of his? This one was way too serious.

That gave him more heartburn. Years ago, he'd taken his opportunity as the valedictorian of his high school class. Gone far away—taken all the scholarship money he'd gotten, plus the endowed candle factory scholarship that paid for room and board for a year, and ran, determined not to be tied down to this town. But maybe he should've been around more for Gia's sake.

He took a bite of the melt-in-your-mouth cannoli. Now all he had to do was convince his dad that serving delectable desserts like this at their restaurant was a good idea. And convince Tessa to say yes.

CHAPTER SIX

Turns out Tessa's mother and grandmother came to work the next day, and Tessa had to listen to Juliet recreate her entire conversation with Jax again. And look a second time at rings on the Internet. Finally, everyone got back to work, but she couldn't concentrate. She added too many eggs to the croissant dough and had to start over. And a bowl slipped out of her hands and shattered all over the floor.

"Is everything okay?" her mom asked.

"I—forgot to eat lunch, and I'm a little shaky. I'm going to run an errand. Be back in twenty, okay?"

She was shaking, but not from hunger, as she walked out of the shop into the bright noon sunshine and straight into Castorinis' restaurant.

Being midday, no one was sitting in any of the booths. But she could hear the clinking of pots in the kitchen.

Leo's Aunt Loretta clutched her chest and gasped.

"Um—hi," Tessa said, trying to pretend she walked into this restaurant every day instead of almost never. "Is Leo here?" She swallowed. His Uncle Cosmo ran out of the kitchen, wiping his hands on a towel, and halted abruptly on seeing Tessa. They both were looking at her like she'd sprouted an extra head or two.

"Leo," Uncle Cosmo called. "Someone's here to…see you."

Leo walked out from the kitchen wearing a white apron, looking like a hot chef.

And now a hot, *very surprised* chef.

But he kept his cool. "Tessa," he said. "What are you doing here?"

"I—I came over to talk to you about…that thing."

"That thing?"

Uncle Cosmo and Aunt Loretta exchanged glances.

"Yeah, you know. The business thing."

Leo's gaze flicked coolly from her to his family. "Uncle Cosmo, I've got the pasta sauce simmering. Can you check it?"

"Sure," Uncle Cosmo said. "Sure thing, Leo."

"I'll help you," Aunt Loretta said, scurrying after him.

Leo nodded toward the back door, then grabbed a bright blue folder off the counter. "Want to talk outside?"

Tessa nodded, stepping outside. In the little space between the two buildings, a blue vintage Corvette sat practically sparkling from the coats of wax Leo must regularly apply. His pride and joy, as everyone around town knew.

Fast cars, beautiful women. A bold plan that could lead them both to complete disaster. But at least Leo didn't hide who he was like Sam had. Tessa had thought he'd been faithful and committed, only to find he'd been neither.

Tessa couldn't help noticing the crumbling pavement, weeds taking advantage of the cracks. "Did you bring me back here because this is a great place to hide a body?"

Leo blushed. From embarrassment? Or because he really was planning on doing away with her? She hoped the former. "It's…an underutilized space."

Yes, it certainly was. She bit her tongue to not say that out loud.

"Once I get my dad on board, I'm going to turn this into an outdoor patio," he said, looking around. "It's going to be gorgeous."

"Great," she said. Old Tessa, the Tessa of yesterday, would have injected a whole lot of sarcasm into that word.

New Tessa was too nervous. And also, she realized, Leo was allowed to have his own vision. His own dreams. She respected that, even if she disliked the rest of him. And she wouldn't mock him.

He didn't seem to notice her mind wandering. "The patio is phase one of my reconstruction plan."

Always with the plans. "What's phase two?"

"I want to use that space between the buildings to expand the restaurant. Once I get people to start coming again, that is."

"Yes. About that. Attracting customers." She swallowed hard, forcing herself to set her sights on that little shop in her mind with black and white tile floors and a pink chandelier.

If she could just focus on *that*, she might get through *this*.

As he thoughtfully scratched the stubble on his cheek, his dark eyes seemed to peer deep inside of her. "The last time we spoke, I believe you were saying something about *balls* and *vultures*."

"I was…hasty."

He folded his big arms. "That right?"

She stabbed the air. "Just for the record, I'm not agreeing to this because you threatened me. I'm agreeing because I believe, as wild as it is, that your plan just might have a chance of working."

And it was the only chance she had.

"But you *are* agreeing." He tapped his chest, like he was mock-touched. "I'm glad you have so much faith in me."

"Oh, I don't have faith in you, and I also don't trust you. But I'll do what needs to be done. For our *families*."

"You sound like you're about to sacrifice yourself on the pyre."

She extended her hands. "This is as good as it gets. I don't do perky, and I don't do chipper. Take it or leave it."

He frowned. "Take or leave *what*, exactly?"

He seemed to want her to say it out loud, probably so he could feel victorious. Well, fine. "Me." She sighed heavily. "I'll marry you, Leo. I'll be your wife."

• • •

If those words sounded strange, forced out through gritted teeth, the ones Leo was about to utter next weren't any less shocking.

"Look." Leo waved the bright blue folder he held, the hallmark of Blossom Glen's biggest (well, only) realty office. "I have an appointment in fifteen minutes with a realtor. Why don't you join me? We could discuss the terms of our arrangement."

Her eyes narrowed suspiciously. "With a realtor?"

He rolled his eyes. "No, with each other. I'm buying a house."

"You're buying a house?" She sounded surprised. "That's a pretty permanent decision."

He tried to shrug nonchalantly. "Call me an optimist. Maybe you could give me some input." She looked wary, so he added, "Yeah. I mean, you'll be living there too."

"I live in a one-bedroom apartment above the garage of a very old Queen Anne. I don't know anything about buying a house."

"Well, you've lived in one, right?" He grinned. "That counts. Plus, I'm looking for something that has the potential to have a great kitchen one day. You can appreciate that." He didn't know why he'd offered for her to come with him. As a peace offering? He guessed it was just his nature to be positive. To start off on the right foot.

That is, if he could bear her quips, one-liners, and all the other ways she planned to torture him.

He walked over to his convertible and tossed the folder into the back seat.

Her eyes strayed to his Nassau Blue car and then back to him before she followed.

The top was down on this perfect day. "I think I've got an extra ball cap in the glove box if you don't want to get your hair mussed." Maybe she was that kind of woman; he didn't know his future wife at all.

She tossed him a frown over her shoulder as she headed to the car. "Isn't the point of having the top down to feel the wind in your hair?"

Oh. Okay, so she wasn't worried about her hair after all. That was kind of refreshing.

She was walking around the car, examining it carefully from every angle. In fact, she seemed to have forgotten all about his appointment. What on earth was she doing?

But at least she looked like she was going to get in the car—maybe. He walked around to the passenger side and opened the door for her before she could change her mind.

"Is this a '65 or a '66?" she asked after he got in himself and closed his door. She smoothed her hand over the white leather seats and the polished wooden dashboard. The interior smelled faintly of wax and lemon oil, which she seemed to appreciate as she took a big whiff. "Beautiful teak steering wheel. Nice seats." She fingered the shiny silver gear shift. "Original gear shift."

She was enraptured by his car. Worse, she seemed to know all about it—also shocking. But also, he had to admit, hot.

"It's a '65," he said, putting the key in the ignition. Actually, it wasn't, but he couldn't resist testing her. One glance told him she was eyeballing every last detail. "You're staring at my stick shift."

"Do you have a problem with that?" she asked fake-sweetly.

He gave an epic grin. "No, because I happen to have a very fine stick." What was it about her that made him want to spar with her right back?

"Some of these old cars don't have the original chrome gear shafts. This one is really beautiful. Shiny." Her gaze caressed the control panel. "Are you sure this is a '65?"

"What makes you think it isn't?" he asked nonchalantly. She couldn't possibly know the technicalities of this answer. Could she?

"Well," she said, "it has vertical front fender vents that look like gills."

"Which is what all '65 'vettes have."

"And '66s," she added. He looked over in disbelief. "But the fact that the word *Corvette* on the hood emblem is centered over *Sting Ray definitely* makes it a '66."

He shook his head, incredulous. "How'd you know that?" His friends didn't even know that. In fact, he wouldn't have, either, unless he'd gone to a vintage-car show last fall. Geez.

She shrugged and went silent, staring at the dashboard.

Curiosity got the best of him. "What are you—like, a vintage car lover or something?"

She gave him a wary look. "My dad used to love old cars. We used to pore over car magazines together. And every fall, we went to the classic-car show at the fairgrounds. He always wanted to own one, but of course they were too expensive. So instead he promised he'd teach me how to drive a stick."

"You never learned how to drive a stick?"

"Not the kind on a car."

He let out a snort. She was funny; he'd give her that. With a biting humor that she pulled out…when she wanted to keep people away.

It didn't seem like Tessa Montgomery allowed people to get too close.

Which was fine with him, because this was a business arrangement. He reminded himself of that as he started the car, which practically purred.

He couldn't resist digging a little deeper. "So why didn't he teach you?"

"When I was seventeen, he helped me buy a used Chevy Astro with a standard transmission. We made a date to practice on that big hill near the apple orchards. But…" She swallowed and looked out at the bakery like it was the most interesting building on the street. "But he had a heart attack. So…we never made it. But I have great memories, and it's still on *my* bucket list."

Without thinking, he touched her arm, which was smooth and warm. She startled a little and looked over at him. In that brief moment he saw the same pain reflected back that he knew far too well himself.

His mom had never lived to see him leave for college. Or graduate high school. Or watch Gia grow up. They'd passed so many milestones without her.

Suddenly he found himself clearing his throat. "I'm sorry." Then he busied himself with grabbing a pair of sunglasses from the visor and putting them on. "So," he continued, "my appointment with Indira is at one."

He kept talking before she could shut him down. "Tessa, I've been thinking a lot about this." He hadn't slept, going over and over it in his mind. "I *know* my dad would loosen up and give me some freedom with my ideas if I was married. And so would your mom. We could make this work. And once we got our businesses headed down the right tracks, we'd both be free, no strings attached. I don't see a downside. This really is win-win."

She turned and looked him in the eye. Her gaze was clear, resolute, and determined. "I get all that." She paused before continuing. "But for right now, can you show me how this thing rides?"

"Sure. As long as we have a deal."

"Only for one reason," she said with a broad smile. A nice smile. One that made him, for some reason, smile right back despite himself.

"And that would be?"

She smoothed her hand over the creamy leather seat. "I'm in love with your car."

He laughed and threw the car in reverse. In love with his car, but she still hated his guts. He guessed he'd take that compromise. For now.

CHAPTER SEVEN

A few minutes later, Tessa found herself standing in front of a large, vinyl-sided ranch with Leo and Indira Mehta, owner of Blossom Glen Realty and a regular customer at the bakery.

How Tessa went from surrendering to Leo's plan to standing here in someone's driveway, about twenty minutes from downtown, was practically beyond comprehension. It was like she couldn't even recognize her life anymore. And that was super scary but also sort of…exciting.

She couldn't let that same weird, addictive energy that flew fast between Leo and her when they sparred make her forget the seriousness of this proposition.

"Thanks for meeting us here, Indira," Leo said, shaking her hand, as pleasant as always.

"My pleasure," she said. "Glad to see you're back in town for good, Leo." Her gaze darted back and forth between the two of them. "Oh hi, Tessa. Are you two looking together?"

"No," Tessa said adamantly.

"Yes," Leo said at the same time.

"What a cute couple," Indira said, unfortunately taking the situation the wrong way. "So I think I know what's going on here. You're on the down low because of your families' feud, right? I totally get it. And you can trust me. I won't say a word."

Before Tessa could set her straight, Indira pushed the door open and stepped back, giving her spiel. "Okay, kids, this is a seventies ranch that needs some updating. It's not as old as the homes in the Blossom District, but it's bigger than a lot of those, so I thought it might be worth a look. And of course it's farther out from town, but there's more yard. You can definitely put your own stamp on it."

"That's code for *needs a lot of work*," Tessa whispered.

"How do you know that?" Leo asked.

"Experience," she hedged. Did years of binge-watching House Hunters count as experience?

They shuffled through several large rooms. "Why does it smell like mayonnaise?" Tessa asked as they entered the kitchen. She tried not to gag. That was enough for her to cross it completely off the list. But Leo whipped out his tape measure and began measuring the lurid, navy blue–stained cabinets. The kitchen was dark and ancient, with tile countertops with dirt in the grout lines. She gave him a thumbs-down sign behind Indira's back.

Tessa looked around at the dirty purple wall-to-wall carpeting, the flimsy materials, the avocado green and orange tile in the kitchen. "Everything in this house has to be redone—the bathrooms, the floors, the landscaping."

"It's mid-century modern," he said.

"More like mid-century *nightmare*," Tessa mumbled under her breath.

He didn't say a thing, but she could swear his mouth twitched.

The next house was a sprawling split-level built in the sixties. "An older couple lived here for forty years," Indira said. "It's tidy but outdated."

"And it's the best price," Leo added.

"There's no charm, no character," Tessa said, looking at the pink-and-mauve duck print in the kitchen. "No moldings, no alcoves, no nooks, no *garden*."

"Ducks are charming," Leo said, pointing up at the wallpaper.

"Ducks *are* cute," Tessa agreed. "Just not on the kitchen walls."

"Wallpaper can be removed," he said in his know-it-all voice.

"From every room?" she countered.

"I have to say, Leo," Indira said, "that Tessa may be right on this one. This would be a major undertaking. You might not have the time to devote to this if you're busy with your family's business."

"One for Tessa," Tessa said.

"One for Tessa," he agreed.

"Wait," Tessa said on the way out. "Why are you being… nice?"

He dropped his voice even lower. "Because I like my balls and want to keep them?"

She snorted.

House three was very large and modern, in a new neighborhood with lots of kids.

"Brand spanking new," Leo said. "Light, bright, airy, and completely updated. Kitchen leaves nothing to be desired, right?"

"Cookie-cutter," Tessa said flatly. "And the rooms are so large they echo."

He groaned. "Are you usually this hard to please?"

"That's not what you said last night, sweetie," she shot back.

Indira laughed, and Leo colored. Tessa couldn't let him get away with that.

"You're blushing," she said on the way outside. "How cute."

He shook his head. "Go ahead. Keep poking the bear."

"Is that what you call your private parts?" she asked sweetly.

He glared. And didn't laugh. At all. "Okay, don't get mad," she said. "I'll…tone it down a little. How's that?"

"I just don't like being poked fun of in front of people. My reputation is important now, especially with the restaurant."

"Well, I'm sorry. I don't like being called *hard to please*." Because it reminded her of Sam.

"Well, I suppose I can tone it down, too," he said in a slightly grumbly voice.

Did they just…compromise?

She stopped on the walkway near the front door. "Also, Leo, this house is huge. Is that what you really want?"

"I can definitely afford it," he said.

"I'm not talking about what you can afford." She waved her hand over the front of the house. "I don't see many things that make a house homey. If you just want a place where we won't ever run into each other, this is it. But frankly, the size makes me uncomfortable."

"I get it. The vibe is definitely not homey. It's more… mansion-y."

"That was uncharacteristically humble of you to admit that."

He stood there assessing her. Like she was a puzzle he was trying to figure out but couldn't. "Thank you."

Indira caught up to them before Tessa could marvel at the fact that they were actually communicating with each other. "House number four is the last one, and it's a beauty. It needs some TLC, and it's not the biggest, but it's cute as a dollhouse. It's in the Blossom District."

That made Tessa's heart jump. She tried to tamp down

her reaction, especially in front of Leo. Indira was talking about the old, charming section of town—the part of town *she'd* choose to live in, if she'd ever be able to save up enough for a house. And if she were going to stay. Which of course she wasn't.

The Blossom District was loaded with old homes, all unique and different. It was fun just to stroll the sidewalks and take in all the charm.

"Ready, honey?" He gave her a little side hug.

"You two are the cutest," Indira said again.

When she turned her back, Leo fake-strangled her.

"Do *you* always act like you're twelve?" she asked when she'd finally wrested free.

He laughed. "No, but I admit, when I put my arm around you back there, I really *was* secretly thinking of strangling you."

"Why does she think we're a cute couple?" Tessa asked on the way to the car after she'd finally wrested free. "All we've done is argue."

"Do you always act like that?" he asked pointedly.

She stopped walking. "Like what?"

"Negativity, negativity, negativity."

That shocked her. *Was* she negative? Had she become accustomed to things not turning out her way?

Maybe she had. "I'm sorry I'm not Mr. Sunshine like you."

"All I'm saying is," Leo continued, "it might be good to look on this as an opportunity. Make the best of it. And let people think we're a couple."

"We never really discussed moving in together." She'd just come along for the ride. Literally.

"Well, since we're in this together, I want your expertise. I want you to look at these awful spaces and envision the most beautiful kitchen that you can. *That's* what I'm looking for."

"All right. I'll give you my opinion." She crossed her arms obstinately. "Uncensored."

Before she could open the car door, he was already at her side, opening it for her. "Somehow that doesn't surprise me."

The final house, a cute century-old colonial with scalloped wood trim and blue shutters, sat on a street with big oak trees planted on the parkway, their roots making some of the sidewalk crooked. Full of charm? Yes, definitely. A money pit waiting for some suckers to buy it? *Absolutely.*

"I love this neighborhood," Tessa said as she took in the cute street. "Lilac lives a few houses down." But Leo was busy examining if the front porch steps were crooked. And viewing a few missing tiles on the slate roof. And checking to see how old the windows were. She could practically see him adding up the dollar signs.

The house was a century old, with a nice fireplace, built-in bookshelves, and wooden floors. It was light and bright, and Tessa felt like it was a perfect little dollhouse. The kitchen had clean, simple white wood cabinets…and zero counter space.

"It's so adorable," Tessa said, looking at the moldings and a tiny little alcove in the hallway that must have housed a phone.

"The kitchen doesn't have an island," Leo said in a practical tone. "And we both love to cook."

"It's large enough to add one," Indira said, glancing around. "And you wouldn't even have to knock down any walls."

Tessa looked out some sliding glass doors onto a brick patio and a cute garden that surrounded it.

"My friend Ginny from Realty Plus showed the house this morning to another couple who are considering it," Indira said. "It was the second showing for them. So if you two like it, you have to act fast."

"You have to love it, Leo," Tessa said. "Try not to feel the pressure."

"You actually know the couple, Tessa," Indira added, stopping to whisper something in Tessa's ear.

It took a minute to sink in. "Oh," she said, going quiet.

"I'm missing something here," Leo said.

"Sam and Marcy," Tessa said quietly.

"I'm sorry, Tessa," Indira said. "I didn't want to—"

"No, it's all right." She forced a smile. "No worries."

Leo was eyeing her with concern, which made her feel even worse. She liked it better when he tormented her. Anything was better than being looked at like *poor Tessa*.

Why did everyone treat her like she was fragile? She wasn't.

Sam hadn't been the right person for her. She knew that. But what he'd done still hurt.

And now he and his girlfriend wanted *this* house.

Suddenly, Tessa needed air. She mumbled something about wanting to see the little backyard and walked through the sliding door. It was just as adorable as the rest of the house, the brick patio lined with flowers bursting in a state of borderline disorder. The patio overlooked rolling green fields. In the distance, she could make out the buildings of their sweet downtown. It was a bright, beautiful sanctuary. A place to make sun tea and sit with Cosette and a good book and unwind at the end of a long day.

The longing for a life of her own resurfaced with a vengeance. A home, kids, pets.

But, she knew now, that had been a bad reason for hanging on to Sam.

Suddenly, Tessa realized that she didn't want Sam and Marcy to have a house that looked like a little dollhouse and would be perfect for a newlywed couple. Not because she somehow wanted to spite them. But because *she* wanted it.

"Hey, are you okay?" a voice behind her said. The devil, back again.

She took a big breath and steeled her shoulders. Used to hiding her struggles from her mother, her sisters, even the whole town, she barely flinched. She even managed a smile.

She was standing in front of an unruly patch of lilies of the valley, their white little blooms tipping over like tiny teacups, the air filled with their sweet, old-fashioned scent.

Leo walked up and stood beside her. "There you are."

"Just enjoying the view," she said. "And all the plants. Irises, daffodils, tulips, hydrangeas, pachysandra…" She hoped the name-dropping would distract him from the truth, which was that she was struggling to keep it together.

He looked around the tiny yard, its brick patio ingrown with weeds, the unkempt garden in need of some TLC. "Looks like the garden's in about the same shape as the rest of this place."

He knocked elbows with her.

That simple, playful gesture slayed her. She was suddenly filled with a longing so intense she felt it might crush her. For love. For a family. For a *life*.

"What if I told you I wanted people off my case for a

while?" she asked.

"Why are people on your case?"

She rolled her eyes. "You *know* why."

If she and Leo married, everyone would back off. They'd be *happy* for her instead of calling her Ice Princess or whispering behind her back. She'd be…normal.

"Screw people," he said. "Who cares what they think? What matters is what *you* want." The intensity of his gaze burned through her, sharp and assessing. "What *do* you want, Tessa?"

"I don't want to be trapped here anymore. I want…out." Her voice cracked a little, containing emotion she couldn't manage to hide. "But I have to fix our business before I can do what I want."

"Then that might entail taking a risk."

She wanted to tell him that she *was* a risk-taker. That she was ambitious and bold. But she wasn't. Not anymore. She was beaten down and…stagnant. But she didn't *want* to be that way.

"Can we talk terms? I don't expect comfort. Or friendship. Just a partnership." She didn't want him feeling sorry for her. "Zero expectations. We save our families' businesses and then part ways, clean and simple."

"Business all the way," he said, his hands in his pockets, staring at a little stone statue someone had left in the garden. "What is that thing? An elf?"

"I think it's a garden gnome." It had a pointy hat and a red jacket, and it was sitting on a mushroom. On his face was a mischievous expression, like he'd just snuck all the cookies from the cookie jar.

A quick glance behind his back revealed…sure enough, he was hiding a chocolate chip cookie behind his back.

That made her smile. It was like a good omen. An elf with baked goods. *A sign*.

"It looks like something from *Lord of the Rings*." He turned back to her. "This is just my opinion, and you'll probably cut me down to size for saying this, but sometimes overthinking isn't good."

"Leo, for God's sake, it's *marriage*."

"I'm not going to lie. It's a leap. But sometimes if you don't jump all the way, you're left hanging from the cliff. You know what I'm saying?"

For some reason, that made her teary.

"We can get along, Tessa. We can be partners. Together we can save our families."

"We *don't* get along. We can *never* be partners."

"Look, people like you. You seem to be nice to everyone… except me. I see that." The corner of his mouth quirked up. "But maybe you're a little *too* nice. Forget that Sam and Marcy looked at the house. They're thinking about it. But we can *act*."

"This is the wildest idea I've ever heard of."

He smiled then. "I'll consider that a compliment." He paused. "But just to let you know—it's going to be all right. How can it not, when this garden is protected by Gnomeland Security?"

She almost smiled at that. "Okay, what do we need to do?"

He was already pulling out his phone. "I'll make the arrangements." *The arrangements*. That sounded like a funeral. Or a mafia hit.

"I have conditions," she said, surprising herself.

He lifted a brow. "Yes?"

"This house. Get this one. If I have to live somewhere with you, I want it to be here." This house gave her a good vibe, a warm feeling. She could see someone being happy here. And for just a few months, she wanted to be that someone.

For the first time in a long time, she wanted something passionately.

"The kitchen sort of sucks," she admitted.

"Well, it's not entirely hopeless."

"There's hardly any counter space. And it needs an island."

He put his hands in his pockets. "I'm pretty good with fixing things. And…I'm okay with this house if you are." He turned like he was going to find Indira.

"I have more conditions," she said.

"Of course you do," he said with a pained expression. "Hit me."

"My mother's dues—they get waived for the entire time we're married."

His thick, well-defined brows knit down in concern. "Will she feel like that's charity?"

"She'll get over it if you sound sincere. It will help with the terrible blow this is going to be to my family. And it will lower her financial stress immediately."

"Done."

"After six months, we go our separate ways, no questions asked."

"Fine. Anything else?"

"I want you to be affectionate in public and in front of my family. So they actually believe this."

"Of course."

"And no fooling around while we're married."

He looked wary.

"I'm not going to be made a laughingstock," she said. *Been there, done that.*

"Then you've got to agree to the same."

She tapped her finger on her lips, pretending like that wasn't going to be easy. As if she had a gaggle of men who were less than eighty lined up all the way to the ice cream parlor to ask her out.

"Fine," she said. "Agreed."

She was so done with *meh.* She was done with settling.

"I have a few conditions, too," Leo added.

"Okay," she said.

"No furry animals, just to make that clear. And I like things tidy, so I'll clean my mess and you clean yours. And sometimes I can have my friends over for sports and stuff."

"So you're a neat freak?"

"No." He paused. "Okay, maybe. I'm not embarrassed to admit I like order."

Now was probably the time to tell him about Cosette. But…well, she was just a sweet little cat. She hardly coughed up any hairballs, so Mr. Neat and Tidy would barely know she was there. Tessa would mention her later. Because leaving her behind was out of the question.

Her eyes narrowed. "Tell me about the *sports and stuff.*" She imagined a gaggle of his raucous friends drinking and eating and yelling at the television, scaring poor Cosette into hiding.

"Every month, my friends and I get together and play cards, smoke some stogies, watch a game—you know, that kind of thing."

Well, whatever. Compared to her list, this was a piece of cake.

He stepped up close. So close she could see the defiant glimmer in his eyes. "You're going to buck me at every turn, aren't you?"

"Only when you're completely out of line." She gave a good long pause. "Which seems to be ninety-nine percent of the time."

"This is a roommate situation," he said. "Equal partnership, equal respect."

"Sure. But just so we're clear, I'm not one of your girl-friends with a sparkling personality who will smile and nod and fawn all over you. If that's what you're looking for in a fake wife, that's not me." His expression told her he recognized that and more.

He held out his hand. She was expecting a *pinch my nose and down the hatch* look, but instead he grinned and held out his hand. "I'm not quite sure what fawning is, but somehow I don't think you'd be into that anyway. Shake on it?"

She looked from him to his outstretched hand. Okay, well, this was it.

She could put up with his grinch-like sarcasm and his awful one-liners because a few months of suffering would buy her freedom. Precious, wonderful *freedom*.

She took his hand. Which was big enough to wrap fully and firmly around hers. And then he shook it. Firmly, purposefully, businesslike.

Except inside, it felt different. Warm, tingly, and charged, her pulse accelerating with the contact.

It was just because he wasn't hard to look at, that was for sure. Her body's reaction to pure male chemistry. *That's all.*

For what seemed like a long time, they stood there, locked in that handshake.

Indira walking out of the slider door broke the spell, causing them to drop hands. "I'm sorry to interrupt, but I have another appointment in a half hour. We can always arrange time to see more another time if you—"

"We'll offer on this one," Leo tossed over his shoulder. "You can start the paperwork."

"That's terrific," Indira said, pulling out her phone. "Did the little gnomes convince you?"

Leo gave Tessa a puzzled glance.

"Gnomes are guardians," Indira said. "They bring good luck."

Well, that was good, Tessa thought, because they were certainly going to need all the luck they could get.

• • •

On a Saturday morning a few weeks later, Tessa was shoving all her possessions into a gaggle of boxes, most of which she'd pilfered from the bakery, when Lilac and Juliet showed up.

She had to tell the two women she was closest to on this continent what was going on—she owed it to them. But how much to get into? Tessa didn't have a deceitful nature. This was only the beginning of the deceit that was sure to ensue from her sham marriage. And she didn't quite know what to do about that.

"What's going on here?" Juliet asked. She looked at the chaos that used to be Tessa's cozy apartment above the garage of the Queen Anne–style house of her landlord, Mrs. O'Hannigan. Lilac was right behind Juliet, blinking in disbelief.

Tessa had just shoved yet another stuffed box toward the door for Leo to pick up. He'd offered to start taking some loads over to the new house today with Jack's truck. She straightened up and greeted her sister and her friend. "I'm moving," she said with a fake smile and a shrug.

"We can see that," Lilac said. "But *why*?" Lilac was looking at the purple couch she'd helped Tessa pick out, the pink beads that hung between the bathroom and the main room, and the bright afghan full of colorful squares she'd crocheted, all to lend a very boho, retro, and colorful vibe.

They'd had good times here. Tessa loved this little place. Now it was all upended, like her life.

Her stomach roiled as she grabbed them by the arms and made them sit down on her purple couch. "Okay, I'm going to tell you something a little unbelievable." She took a breath to try and calm down, recognizing that she needed to spill and get this over with before she had a heart attack. "This might be a little shocking, but I need you to trust me on this. And you have to promise me you won't tell a soul."

She hadn't meant to be dramatic. But this was important. And she couldn't do this without them; she just couldn't. She took another big breath. "I hope that no matter what you think, you'll still stick with me."

"Are you sick?" Lilac went pale, which looked especially pronounced against her violet-hued hair and bright flowery outfit. "Is it cancer?"

"Is it your mental health?" Juliet added. "If it is, I'm proud you've sought help, and I'll do whatever it takes to support you."

Cosette, her little rescue cat, who was mostly furry yellow but with a little gray, too, darted out from her bedroom and scrambled across the floor, chasing the dust bunnies that had kicked up when she'd dragged out some storage boxes from under her bed. Cosette batted enthusiastically at one like it was a mouse, oblivious to the tension in the room.

"I've reconnected with Leo. Leo Castorini." She avoided looking at Juliet, whose mouth had dropped open. "We… we're in love. We bought a house. And we're getting married. Tuesday at noon. Will you both come and support me?"

No one said anything.

"It *is* a mental health issue," Juliet said. "We've got to get you out of that bakery."

Just then, Leo showed up in her doorway, wearing a ball cap backward on his head and a gray Pacers T-shirt. On the one hand, her relief to see him was palpable. On the other, she couldn't believe that she noticed he looked…hot.

"Hey," he said without batting an eye. While she was freaking. The heck. Out. "Ladies."

"You remember Juliet and Lilac," she managed.

He planted a firm kiss on her lips. Except it made an awkward smacking sound. But also made her lips tingle and sent her already skyrocketing pulse through the roof. That was when she noticed that he smelled really good. Even the spot where he'd grasped hold of her arm was tingling. She rubbed the tingles away.

"Are these boxes ready to go?" He looked at the ones she'd dragged outside the door.

She grabbed a roll of packing tape and herded him quickly out to the landing. The door closed on its own behind her.

"How's it going in there?" he asked with a smile on his beautiful face.

"Great. Considering I just told them I'm moving and

getting married to someone I didn't even speak to last week—in twenty words or less."

Leo held out his hand for the tape. "Take a break and tell me if you want these boxes labeled," he requested, ignoring what she'd just said. The open boxes in front of him contained all her books, mostly. And whatever else she could conveniently toss inside.

"You can just seal them up," she said.

He blinked.

"What?" she asked. "What is it?" Because she really had to get back inside and deal with things.

"I have a great labeling system," he said. "Blue for clothing, red for essentials like kitchen stuff, and green for hobbies." He pulled three markers out of his back pocket.

"I bet you alphabetize your books on your shelves."

"No, I arrange them by color," he said without skipping a beat. "What's in here?"

"Stuff," she hedged, too stressed to argue with him. "I—I'll sort it out later."

He hovered his marker over the box, eager to establish order with a few color-coded slashes. "May I?" he asked, wanting to see what was in the box.

"Go for it."

He riffled through the box. "Let's see. Hmm, not just cookbooks."

"Are you surprised that I actually read other kinds of books?"

He looked too interested in what he was finding to answer. "*Hamilton* by Chernow," he said, looking over the back cover.

"Did you read it?" she asked.

He flashed a grin. "I saw the musical. Does that count?" He picked up another book. "*The Godfather*?"

"I'm studying Italian families."

He laughed out loud at that. "Well, I've studied some French works in my time."

"Oh yeah? Which ones?"

"*The Hunchback of Notre-Dame*," he said with a mischievous look that told her not to believe him for a minute.

"You've actually read Victor Hugo?"

"Actually, I saw the movie. Does that count?"

She shook her head. "I really can't agree to live with you if you're one of those people who thinks the movie's always better than the book."

"I don't think that, but I'm an overachiever. I always try to read *and* watch."

She crossed her arms. "You say overachiever, I say a good BS-er."

"Ha! Good one." He was chuckling—and giving her credit for winning that round.

Their gazes locked. It occurred to Tessa that he might actually be distracting her on purpose. Nah, that would be too nice. "I've got to get back in there."

"I'm going to stop and make sure we have plenty of cleaning supplies. And I bought us a new vacuum. Consider it a wedding present," he added with a smirk.

"Yay," she said, deadpan, clapping a little.

"Oh, and I took care of the rings. For the ceremony. Unless you want a say?"

Rings and a vacuum, both in practically the same sentence. That was scary.

But not as scary as their impending wedding, just days

away. Merely the thought made her nauseous. "Thanks. I'm sure anything you picked is fine."

"All right then," he said with a definitive nod. "Good luck in there. I'll be back later with Jack's truck. And hopefully Jack, too."

She walked back into her apartment to find her friends gathered at the window, where they'd clearly been watching her.

"You weren't kidding, were you?" Juliet still sounded like she was in shock.

"No," Tessa said carefully. "I wasn't." She found herself rubbing her arm where Leo had touched it.

Lilac was scrolling through her phone. A bad sign, because it usually meant she was consulting the stars. This is what happened when you had a best friend who believed she'd been born in the Age of Aquarius.

"This is unbelievable," Lilac said.

"I know," Tessa said, "I know it's sudden, but—"

"No, I mean your horoscope." She proceeded to read from her phone. "Mars is orbiting around Neptune today, and the illuminating sun is interacting with the North Node of fate."

"That sounds really ominous," Juliet said.

Lilac looked up. "It means your life is about to be seriously shaken up."

For once, she had to agree—Lilac's horoscope was spot-on.

CHAPTER EIGHT

On the day of his wedding, on the ides of June, Leo took half an hour to dress. Considering it usually took him five minutes max on his worst days, that was saying something, but he wasn't sure exactly what. At first, he put on a black polo and khakis. The black seemed ominous and the khakis too casual. Next he tried a shirt, tie, and sportscoat, which felt more like he was attending a business lunch than his wedding.

He finally settled on black pants, a white shirt, and a striped tie, the bright blue of which, he noticed with chagrin, was a good match to Tessa's eyes. That almost made him change it, but by then he was running late. Worse, while he was tying it, his hands were shaking so much he could barely finish. And to top it all off, when he looked in the mirror, he saw his mother behind his shoulder.

"It's okay, Ma," he said as he threaded the last loop through and tugged on it. His voice cracked despite himself. "I'm doing this for all the right reasons—you'll see."

She gave him that look. That *you can't fool me* look that made him feel guilty, almost always for good reason. No one had known him like his mom. Leo loved his dad, but…well, his mom just got him emotionally in that way that moms often do, and he really missed that.

When she was fighting the cancer, he used to sit by her bed and read to her. It would get both their minds off sadder topics. They both loved thrillers. His mom would literally sit forward on her pillows in anticipation of the next surprise twist. She'd jump at the frightening parts and *oooh* and *ahhh* at the romance between the PI and the woman accused of murder whose life was in danger because she knew too many secrets. And when the danger was finally over, she'd collapse back on her pillows and sigh, exhausted but happy.

Once, when they'd just finished a book, she grabbed his hand. "Leo, I'm not going to be here to see you marry, but I *will* see you. Do you hear what I'm saying?"

"Don't talk like that." He'd shrugged away her hand in the way that teenagers do. "You're going to make it through this."

But they both knew she wouldn't.

He didn't care about marriage, Leo told himself. Life had shown him that loving someone was…painful. He liked keeping things light.

"Look at me, Leo." His mom had curved her hand under his chin, forcing him to look her in the eyes. "Smile your beautiful smile. Don't be sad. Be strong for your dad and sister. And for me. I'll be watching."

His mom herself had told him to keep smiling, to keep pushing through with as much optimism as possible. She'd understood how difficult it was going to be for all of them to lose her. She'd been trying to prepare him for the pain.

He knew now that nothing could prepare you for pain like that.

He still missed her, but he'd taken her words to heart. That was the way he attacked everything—with all he had, always looking on the brightest side. Even though, he had to admit, he'd lost his faith in some things, like magical happily ever afters. Life was too hard to expect those.

What was left was doing the best he could, for his dad

and for Gia. And doing it with a smile on his face, for their sakes.

"It's okay, Ma. I got this," he told the mirror. "You'll see."

He silently vowed to himself—and to his mother in the mirror—that he'd do everything possible to save the restaurant. That was the whole point of this marriage, plain and simple. It was secret, would serve both of them, and had a bit of an illicit tinge. There was a name for that. A Sweetheart Deal.

Despite the romantic name, it was just...business.

He'd be so busy focusing on that that he wouldn't have time for distractions like this darn attraction to Tessa. So he made the last firm tug on his tie, grabbed his suitcoat on impulse, because if you're going all the way, you might as well go all the way, and left.

Fifteen minutes later, he was standing outside of the office of his best friend, Jack, who was the mayor...no Tessa in sight. Tessa, that stubborn woman, that perpetual needle in his side—who'd refused to let him pick her up. She wanted to do it *her* way, whatever that meant. He'd finally just said *fine*, so long as she showed up. On time.

A quick scan of the municipal parking lot failed to turn up her somewhat beaten-up blue Ford Fiesta. It appeared that on top of her obstinance, her opinions, and her bucking him at every turn, the woman was apparently not punctual, either. Which was going to make his life absolutely hell for the next six months.

When he got to the fourth and top floor of the municipal building, he found Jack sitting at his desk, in front of bookshelves stuffed with biographies of famous leaders—Churchill, Roosevelt, Gandhi, Martin Luther King Jr. On a table against the wall sat the full-scale model of downtown Blossom Glen that he kept adding to in his spare time, compliments of his architecture degree from MIT.

Jack had left town and come back, bringing with him a fresh perspective that often benefitted their home town. And if he'd done it, maybe Leo could, too.

And there was Tessa, sitting in a chair wearing a lacy dress, bright pink heels on her feet, *laughing*.

Adjectives to describe her came to mind—but "punctual," while it could have made the top of the list, didn't even break the top ten.

Pretty. Great legs. *Hot.*

Okay, delete that last one.

The last time he'd heard her laugh like that was probably in high school when she'd beaten him out with the high score in AP Calc.

It was…nice, her laughter. And sort of musical. The kind that made you want to join in and laugh, too.

Nerves made him straighten his tie and clear his throat. A sense of relief flowed through him that he'd been spot-on about ditching the khakis.

"Hi Leo," Jack said, glancing up and gesturing him in. "Have a seat." As Leo walked to the front of Jack's desk, his friend was frowning.

Leo ignored the displeased look as best he could. As he dropped into the seat across from Tessa, he noticed she smelled good. Like flowers. What he imagined meadow flowers to smell like, not fancy ones.

And speaking of flowers, she didn't have a bouquet. On her wedding day. He hadn't even thought to bring one, and she somehow didn't seem the type to get one for herself. For some reason, that made him feel sad.

Just business, he reminded himself. *Don't make it personal.*

"I'd like to know what's going on here." Jack removed his long legs from the top of his desk and sat up in his chair, glancing back and forth between both of them, then riveting his gaze onto Leo. "Tessa doesn't seem inclined to explain much about why you two want to get married today. How about you?"

"Because we're busy tomorrow?"

That got a balled-up piece of paper tossed at him.

He'd purposely told Jack he had official business but didn't get into what that was on the phone—for obvious reasons. He telegraphed a warning look in Jack's direction that was supposed to mean, *Ask no questions. Just do your job.*

But Jack, the second-most obstinate person he knew, didn't seem to get that memo. "I've just spent the past fifteen minutes trying to talk Tessa out of this. I *am* your best friend, unless you've gone and gotten another one in the past week. What the *hell*, Leo?"

He tried for a nonchalant shrug. "We fell in love fast. We want to get married. That's it." Was unemotional and deadpan convincing enough? Because that was the best his nerves seemed to allow.

Jack looked at him with piercing blue eyes that never missed a trick and combed his fingers through his thick head of hair. "Are you really sticking with that story?"

Leo had never kept a secret from his best friend before. But if he told Jack the truth, he would never agree to marry them.

"As of two weeks ago, you were chatting up some woman at the Tin Cup in Cloversville." Okay, now he was playing dirty. Tessa's face colored, and that made Leo feel bad. Even though this soon-to-be-marriage was as fake as reality TV.

He had zero emotional attachment to Tessa. But what woman wanted to hear that her fiancé had been flirting with someone right before their wedding? Especially someone who'd been cheated on by that ass Sam, who'd wanted Tessa ever since high school and, from what Leo had gathered, had zero emotional growth since then. Why she'd finally given in and dated him these past few years baffled him.

He reined in his wandering mind, but one glance at Tessa herself distracted him again. She looked…she looked really nice. She wore a very pale pink lacy dress with a bright pink sash around her waist and some seriously sexy bright pink shoes. She had pretty ankles. Shapely calves, too, like she might be a runner or something.

And her hair was flowing loose and wavy around her face. Not her usual messy bun accompanied by the typical trail of flour on her cheek. Although he didn't mind the flour. It was the mark of a hardworking person—and was also kind of cute. But this look…this feminine Tessa…completely threw him.

When their gazes snared, he actually sucked in a breath because she looked worried and a little fidgety and…beautiful. There was no other word. He couldn't even lie to himself.

His nemesis was *beautiful*.

His mouth went dry. Not from attraction. Not that. Because he was robbing her of a real wedding. What if this harebrained idea failed? What would the fallout be for both their families? And he hadn't thought of this before but… what would it be for *them*?

No attachments, he reminded himself sternly. Business only. He'd make *sure* of it.

If she fell for him…well, that would throw everything off. He didn't want entanglements or hurt feelings. He'd fended that off before with women in the past.

And of course, *he* would never fall for *her*.

"So, Leo," Jack said, leaning back in his chair and tapping his fingers on the armrests. "I can see by that smitten look on your face that you might be in love with her." He addressed Tessa. "But no way are you in love with this clown." Back to Leo. "Cloversville?"

Leo opened his mouth to answer, but Tessa spoke instead. "That," she said coolly, waving her hand dismissively in the air, "was the past. A lot has happened since then, and we're totally in love." She levelled her gaze at Jack. "Can we please get on with this now?"

Jack looked at her sympathetically. "If he knocked you up, you don't have to marry him. You know that, right?"

Leo rolled his eyes. "She's not knocked up."

Jack responded by frowning deeply. "I don't want any sort of coercion here." He leaned over his desk. "Tessa, honey, don't do it."

"Oh, for the love of…" Tessa *honey*? Just how well did Jack know her? There were times when his Texas-born-and-raised friend was just too much.

Jack assessed Leo carefully. "I've known you since you were four, and I get how you throw yourself into anything with all you've got. But this…this is just…hard to stomach."

Leo felt a little torn. He caught Tessa's eye, and she seemed to agree silently that this was between the two of them.

"Neither of you is going to say anything?" his friend asked.

"Just do it, Jack—please," Leo instructed.

Jack's gaze drifted back over to Tessa. "Tessa?"

She smiled at him in a sweet way—a way she never smiled at Leo. She leaned across the desk and patted Jack's hand. Patted his hand? As in, *touched* him? Why were these two so friendly, anyway? "It's okay," Tessa said. "I'm not being coerced"—she tossed Leo a wink—"too much."

Leo stood and tugged at her elbow to help her up—and to get her away from Jack. "You heard her, Mayor. Let's do this."

A minute later, Leo was standing next to Tessa in front of the big palladium window that overlooked their hometown. As Jack dug up the words to the ceremony on his phone, Leo looked down on Main Street. The candle factory. The florist. The hardware store. The year-round Christmas shop. The art gallery, the antique stores, and the craft brewery. The green fields and rolling hills and the steeple in the distance. The sights of his growing up.

He really hadn't spent much time imagining himself marrying. Maybe in New York, at a big venue. But even then, he never dwelled on it, figuring that, if it ever happened, it would occur at least a decade down the line.

Never in a million years had he imagined that he'd be here, in Jack's office, in his tiny hometown, with a woman he barely knew. Who, despite her expert use of biting sarcasm, was trembling at his side.

"Do you have a ring?" Jack asked with a heavy sigh. "You'd better have a ring."

"I have a ring," Leo said calmly. He hadn't thought of

flowers, but he wasn't a total newb.

Tessa's gaze darted over to his. He forced himself to give her an I-got-this-covered kind of smile. Because one look in her eyes told him his Ice Princess was freaking the heck out. He'd never seen her like this before—pale, clammy, sweating. *Vulnerable.*

Suddenly, she disengaged her elbow from his. One glance revealed her suddenly puce complexion. "Excuse me, I—" Covering her mouth, she bolted from the room.

Leo moved to follow her, but Jack held him back. "Give her a minute." Being the new mayor was making him entirely too bossy. Jack still hadn't let go of his arm. "Tell me what's going on right now, or I'm not doing this."

Leo sighed and met his friend's concerned gaze. "This is the only way we can save our businesses."

Jack shook his head. "Leo, this is diabolical, even for you."

"Look, I—I know you want a better explanation, but I just need you to trust me on this." He looked his friend in the eye. "It's a marriage in name only. And you know me well enough that I wouldn't do something like this lightly, right?"

"Right, but there's got to be a better—"

"There *is* no other way." He shook himself free. "I'd like you to marry us, but if you won't, we'll just go someplace else."

Then Leo ran down the hall to the ladies' room.

• • •

Tessa hugged the porcelain bowl, her stomach churning violently. She unwound a long tail of toilet paper and wiped her tearing eyes as she knelt on the old-fashioned pink and white tile on the ladies' room floor.

At least I have a few minutes to be alone, she thought as she took in deep gulps of air to steady her spinning head.

This is no big deal, she told herself.

This wasn't really a marriage. It would all be worth it in the end. It was just for a couple of months.

As soon as she ran out of positive affirmations, she heard the door squeak open.

"Are you all right?" Leo's voice was full of concern.

Yes, he was tenacious, if she didn't know that already, but he'd followed her *here*? If the women's restroom wasn't safe, what was?

"I'm…okay," she managed, blowing her nose and rocking back on her shoes. "I'll be out in a second."

Except she wasn't okay. She was freaking the hell out.

What had she been thinking, dressing up for this, like it was a real wedding? She should have worn that biker chick T-shirt Juliet had brought her from Daytona a few years back that said *Make Love on a Harley*. Something badass. Because she was feeling anything but.

She realized Leo was still there, as evidenced by the heavy sigh he'd just expelled. A sigh of impatience? Or one of discomfort at being trapped in the ladies' room, full of tiny pink and white tiles, little baskets of feminine supplies, and a purple plastic flower arrangement between the sinks?

"Don't worry about me," she said, trying not to let her voice shake. "I'm fine. Just go."

Where was Juliet? She was the worst maid of honor ever. And no, she hadn't told Leo Juliet was coming. But too bad. She wasn't going to get married without her sister, even if this *was* a sham marriage. She needed someone on her side who would support her no matter what. Whose presence would calm her enough that she could go through with this.

Despite all their differences, that was her sister.

"Come out here," he said insistently but not unkindly. "I have water."

"I'm fine. *Really*." She was *not* going out there with puffy eyes and streaking mascara looking like Frankenstein's bride. *No. Way.*

"Tessa?" he said. She heard him pace back and forth in front of the stall. She wanted to answer him, except for some reason she started to cry. Silently, of course. But she couldn't seem to stop.

Then Leo said, "I'm coming in." She heard the thud of his hands hitting the stall door. At the same time, the bathroom door squeaked open again.

"Excuse me, young man," a woman's voice said, "but what do you think you're doing?"

Oh no. Who…?

"Oh, hi," Leo said. "I'm just talking to my…fiancée."

"Well, I'm in charge of this restroom, and you need to leave right now." It was a woman with a gravelly voice, like maybe from smoking cigarettes. "Are you okay in there, honey? If you aren't, just say the word. The police headquarters is right down the hall."

"No, ma'am, you don't understand," Leo said. "It's just— hey!"

A scuffling ensued. Was that the sound of Leo being dragged away?

The woman's voice was more distant now, echoing in the nearly empty restroom. "You can wait for her down the hall on the bench where all the couples sit, if and when she decides to come out and marry you. But until then, you need to get your butt out of here, pretty boy."

What on earth was going on out there? *Pretty boy?*

Tessa scrambled up and opened the door to see a middle-aged woman in a cleaning uniform, holding a large mop like a gun and aiming the head at Leo. Leo—big, tall, broad-shouldered Leo—was cornered between the wall and the sinks, hands up in surrender, a water bottle in one hand.

Being held hostage *by a mop*. On their wedding day.

Oh dear.

"It's all right," Tessa said. "He was…helping me. He's not dangerous."

Except somehow he was. He'd convinced her to do this, after all.

Tessa turned to the woman, who stood beside a cart stocked with toilet paper, tampons, and paper towels. "Would you mind giving us a minute?"

"Okay, but if you need something, you just give a yell. Okay?"

"Thank you," she said gratefully.

As soon as the door shut, Leo straightened his coat.

She almost cracked a smile, but he seemed a little agitated. So no mop jokes. For now. She nodded at the water bottle. "Is that for me?"

"Drink up," he said, handing over the ice-cold bottle.

She did, desperate to stop the acid burn in her throat.

Suddenly she heard a chuckle. She gave him a look that could kill.

"What? What could possibly be funny?"

"I'm sorry," he said, rubbing his hand over his mouth as if to wipe off the smile. "I can't believe you actually did something I said."

She drank again, a long draught, then wiped her mouth on the back of her hand. "Yeah, well, don't count on that becoming a habit."

"If it means anything to you, I'm sorry about this."

She flicked her gaze up to his. He did look sorry. And far too handsome. She'd always had a weakness for men in dark suits.

Whatever criticisms of him she harbored, she had to hand it to him that he'd come after her. In the ladies' room. *And* survived an attack by the tampon lady.

"I'm ready," she said.

He pulled a box out of his pocket. "I have the rings. Okay if I give mine to Jack to hold for the ceremony?"

"Sure. Of course."

He opened the garish pink restroom door with a flourish. "After you."

As she passed by him, an errant thought sent a shiver down her spine, and it suddenly occurred to her why she was upset. It was because whatever happened, she was leaving her old life behind. Not just her little apartment, her routine, her way of life, but *everything*.

She was entering new, uncharted territory—with the bakery, with Leo's family, with Leo himself—that would alter her life. Not just for six months, but *forever*.

CHAPTER NINE

When Leo reentered the office, Jack was bending over his model town with a tiny toy car in his hand. If Jack was actually pretend-driving down the pretend-streets of the pretend-town, that might possibly be cause to reassess their lifelong friendship. But not until he married them first.

"Shall we get started?" Leo took hold of Tessa's hand. He felt an urgency to get this over with before something else happened to stop them.

"Okay. Here we go again," Jack said, grabbing his phone again as they reassembled in front of his desk. "Tessa and Leo, we gather today to—"

A knock on the door had them all turning. Actually, it was more like ferocious pounding before two women burst into the room.

One of the women, a redhead, stormed up immediately to Jack and tapped him on the chest. "What kind of mayor are you?" she demanded. "How dare you marry my sister without a witness?"

"Hello, Juliet," Jack said with strained patience. "We're in Indiana. None needed."

She tossed him a scowl. Then, turning to Tessa, she said, "I'm sorry I'm late. I—I have your bouquet." She held out a small round bouquet of tiny white flowers, tied with a bright pink ribbon.

The other woman, who was blond, ran over to Tessa. "I'm here!" she said, throwing her arms around her. "You look beautiful." Her eyes overflowed with tears.

Leo realized with a bit of a shock that that had to be Tessa's youngest sister, Vivienne. His last memory of her was of a big-eyed little girl eating a chocolate cone with ice cream dripping down her chin.

Yeah. It had been a while.

The door opened again. Lilac Krause, who Leo knew was the town's children's librarian, stood there in leggings and a smock-like shirt covered with sewn-on silk flowers. "I'm not late, am I? I just ran over from toddler story time."

Leo turned to Tessa. "You called her, too?"

Tessa shrugged and gave Lilac a little wave. "She's my best friend."

"We'd better get this going before the whole town shows up," Leo said under his breath.

Tessa was crying and hugging people. "Viv! You came from *Paris*?"

Vivienne gripped Tessa's arms tightly. "I-I was on the way back anyway, can you believe it?"

"You were on the way back?" Tessa said incredulously. "But why—when?"

"Everything's fine. I just…missed everyone. It's a little strange, but Tessa, I was thinking that maybe Dad had something to do with this, you know? Maybe he didn't want me to miss your wedding."

That made Tessa tear up. Actually, it created a chain reaction of tears as everyone cried together. "Oh, Viv," Tessa said, hugging her sister tight.

"The karma of the universe," Lilac said solemnly. "There are no accidents." Which created another avalanche of tears.

"Juliet filled me in on everything," Vivienne finally said.

"Tessa, don't marry him!"

"We know what you're doing," Juliet said with all the conviction of telling a patient on the ledge not to jump. "*Don't do it*."

Aw, no. This was just what he'd hoped to avoid. Three sobbing sisters.

"And you," Juliet said, whirling on Leo next. "My sister would *never* marry you willingly! You used to laugh at her in high school. You *tormented* her about those ridiculous GPAs. How *dare* you bully her into this?" She turned back to Tessa. "Did he threaten Mom in some way? Because I don't know what else could possibly make you do this."

Leo raked his hand through his hair, took a few deep breaths, and faced Tessa.

"You're right," Tessa said to Juliet.

Okay, this was it. He might as well pull up a seat and join Jack in playing with the Hot Wheels because it was over. Decimated by sisterhood.

"You're right that this looks…suspicious." Tessa spoke very calmly, like the eldest sibling that she was. "And you're right that this is about the bakery. We *are* going to save it." Her voice wavered a little at the word *save*. "And the restaurant. As a team. But you've got it wrong." She turned to Leo, looking him square in the eyes. "I—I'm in love with Leo. And he loves me, too."

There were gasps as all eyes shifted to him. Tessa's were imploring him to stick to the script. She stood there, spine steeled, resolute. He'd give her that.

He swallowed and blocked out everyone but Tessa. She looked…miserable. And resigned.

He couldn't do it. He couldn't go through with this.

"Tessa, I—"

"Tell them, Leo," she urged, her voice more steady. "Tell them. About *us*."

"About…us?" He didn't have a clue what she was asking him for.

She took up both his hands. Hers were clammy and cold, but they gripped his like a vise. "We've always competed with each other, but that's because we're equals. Family is always the most important thing—to both of us. We've agreed to help each other achieve our dreams." She turned to her sisters. "And…and somewhere along the way, we fell in love with each other."

"Did you write those vows?" Jack patted his pockets. "Because I didn't get a copy."

Jack was right. The words were touching. And beautiful. They filled him with regret that they were wasted on a sham marriage.

He turned to Tessa's sisters. "I know you're afraid we're doing this for the wrong reasons. And it's going to be a shock to our families. But we wanted to do this before they could object. And we'll have a real wedding…next year."

"You're going to have a real wedding?" Juliet asked in a surprised tone.

"Yes, of course," Tessa said. "And you'll both be my bridesmaids."

"In the church?" Vivienne asked. "With the whole family?"

"Yes, Viv," Tessa said, looking at Leo. "In church."

He got what she was trying to do. Well, the part about family and helping each other to achieve their dreams—that was something he could hang his hat on. And it made this whole fiasco seem not quite so bad.

"All right then." Tessa gave him a nod as they lined up again in front of Jack. "No more distractions; let's do it."

"Repeat after me," Jack said. "'I, Leonides Leonardo Castorini.'"

"I, Leo," he repeated, "take you, Tessa Elizabeth Montgomery, to be my wife…"

And the rest, he didn't really remember, because his mind was wandering as he repeated the words. To her sisters, crying, but not from happiness, and to Tessa herself, who managed to get through the vows without crying but was looking a little green again.

Which really hit a guy's ego where it hurts—the realization that marrying him was so terrifying to his new wife that she pukes.

Then Jack handed over the rings.

Tessa caught sight of some sparkles, her eyes widening. "That's it?" she asked, her voice hoarse and barely audible.

"You don't like it?" he asked, his heart accelerating. He cleared his throat—damn frog.

She stared at the ring, which was platinum, surrounded by tiny diamonds alternating with sapphires. "I was expecting—something different."

She didn't care for it. Which disappointed him more than it should have. "We can exchange it for something that's more to your liking. More modern."

"It's beautiful. But expensive."

Wait a minute. She was objecting because she thought it cost *too much*? "We sort of skipped the engagement, so I wanted to make sure you had a nice ring, and there was no time to discuss it. Like I said, if you don't like it—"

Jack was standing there, his eyes darting from Tessa to

him and back again, not sure what to make of the fact that they'd essentially stopped the ceremony to have a discussion about rings.

"I really like it," she said, her deep blue eyes looking big and maybe a little frightened. "It's stunning."

Leo nodded. "Great."

She was contradicting everything he knew about her. Nothing about her was passionless. Or wily. Or deceitful. Which was a shame, because it made him want to like her. A lot.

Meanwhile, Juliet and Vivienne were standing there, their expressions alternating between shock and disbelief.

Jack cleared his throat. "Okay to go on?"

"With this ring, I thee wed," Leo repeated after Jack. He slipped the ring onto Tessa's icy finger. "And pledge you my love now and forever."

One glance in her eyes made him see things he'd rather not see—sadness. Confusion. *Dread.*

And it was then that he realized that this was not a game. Their scheme involved playing with people's lives. Lying to the people they loved.

Jack handed her a plain band. She repeated the same words and slipped it on his finger, her words and her gaze not wavering.

"You may kiss each other," Jack said.

"You won't regret this," Leo whispered before meeting her halfway for the kiss.

He didn't get as far as her lips. Because suddenly someone shouted, "Stop the wedding!"

• • •

Tessa's mother and grandmother, Leo's father, and Gia had squeezed into the now crowded room.

"No," Tessa whispered. A quick glance over at her sisters showed that Vivienne's cheeks were blazing, a telltale sign. "Viv, you didn't."

"I'm sorry," she said. "I just panicked. You wouldn't get married without Mom, would you?"

Next to her, Leo groaned. She followed his gaze to the door, where his other best friend, Noah, stood, carrying a straw basket with a handle and wearing a white tux with a black bow tie. Which officially made him better dressed than Leo. And Tessa. Combined.

"Hey, everyone," Noah said, smiling. "I brought everyone Summer's Night pillar candles." He held out the basket so Tessa could see a cluster of candles, each tied with a raffia bow. "For wedding favors." He took in the shocked faces of their parents. "Okay, maybe a little later."

"They're really sweet, Noah," Tessa said. "Thanks." Not only was Noah a good friend of Leo's, but he was also a head designer at the candle factory, which explained the party favors—which, under normal circumstances, Tessa would be really excited about.

"They smell fabulous," Lilac said, picking one up and sniffing it.

"I told you to come quick," Jack said under his breath, "not to bring presents."

"They're not presents; they're welcome gifts," Noah said. To Tessa, he added, "You are totally rocking that pink theme. If I had known, I could have coordinated the ribbons."

"A last-minute decision," Tessa said.

Tessa's mother scanned the room, noting her other

daughters huddled together, then zeroed in on Tessa. "What's going on here?"

Tessa cringed. She opened her mouth to speak, but Leo's father stepped up. "Leonides, what is the meaning of this?"

Something made her step forward. Maybe it was the fact that Leo hadn't let go of her hand, which reminded her that for better or for worse, they were in this together. "We got married," she said, holding up her hand. She had to admit, the ring *was* stunning. It almost made her forget this horrible scene.

Tessa's mother clapped a hand to her mouth, and not in a good way. Leo's father gutted his son with a look. Gia gasped. Tessa's grandmother narrowed her eyes at Leo like she could practically see remnants of Ancestor Guido's blood circulating in his veins.

Leo put his arm around Tessa. He felt stiff as a corpse. "We were just about to tell you all the good news."

"You got married in secret without telling us?" Tessa's mom said. She looked more hurt than angry.

Leo started to speak, but Tessa beat him. "It was only because of the feud, Mom. We wanted to come to both of you already married so there would be no argument or discussion." Why did she sound so calm when inside she was freaking out?

Leo looped his arm in hers, making sure to squeeze her hand. "Exactly," he confirmed. "We didn't want the feud to stop us."

Leo's dad looked at Tessa. "You're a wonderful girl," he said. "But you're a Montgomery. And Montgomerys and Castorinis don't mix."

"Exactly," Joanna said, folding her arms across her apron,

which she hadn't taken off, probably because she'd barreled over here in a panic. She swung her gaze to Tessa. "Are you sure you're not pregnant?"

"Of course not," Tessa said as if sex with Leo would be more distasteful than castor oil. But somehow, she didn't think it would be.

And why was she thinking of sex at a time like this?

"It's not sudden," Leo said, looking lovingly at Tessa, "because when you know, you know." He turned to his dad. "You and Mom knew."

"And you and Dad knew, too," Tessa added to her mom. "You've always told me that when it's right, it's right."

"I can't abide by this." Her grandmother wrung her hands. "Any family but theirs, Tessa!"

"What's that feud about, anyway?" Gia asked, examining her nails. "It's ridiculous."

"Gia, it's not ridiculous," Leo judiciously rushed to say. "It's just…longstanding. And maybe we can resolve it over time. Because now we're all family." He fake-smiled. But no one smiled back.

"Oh *mon Dieu*," Tessa's mom exclaimed.

"Have you done it yet?" his dad asked.

"Done what, Dad?" Leo asked. "Made it official? Yes."

"I think he means, is the marriage consummated yet?" her mom asked in a panicky voice as she clutched the edge of Jack's desk. "Because maybe we can reverse it."

"Mom!" Tessa exclaimed.

"What's consummated?" Gia asked, crinkling her nose. "Isn't that an entree?"

"That's *consommé*," Vivienne answered. "It's a French broth."

"Let me see that paper." Leo's dad accosted Jack, who had taken a seat behind his desk. But Jack suddenly gripped it with both hands.

"It's official, Mr. Castorini." Jack tucked the marriage certificate efficiently under his desk pad and folded his hands over it. "The only thing that will take it back is divorce."

"Oh *Dio mio*," Leo's dad exclaimed, sitting down on one of the extra chairs against the wall and rubbing his forehead.

"I feel faint." Tessa's mom collapsed beside him.

"Does somebody have water?" Juliet asked. Jack reached into a mini fridge behind his desk and pulled out a few bottles for Juliet to pass around.

"You wouldn't happen to have anything stronger in there, would you?" Juliet asked.

Tessa would have seconded that, except then Leo's dad said to her mom, "I think very highly of your daughter. She's a talented baker and a good person. It's just her *family* I'm worried about."

Her mother crossed her arms. "I just hope your son will be more faithful than his great-great-grandfather."

"Guido Castorini was not unfaithful," Leo's dad said. "He simply chose not to marry your deceitful ancestor, who wanted him for his money."

"He went on to father twelve children with three different women," Gram said.

"Gram!" Tessa said. She caught Leo's eye. And strangely, in the middle of all this confusion, he looked like he was holding back a laugh. Which had an odd effect of making her feel that he was seeing the ridiculousness of all of this, too.

"I'm sorry, Tessa," her grandmother said solemnly. "But it's the truth."

What *was* true was that her wedding day had officially turned into a farce.

"Well, everyone might need a little time to adjust," Leo said in a level voice. "But in the meantime, we've had a long day, and we're going home."

That made Leo's father perk up. "Home? Where's home?"

"We bought a house," Leo said. "In the Blossom District."

Gia jumped up and clapped her hands a little. "Oh, that's so close."

"Hold on a second, people," Jack said, standing and waving his hands. "I need Tessa and Leo back up here."

Too weary to do anything else, they obeyed his summons.

"You may now kiss…each other," Jack said.

Leo looked at Tessa. She barely knew him, but she saw something in his eyes. A steady conviction. Determination.

He was telling her silently, *let's make this convincing.*

She gave a silent nod.

And then he went in for the kiss.

His lips brushed hers lightly, tentatively, and she thought he was going to pull back and be done. But instead, he leaned in enthusiastically, his hands grasping her face in the way people kiss when it really *means* something.

Their lips met full on. His were soft and warm, and his hands were strong and gentle, and she had to grasp onto him—yikes, the lean, hard muscle—for balance.

He kissed like his personality—confident, smooth, and easy.

As he angled his jaw to kiss her more thoroughly, she found herself kissing him back, getting lost in his taste, in the feel of his mouth, of the way he lowered his hands to her waist and pulled her into him. Or did she do that herself?

He broke the kiss seconds later, pulling back. In front of her families, it was probably a solid PG.

Yet the effect was definitely *not* PG.

Because Tessa was not very clear about time and space. She felt dizzy and weak, sort of like she did in the bathroom earlier, the room spinning around her. Whatever Leo had just done with his lips, he'd made her forget all about this horrible arrangement for ten seconds. Or a year. Or however long it had lasted.

As she caught her breath and her balance, she realized that there was a lot she didn't like about Leo, but their chemistry apparently was a time bomb. A sleeping bear that must never be poked again.

Duly noted.

She was left looking into the shocked faces of her sisters, who were staring, mouths agape. Juliet was biting her nails, and Vivienne was tearing up.

As Leo moved off to talk to Gia, Jack gave Tessa a hug. "I don't know what's going on here," he said as he pulled back, "but I just wanted to ask you to please be patient with my friend Leo."

"Patient?" Of all things. "Couldn't you just say congrats?"

He chuckled. "Leo is… I honestly don't think Leo has ever thought seriously about what he wants—besides his career. You're going to force him to do that, whether he likes it or not."

"Jack is right," Noah said. "Leo's never talked about having a wife."

And now he had a wife and a cat that he didn't even know about yet. "Well, thanks, guys, for the advice," she managed, until suddenly Leo was at her side, steering her toward the door. She resisted.

"What is it?" he asked, his face pained.

"I have to throw my bouquet."

He gave her a look that said *really?*

"It's bad luck if you don't."

He dropped his voice. "Maybe you could define what bad luck is for a marriage that's only going to last for six months."

She ignored that. "Okay, ladies. Turn around."

"Tessa, no," Vivienne complained. "This is old-fashioned. It's weird."

"No it's not," Juliet said, elbowing her sister and extending her hands. "Throw it to me, Tessa."

"Just be grateful we're not doing the garter thing," Leo mumbled.

Tessa shot him a look. "That's misogynistic."

"Or the lap dance," Noah said.

Tessa startled. "The what?"

"You know," he said. "Where they give the bride a dollar."

"That's called the *dollar* dance," Jack said. "Geez."

Tessa tossed her little bouquet. There was a polite scuffle. And when all the heads bobbed up, the catcher was…her mother.

"I'll press the flowers for you," she said, holding it up.

She wanted to tell her not to bother—that she didn't want to commemorate this day at all.

"Bye," Tessa said, hugging her sisters one last time. "Talk soon, okay?" Then Tessa gave Gia a squeeze, too. Leo's sweet little sister. Tessa didn't want Gia to think Tessa was any threat to her relationship with Leo.

"Now we can be sisters," Gia said. "And you won't have to sneak cannoli to me. I'm thrilled."

Tessa hugged her back, getting a little teary. "Now we *can* be sisters."

Then Tessa's sisters walked over and hugged Gia, too. Because her sisters might individually be pains in the rear, but no one could say they weren't welcoming.

At least something good had come of this. And now it was time to go home.

Leo offered her his hand, a look of relief on his face that this was finally over, and she took it as they both walked out of the door.

They'd done it. They'd gotten married. And *that* had been the easy part.

CHAPTER TEN

It was done.

A thick, heavy silence descended as Tessa got into Leo's 'vette and the whirlwind events of the day sank in. If this were a real wedding, their family and friends would've tied cans to the rear bumper. There would be cheering and happy tears and *noise*. And real kisses, not just fake ones that sealed a deal. Even if the fake one made her stomach pitch and her heart pound nonetheless.

They were both quiet in the car on the way to the little house. She'd have given anything to retreat to her cozy garage apartment, sink onto her purple couch with her pink-and-green crocheted afghan, inviting Cosette to curl up on her lap while she watched Netflix and sipped a glass of wine. Instead, she'd be sifting through boxes for her sheets and trying to find Cosette, whom Juliet had brought over earlier, along with a few things for the fridge. She was probably hiding somewhere, shaking and completely confused.

What have I done?

Vaguely, she realized she'd never gotten around to telling Leo about Cosette. But who wouldn't love the sweetest little cat in the world?

Leo pulled his car up the little gravel driveway, got out, and walked over to the side door, sifting through several keys on an old ring.

Tessa came up behind him. "Wait," she said.

He turned to look at her. He had circles under his eyes. His thick, wavy hair was boyishly tousled after the long day, making him look very approachable and a little vulnerable.

You'd better be careful, Tessa cautioned herself. This day had held a roller coaster of emotions. It would be a shame to think that Leo was someone else just because he'd talked her out of the bathroom.

He straightened out, the keys clinking. "What is it?" he asked, not unkindly.

She hesitated. But she decided she was going to speak her truth. And maybe she'd been hanging around Lilac too much, but this particular truth was important to her, if somewhat out there. *New life, new truth* was her new motto. "It's tradition to enter through the front door."

To Leo's credit, he didn't heave a disgusted sigh. Just lifted a brow in question. "Tessa, have we done *anything* the traditional way?"

Thank goodness it was almost dark, because she felt her cheeks heat. "Well, this may be a sham marriage, but I don't want bad luck. We're starting something here, and I think we should do it right."

He leaned his long frame against the doorjamb. "I believe a person makes their own luck."

"I believe that, too," she said as he turned back to the lock. She added in a quiet voice, "But I also believe in tradition."

"Fine," he said, pulling the key out of the lock, this time with a *very* heavy sigh.

They congregated a minute later at the teal front door, a lovely color, but needing a good coat of paint. Leo turned the key, but before he could open the door, she tapped him on the shoulder.

"What is it now?" He was past trying to disguise his irritation.

She closed her eyes and swallowed. She wasn't going to hold back on who she was. "It's bad luck unless you *carry* me in. It's *ancient* tradition," she said. "Carrying the bride over the threshold keeps her away from the evil spirits on the floor."

"And so the groom has to walk through them? Nice. And what if I trip and fall? That's definitely bad luck."

She shrugged. "I didn't make the rules."

Something glinted in his eyes. "I thought that custom began because most people back then married by capture, so the bride was dragged or carried in."

"That's really disturbing," she said, rolling her eyes. "I'm not sure what 'marry by capture' is, but maybe I'll just walk in after all."

"I wouldn't want any bad luck to infect our business ventures." He bent to scoop her up but hesitated at the last second.

"What is it?" A horrible thought crossed her mind. "Oh no. Let's just forget it." This was *so* embarrassing. He was sizing her up, probably worrying about breaking his back in the process of picking her up.

Mortification crept into her cheeks, and she turned away. But he caught her arm. "What is it? What just happened?"

"Just forget this. Like you said, it's just…you don't have to carry me after all."

"Forget what? What did I miss?"

She sighed. "I get it that I'm not exactly a tiny size." *Svana's size* popped into her head. Which was crazy because she'd never even seen Svana. And why should she care, anyway?

He laughed. *Not again*. Why did he always do that?

Her anguish turned to outrage as she crossed her arms. "Are you *laughing* at me?"

He said very gently, "Tessa, I'm not laughing at you. I just—I just don't get how someone as stunning as you wouldn't be happy with having some curves."

Before she could say anything, he'd scooped her up—but not in the traditional newlywed way. Instead, he hiked her over his shoulder.

Which was appropriate, considering this upside-down day. This upside-down *marriage*.

She gave a little yelp as he whisked her through the door, closing it behind them with his foot, and stood for a moment in the dark room, lit only by the stars and the distant streetlight. Her hair fell out and hung down in an unruly curtain, making her part it with her hands to see anything.

When he deposited her upright in the middle of the living room, amid all their various boxes, couches, lamps, and wall art, she was dizzy.

And maybe not just from being whisked through the door, caveman-style.

He smiled, dusting off his hands.

"That was very untraditional," she said, a little out of breath.

"And yet I carried you over the threshold."

"Yes, you did. I suppose we're going to do this marriage our own way."

Before she could react, he flicked on their only light—a bare overhead bulb—illuminating the waist-high pileup of boxes around them. There were her purple velvet couch, her multicolored patchwork ottoman, and her teal chair. In stark contrast to her boho hippie furniture sat Leo's leather couch and clean-lined, expensive glass-topped tables, looking very clean and mid-century modern. And—very out of character—the most giant oak desk she'd ever seen, complete with a hutch full of drawers. It was already tucked into a little nook under a window overlooking the backyard.

"That thing is *huge*." Yet the space seemed made just for it.

"It was my grandfather's." Leo grabbed the matching chair, brought it over to the desk, and sat down. "It's got some really cool features."

He ran his hand lovingly over the beat-up wooden surface. "It needs some TLC, but I'm going to work on it. Watch this." He tapped a small drawer in the center of the hutch, causing it to spring open.

Tessa laughed. "That's amazing."

"That's not even the best part." Leo opened the drawer and pointed inside. In the back was *another* hidden drawer.

"Exactly what did your grandfather do that he needed secret drawers?" Tessa asked.

"When he first started out, he had a pizza shop, and he used a sauce recipe his family brought with them from Italy. Except until the day he died, he wouldn't give it to anyone."

"No one?"

"Not a soul."

"So did he hide it in the drawer?"

A long, slow grin spread over his face. "That's the best part. He left a letter for my dad with the recipe, telling him to use it as he wanted. That it was a symbol of our family's creativity and adaptability. That food feeds people but it also helps us make a living. And he left some photos of him and my grandma." He reached into the drawer and pulled them out. "She was the love of his life."

Tessa examined the old photos of a young couple, laughing, with their arms around each other, clearly very much in love.

"Together they started the restaurant. One of my dad's dreams is to make pizza again." He looked a little dreamy, like maybe that was part of his dream too. "Someday, maybe."

A pang hit her as she wondered if great loves could happen to people like her. "That's a wonderful story. These are sweet."

She handed the photos back, and he replaced them carefully in the secret drawer. "In her later years, my grandma got Alzheimer's, but Gramps visited her every day."

One thing was clear: Family was important to Leo Castorini. Regardless of his ability to make a quick sham marriage. "Funny how our families are both so family oriented, yet they let the feud go on for so many generations."

"I've tried to understand that for years. It's beyond me." He sat leaning his elbow on the desk and looking at her, amusement suddenly lighting up his eyes. "By the way, you looked pretty today. So learn to take a compliment, okay?"

He seemed serious for once. And he was being…nice. "Okay," she managed.

Maybe it was the emotion of the day, or the fact that her life had turned as topsy-turvy as a jar of marbles that had spilled and scattered and rolled everywhere, but she found herself staring at him. Swallowing past a lump in her throat. Wanting to…confide in him? Kiss him? Murder him? All *three*?

And then a little yellow blur flew by, meowing loudly.

She scooped up her cat and snuggled her against her

cheek. "Cosette! You poor thing!" She was glad for the spell to have broken. Glad for the escape.

Kicking off her too-high heels, she walked into the kitchen, looking for the box where she'd packed away the cat food.

"You have a cat?" Leo said it as if he had said, *You have a mountain lion? Escaped from an illicit animal farm?*

"She's very well-behaved," Tessa rushed to say. "And clean. You'll barely notice she's here. I—"

Tessa could tell him all kinds of things to make him sympathize, but the truth was, Cosette was a dealbreaker. Tessa wouldn't have gone anywhere without her.

"Oh," he said, sounding a little disappointed. Or was he angry? She couldn't tell.

"I've had her ever since my dad died. We found her out the back door of the bread shop, part of a whole litter of kittens. She's very sweet and affectionate." The cat and he were having a stare down, Cosette sitting on the floor, calmly winding and unwinding her tail around herself, and Leo, looking back at her like she was the devil. "It's okay to pet her," Tessa finally said.

"I'm not much of a cat person," he said. He glanced at his phone. "Listen, it's been a long day. I'm going to get settled. And I have to go out. Do you need anything?"

He suddenly sounded tight and formal. She thought of asking him if he wanted her to whip up some eggs and toast—all that they had in the fridge. But he suddenly seemed like he was in a hurry to get away.

"No, I'm fine." Tessa was realizing she had no idea where she'd packed the cat food. And her mattress was standing against the wall in the guest room, blocked in by boxes.

Weariness felt bone-deep. Where did she even begin?

"Okay, well…see you later," he said and headed out the door.

A terrible thought occurred. Was he going to see Svana? Even though he'd promised not to sleep with anyone else? Just like she'd accidentally-on-purpose not mentioned Cosette?

And, more importantly, *why* was that a terrible thought?

She suddenly felt foolish about the threshold thing. Being carried into the house did not make this a real marriage or even a friendship, no matter how boyish his grin or how appealing that thick, wonderful head of hair was.

Living with him in this adorable little place was not playing house.

They were on a mission. Project Save the Bakery/Restaurant began tomorrow.

And she'd better not forget that.

• • •

Leo's eyes were itching so bad he wanted to—well, he wanted this day to be over. They were also swelling up. And tearing. And his nose was running. And he'd sneezed at least seven times since he'd gotten into his car. At this point, even *he* was having trouble staying positive.

If he didn't get on some antihistamines right now, he was going to wake up tomorrow with his eyes swollen shut and covered with hives.

And did he ever refill that EpiPen?

He couldn't tell Tessa any of that after the day they'd just had, and after all he'd asked her to give up in order to make this arrangement work. It was clear she loved the animal, and he couldn't stand to upset her after everything he'd asked her to give up. She'd looked a little hurt by his inattention to her cat, but staying would have sent him into anaphylaxis right smack in the middle of that old living room.

Even worse, Tessa was throwing him curveballs in ways he'd never expected.

She'd had the courage to go on with the ceremony when he'd faltered. She was superstitious. All her wildly colorful boho/hippie furniture clashed with his.

What should he expect from someone who named her cat after a character from *Les Mis*?

She was the worst possible wife he could have, because just looking at her pretty curves and her long wavy hair, beautifully disheveled like that, made him…well, made him think of her in very unbusinesslike ways. And that was a very, very bad thing.

Note to self: *Never carry your wife over the threshold again.*

As he drove to the 24-hour drug store off the highway, he made himself think of just how aggravating she was. Except today, she'd *cried* when her sisters had shown up. And that moment in the bathroom—she'd looked scared and alone. Yet she'd somehow managed to convince everyone their marriage was for real.

All of these things surprised him in a way he did not want to dwell on.

He walked into the brightly lit pharmacy and bought two different kinds of antihistamines, nasal spray, and some Benadryl just in case. And some water to wash it all down.

A drug store…on his wedding night.

He thought of the shock and surprise on the faces of the people he loved. His friends, his dad, his little sister. This game they were playing…it was real. It had consequences.

He was determined to place all his focus on turning both businesses around. All he had to do was play by the script he'd already written and see this through. And take a lot of anti-cat drugs.

That would leave him no time for distractions. Especially those coming from his pretty new wife.

CHAPTER ELEVEN

"How's married life?" Vivienne asked a few nights later when she stopped to visit Tessa in the bakery. Tessa was starting to think that maybe she couldn't call what she was doing sneak baking anymore, since everyone on the planet seemed to know *exactly* where to find her.

Tessa smiled. "A big change." She hated lying to her family about her marriage. But what she'd just said happened to be 100 percent true. Even though she'd barely crossed paths with Leo since the wedding, since they were both so busy preparing to launch the next part of their plan, it was clear that both their lives had completely changed.

That included everything from having a strange coffee press and a real knife set on the kitchen counter to seeing boxer briefs in clothes baskets and smelling the spicy scent of mentholated shave cream in the bathroom. His shoes were always carefully lined up at the door, and he often spent his time before bed poring over work at his big desk. But besides being roommates, they'd had little other interactions.

Tessa nodded toward a counter stool. "Pull up a seat."

"Are you angry with me?" Vivienne asked. "That I told Mom?"

"Of course not." Tessa couldn't help smiling a little because Vivienne suddenly reminded her of when she was a little girl, coming to Tessa with her troubles. Even though now Viv was twenty-eight and all grown up, Tessa could tell by the way she was shifting her phone from hand to hand and looking around that she had something on her mind. She'd had that very same tell since she was twelve.

"I know the surprise ceremony was a little shocking for everyone," Tessa said. "But I'm so glad you and Juliet were there." Truthfully, she might not have made it through without them.

"And no one even ended up killing one another," Vivienne said with a little chuckle. "I've always liked Leo. I'm glad you guys worked things out. I always thought maybe you two would get together one day."

"You did?" Vivienne was just fourteen when their dad died and Tessa had started her senior year. It seemed to Tessa that her relationship with Leo would be the last thing Viv would remember from back then.

"Yeah. You two had this competition thing going that was really…hot. He was always overly interested in what you were doing, and you two were constantly going at it. Your chemistry's always been off the charts."

Funny that Vivienne would remember it that way. For a short time, Tessa had thought that, too. Until Leo had shown he hadn't really been interested in her at all. To be fair, she'd hurt him first. But she'd had no other choice.

With relief, Tessa noticed Vivienne looking distractedly at her phone. Hopefully that would mean no more questions.

"What are you making?" Viv scooted up to the counter and stuck her finger in the icing bowl. She was always the icing licker of the bunch. "Buttercream," she confirmed by taste test.

"Your taste buds are correct. This is *dacquoise*."

Vivienne examined the layers of cake. "I see frosting and sponge cake."

"The layers are hazelnut sponge cake, and the icing is espresso-flavored."

"How do you get the layers to line up so perfectly?"

"Ha! That's the problem. This is the third time I'm making it this week."

"It's beautiful, Tessa. It looks just like the ones in Paris."

"Thank you." She forced herself to take the compliment for once. But what she was doing now was a lot more important than baking for stress relief. The recipes she was experimenting with had stakes attached. People dining in Leo's restaurant would *eat* them, not just admire how pretty they were on YouTube.

"What do you do with the ones that don't work out?" Vivienne asked. "I wish gluten didn't hate me so I could help you with the leftovers."

"Sometimes I take them to one of the churches to serve at meetings, or if I bring them on a Thursday, Mr. Cartwright drives them to a domestic violence shelter in Indy."

"You're always thinking of other people."

"No, just being practical." That's who she was.

Not that she would begrudge her beautiful, sparkling youngest sister her glamorous Parisian life. It was just that Vivienne was a constant reminder of what Tessa's life wasn't. But she was too busy to really think about that now.

Tessa smiled. "Thank you for helping out in the bakery while you're home. I know it's a chore for you, but I want you to know it's meant a lot to me to have extra time to practice my desserts."

"I'm glad I can help in a small way." Tessa felt Vivienne's gaze on her as she iced a layer. "Because I haven't exactly been here to help the family, have I?"

Tessa stopped icing. Vivienne's blue eyes looked troubled. "You weren't *supposed* to be here, Viv. You have a life somewhere else."

"I was spoiled. I begged to go to Paris. You made sacrifices that enabled me to do that." Viv's voice was low and quiet.

Opportunity had knocked for Vivienne, and yes, they'd all sacrificed for her to take it. Although at times the fabulous photos from France had burned straight into Tessa's soul. "That's what families do, Viv."

Vivienne tapped her phone on the worn wooden counter. "I—I just want you to know that everything you did for me wasn't in vain."

Tessa reached across and grabbed her sister's hand. "Of course it wasn't. Everything worked out. You're a talented artist. One day we'll see your work in a gallery." She squeezed her sister's hand. "I'm so proud of you."

To her surprise, Vivienne swiped at her eyes.

"Are you okay?"

"I'm fine." She gave her sister a watery smile. "It's just that I see how hard you're working on your baking. And now you've found an incredible guy. And you're trying to mend fences. Everything you've accomplished, you've done right here in Blossom Glen. I'm just so happy for you, Tessa."

She was talking like *Tessa* was the one who had it all together, not her. Ha. That was ironic. Because every day Tessa woke up wondering if she'd *ever* have it together.

Tessa got up from her stool and walked around to hug her sister. "You sure you don't want to talk about anything?"

While Vivienne hesitated, Tessa felt a twinge of guilt. Asking if her sister wanted to talk when she herself was holding any number of secrets seemed really dishonest.

Vivienne let out a sigh. "No, I'm just—I'm just emotional about being back home, I guess. I missed you. And I wish I could do something to help. More than taking shifts."

Vivienne swiped at her eyes again. What was making her so emotional?

"You have no idea what a help it is to have you working in the bakery. I know how much you dislike it." Not to mention Viv couldn't eat any of the wonderful things they made. "I mean, taking two businesses on the brink of financial ruin and two families who haven't talked in a hundred years and trying to make everything work out…yeah. It's a lot. But because you're here, I can focus on baking. And I'm so grateful for that."

"'Act like you have nothing to lose,'" Vivienne said. "That's what you've always told us."

Had her overly cautious self really said that? "So you really were listening, way back then, huh?"

Vivienne, seeming anxious to change the subject, picked up Tessa's light ring. "What's this for?"

Tessa felt herself blush as she walked back around the counter to tend to her cake. "I—well, I started a little YouTube channel. To document my baking. As a way to challenge myself, mostly, to keep trying new things." She pulled out her phone and handed it to her sister. "Take a look."

"*Contessa Bakes*. You have five hundred subscribers. Interesting." Viv was tapping the phone vigorously, scrolling through, looking at her poor-quality videos, no doubt, and comments from the small handful of her followers who followed her baking escapades.

Tessa shrugged. "It's just for fun. Some people are

interested in baking techniques. Some love French cuisine or France. And others are seniors looking for a little entertainment. Honestly, posting keeps me on my toes, because people ask me questions about how I make stuff, what exactly the pastry is, the history of it, all kinds of things."

"Who's Mrs. Roseberry? She comments on every video. And she posted a pic of her cat." She held up the phone to Tessa.

"Oh, her husband died last year," Tessa said. "He was French. She's actually from South Bend. She says she's going to stop by and meet me sometime."

"That's nice. How about DrLongschlongMD?"

Tessa grabbed her phone and did what she needed to block the person. "I do get the usual creepers. But mostly it's a nice little group of people. It's just…fun." She didn't mention that it helped with loneliness. And made her feel happy because she got to share her love of baking. Which she somehow *needed* to do.

Tessa put down her phone. "Anyway, I don't have time to build my channel properly. I'm too busy trying to learn how to make new desserts."

"No, Tessa," Vivienne said emphatically. "This is actually the *perfect* time to keep posting. Do you know why? You're on the brink of doing something exciting, of putting your creations *out there*. And you're a newlywed. Have you told your people that? You *need* to keep documenting what you're doing." She tapped the phone against the counter. "I could help you."

"That sounds like a lot of work and time." Time Tessa didn't have. "Plus, I'm not very camera friendly. I mean, look at me. I've been working all day, and I'm a wreck. Honestly, I was just doing it for fun." Tessa pocketed her phone. As if that would table the discussion.

"You're looking at this all wrong." Vivienne spoke with her hands, clearly excited. "People love honesty. They love chitchat. They love…love stories. They don't care that you're not wearing lipstick." She grinned. "Plus, what you're doing here could actually help our bakery. *And* Leo's restaurant."

"You're kidding, right? I mean, all I have is a phone holder with a light ring. I can't afford special equipment, and I don't have time to learn about that technical stuff."

Viv smiled smugly. "That's why you have me." She held out a hand. "Now surrender your phone. We can start right away."

"Viv, I'm a mess! Look at me! How about we put *you* on camera?"

"You're adorable. Especially with the flour on your apron. And besides, if you attract new subscribers, you might actually make some money from your channel."

Money? Tessa surrendered to Vivienne's enthusiasm. "Okay, fine. Whatever you think."

"Great." Vivienne looked excited—and pleased. "Now as a reward, I get to lick the bowls."

"Deal." Tessa would do it. Because it was desperate times. And what did she have to lose?

CHAPTER TWELVE

Leo walked into the bakery on a "busy" Tuesday afternoon to find Tessa chatting with Arthur Gladwell and Beatrice Hawkins, two of the tenants at the senior complex he managed. As the bell tinkled above the door, Tessa looked up and saw him and did a double take.

"Hey, Tessa," he said with a wave.

"Hey there, Leo." She gave him a wave back and lost her balance with a heavy baking sheet, which clattered to a counter. Which made her blush furiously. Cute.

"Oh look, it's the newlyweds," Arthur said.

"That certainly was a rush-rush wedding," Bea said *sotto voce*, nodding solemnly. "Are you sure you don't have a bun in the oven?"

"The only buns in the oven are some ficelles, if you're interested in those," Tessa said, pointing to the long, thin breadsticks in the case.

"Hey, Arthur." Leo bent to pet Arthur's dog, Millie, who jumped up to lick his face. Which helped him ignore Tessa's furious blush. "And Bea. Nice to see you both."

"Hi, Leo," Arthur said as Tessa packed up his lunch. "The new remodel in our building is fantastic. It's like living in a brand-new apartment."

"I love the fresh paint," Beatrice said. "And the new stainless-steel refrigerator. Thank you, Leo."

"Glad you folks like it." Leo gave Millie an extra belly rub and stood.

"Wait a minute, Bea," Tessa said, tiny lines crinkling her brow. "You two are…talking." She gestured between Bea and Leo.

"Of course we're talking." Arthur pointed a thumb at Leo. "Although I'm a little jealous *this guy* asked you to marry him first."

"No," Tessa said. "I meant Bea and Leo are talking. Bea, didn't you say seniors were being evicted from your complex? By the *management*?" She raised a brow at Leo.

Arthur laughed. "If you call *evicted* the fact that some of us had to take turns spending the night across the hall in the model unit while our places were being painted and new fixtures put in."

"Oh, I might have exaggerated that just a little," Beatrice confessed, flapping her hand dismissively. "I must admit, I *was* a little discombobulated about leaving my apartment for two nights. But it was worth it."

Arthur picked up his bag and patted Leo on the back. "You got yourself a good one there. Treat her like the diamond that she is." With a wink to Tessa, he tugged on Millie's leash and helped Bea out the door.

"Arthur's very fond of you," Leo said as the door shut.

"Well, I'm very fond of him, too. He's one of the people who've helped us stay in business."

"I think he comes in for more than the egg croissants." Wait. Did he just sound jealous of an eighty-year-old who might be a little enamored of his fake wife?

She shrugged. "Well, who doesn't like company?"

Leo leaned against the bakery case and stopped the small talk. "You thought I was *evicting seniors*?"

"Maybe?" she said in a very quiet voice. He shot her a

frown. "Okay, *yes*."

He touched his chest with a dramatic gesture. "That's cold, Tessa. Really cold."

She pressed her lips together and shrugged.

That wasn't good enough. Somehow he felt a strong need to do more than joke about this. "You actually thought I was a cutthroat landlord who would stop at nothing to get what I wanted." He couldn't help pressing the issue because…because he wasn't that. And for some reason it was important that she knew it.

She fidgeted by smoothing down her apron. She was also blushing, which made him feel a little better. "I'm sorry," she said. "I mean, in my defense, you always *have* been very goal directed. And Bea said—"

"There's a big difference between *goal directed* and *cutthroat*," he said. "I'm not the villain you think I am."

"That's exactly what I'm afraid of," she said with a half smile. "But maybe I'm not who you think I am, either." She'd put her hands up on top of the bakery case. Nice hands. Hardworking hands. After work, she always put lotion on them that smelled like roses. She kept a million jars and tubes on her sink top. She was on the messy side, often tossing her clothing over chairs and on the closet floor. Yet their kitchen was always neat as a pin. She left romance novels in stacks lying open in various places around the house, especially in their living room. And she loved plants.

And wait. Did she just say she was afraid of knowing he wasn't a bad guy? Interesting. "How do I think wrong about *you*?" he asked, trying to stay on track. And forgetting why he'd come in here in the first place.

"I think you feel that I'm uptight. Not a risk-taker." She

gestured around the faded bakery. "Stuck here."

He leaned a little closer, his gaze holding hers, and dropped his voice so her mother and Vivienne, whom he supposed were in the back, couldn't hear. "I think we've both taken a pretty big risk."

Her eyes were blue like the sky on this perfect June day. For a moment, he was at a loss trying to describe their color. Sapphire? No, too dark. Nassau Blue like his 'vette? Closer.

"And I'm working as hard as I can to make that risk pay off." She straightened out and fidgeted with her apron ties, breaking his gaze. "Do you mind if I ask you another question?"

"Sure. Anything."

"Are you still seeing Svana?"

"No," he said, looking her square in the eye. "Not for months."

She nodded as she busied herself adding more bread into the bakery case.

She seemed like she was trying to figure out if she could trust him. He had to admit, she was harsh on herself, using words like *uptight* and *stuck*. And he was coming to find that she was like one of those fancy cakes she was always trying to perfect. Every time he talked with her, he found she had more and more layers. Complicated. And far more interesting than he liked to admit.

"Can I get you a sandwich?" she asked, moving on to safer subjects. "I make a killer hummus and veggie on rustic loaf."

Before he could answer, Tessa's mom walked out of the back room.

"Leo," Joanna said, wiping her hands on her apron. "Thanks for coming by. Can I show you what I need moved in the back room?"

"You came to help my *mother*?" Tessa asked.

He answered that by lifting a brow as if to say, *What's wrong with that?* Did she still think that he was going to make good on his threat about charging her interest? Which he'd just said because he was desperate, anyway.

"I'll just keep him a minute or two," Joanna said, taking his arm and purposefully steering him to the back.

He followed her through the oven room to a small room full of boxes. It also contained extra bread racks and giant sacks of flour. Not to mention a battered old table and two large, very solid-looking doors made of dark wood leaning against the wall.

"These are the original front doors to the bakery," Tessa's mother said. "They weigh a ton. Could you maybe haul them out? They're so heavy, I thought you might bring your friend Jack and move them out for us."

"Sure, no problem." Leo walked over to examine the doors. They were paneled and made of solid wood, probably walnut. Stained a dark color and clearly weather-battered. But they had a nice grain. "Nice craftsmanship," he said.

"They're over a hundred years old—a part of the bakery's history. It's a shame we can't use them anywhere."

"They are beautiful," Leo said, running his hand along the surface. "Or at least, with some TLC, they could be again."

"Tessa asked me to clear out this room so that she could store some baking things back here. She's asked me again for a shelf for her pastries, but between you and me..." She looked around surreptitiously and closed the door. "I think it would be better for her if she started her own business. Our bakery is a traditional boulangerie—it's never carried sweets in its entire history, and one shelf certainly isn't going to make her any money."

Leo's neck was prickling. Because Tessa's mom was fidgeting her hands in the exact same way Tessa did when she was nervous. And he got an uncomfortable sense that she'd brought him back here for more than just moving old doors. "Have you talked to her about this?"

He did *not* want to discuss this behind Tessa's back. They were partners in this effort, and he wasn't about to make any decisions without her.

"Well, I was actually hoping to talk to you for a moment."

Oh no.

"I don't know what she's told you, but when we lost her dad," Joanna continued, "Tessa held us together. All of us. And in doing that, she missed her chance."

"You should talk to her about this, Joanna. I think she feels—"

Before he could back politely away, Joanna thrust a piece of paper at him. "I want to sell you and your father the business."

Stunned, he let the paper drift to the floor. "What? Why?" No. Absolutely not. He did *not* want this. He held his hands up and backed away a step. He *really* did not want to take part in something that did not involve Tessa. Something serious and important.

And why on earth would her mom be trying to sell him their bakery?

Joanna picked up the paper and insisted he take it. "I know your father wants to have the ability one day to bake his own bread for the restaurant. And he'd probably like to put in a wood-fired oven for pizza, too. This would be the perfect space. I would just ask that you'd keep me on as an employee until I could make another plan."

"There's really no need—"

"Tessa's *going* to get accepted into pastry school." She clutched a religious medal on a gold chain around her neck. "And when she gets in, I don't want there to be anything holding her back."

"Have you"—Geez, he really did not want to get involved with this—"Have you considered taking out a loan?"

She snorted. "Not the way the business is doing now. I'd never get one."

"Look," Leo said, "I—Tessa and I don't have secrets." They'd concocted this plan, and they were on the same side, with the same goals. He tried to hand the paper back. "Why don't you sit down with her and talk this through?"

Joanna shot him a look that appeared way too much like Tessa at her most stubborn. "Because she would get upset, of course. I want the money to be ready for her when she needs it. So show this to your father, okay?"

"Leo, your lunch is ready," Tessa said, appearing in the doorway with a little bag and a coffee.

Before Leo walked out into the bakery, Joanna grasped his arm firmly and dropped her voice. "Please, not a word about this to her," she pleaded. "She'd never allow it."

"Joanna, I—" He knew Tessa would be upset—very, very upset if she learned her mother was trying to sell off their century-old bakery. The one she'd just fake-married him to save.

Her eyes took on a pleading expression. "Please, Leo. For Tessa."

"Leo, are you coming?" Tessa called from the front.

He heaved a sigh. "Okay, fine."

Joanna smiled and hugged him, then held him at arm's length. Her eyes filled with tears. "Thank you, Leo," she said. "I'm so grateful."

Leo was left staring at the doors, his mind whirling. Joanna was *grateful* to him for allowing her to sell him the bakery? That was like thanking him for helping to ruin everything the Montgomerys had worked for during the past hundred years.

The doors—solid, unyielding, and large—seemed to mock him for that.

"Be nice to me, or I'll make you into a kitchen island," he said in jest.

And then an idea hit him. A kitchen island. For Tessa. What a great—and needed—surprise. And a meaningful one, that she could bake her creations on something that was symbolic of her family's livelihood.

Yeah. Selling this bakery that had been in the family for generations to finance Tessa's education was a terrible idea. There *had* to be a better way.

Leo walked out into the bakery to find Sam Donovan chatting up Tessa. "So we bought this house on the west side that's got wallpaper all over the place. There are, like, ducks in the kitchen. Do you know anything about removing wallpaper?"

Leo's gaze locked with hers, and he knew they were thinking the same thing. That Sam was in for a whole lot of wallpaper removal in that house.

As Sam droned on about the woes of home ownership, Leo walked over to Tessa and draped an arm around her shoulder. "Hi, Sam. Did I hear you congratulating Tessa on our marriage?"

"Oh. That's right. Of course. Congratulations. I, um, I was just asking her if she knows anything about removing wallpaper. Marcy's tearing down two walls, but I have to somehow figure out how to get the ducks off the other two standing ones."

"That right?" Leo nuzzled Tessa's neck, not too aggressively, but he *was* a little worried she'd haul off and slap him—or worse. But she actually stretched her lovely neck a little to give him better access. Either she was playing along with him or she was liking what he was doing.

Probably the former, and he'd get a tongue lashing as soon as Sam left. Which had better be soon.

And as for himself…well, he was just doing it to prove a point.

"Well, I—I'd better be heading out," Sam said, looking uncomfortable as he edged toward the door.

"The hardware store has a steamer you can rent," Leo called as Sam looked back, and he made sure to cast an adoring gaze at Tessa.

"Why did you do that?" she asked once Sam was gone.

"Are you angry?" he asked in a low voice, in case Joanna happened to be listening.

"No— Yes— I don't know." It seemed like he wasn't the only one who was a little discombobulated.

"I was just trying to let him know what he's missing."

"What's that supposed to mean? Are you teasing me?"

That guy really did a number on her. "I'm not teasing you. I just hate assholes who treat people badly. And I don't know if you want my opinion or not, but good riddance." He dusted off his hands.

"Oh. Well, thank you." She looked at him with a penetrating gaze. "I forgot to tell him about us getting the house they wanted."

He realized with a start that he wanted to believe that *he'd* been the reason she forgot. "We were too busy pretending to act like newlyweds," he said. "Besides, they'll find out soon enough. And as far as I'm concerned, we saved that house from them."

"I think you're right. Anyway, your antics certainly got him out of here quickly."

"Happy to help."

"Oh, I nearly forgot." She pulled out a brown bag and a coffee cup. "I hope you like this," Tessa said. Then, she added, "I mean, I *know* you like a cappuccino with an extra shot of espresso and lots of whip."

"Perfect," he said, taking off the lid to find a steaming, cinnamon-smelling coffee with an intricate leaf design folded artistically into the foam.

"Did I guess right?" she asked in a whisper.

He smiled. "I'm used to plain black coffee, so this is a treat." The paper from her mom felt like it was burning a hole through his pants. He wanted to toss it out right now and never mention it. Ever. Also, the scent of Tessa's shampoo was still clinging to him, which was disconcerting. "What time are you coming home?"

"I get off at two," she said, "but I'm going to stay and try a few new recipes, so it will be a late night tonight."

"Okay, well, good luck. See you later." Wait—did he just ask her when she was coming *home*? That was a weird thing to say. Over his shoulder, he called, "Bye, Joanna. I'll bring Jack around later to help get those old doors out of your way, okay?"

"Thanks, dear. Appreciate it!" she called from the back room.

He did not want to tell his dad that Tessa's mom wanted to sell the bakery.

And he *definitely* didn't want Tessa to find out.

But maybe she wouldn't have to.

If Tessa made the bakery successful — *really* successful — his dad wouldn't be able to afford their business. And Tessa wouldn't need her mom's money. And her mom wouldn't need to sell her business.

Problem solved.

He'd do everything in his power to make that happen.

Except that shaky house of cards depended on an awful lot of *ifs*.

• • •

At eight thirty that night, Cinnamon Toast Crunch was calling Tessa's name. Bone-deep tiredness made her want to grab a bowl of her favorite comfort food, then crash for the night. She walked in the back door to find Leo in the kitchen, steam rising from a big pot and bright-colored vegetables scattered about the counter. "Hey," she managed, stifling a yawn. Good thing she was too exhausted to worry about any Leo-initiated tingles hitting her tonight.

"Hard day?" he asked as he quickly and expertly chopped an onion. "Dinner's almost ready."

Wait. He was *cooking dinner* for her? Waiting to *eat* with her? How…unexpected.

"Long day," she said. "But all good. By the way, my mom

couldn't stop singing your praises all afternoon."

"She was pretty thrilled that Jack and I got those doors out of the storage room."

"And then you spent another half hour cleaning and sweeping. She's your fan for life."

"I'm glad to hear she's not holding the feud against me. That means our plan is making a difference." He looked up and grinned, which sent a wave of tingles instantly spreading all through her. And the dreaded flush rushing furiously into her cheeks. Ugh.

There was an unidentifiable vegetable that looked like an onion, only more oblong, sitting on a cutting board. Surrounded by garlic and baby lettuce and oranges, a partially-grated hunk of parmesan and…a bottle of vodka.

Hmmm. "Trying a new recipe?" she asked.

"Nope. Making a tried-and-true one." He stopped chopping and stood up, which brought them face to face in the tiny kitchen as Tessa herself reached up to the cupboard. Tessa looked up—way up—into his eyes, which held a tinge of amusement. Over his gray T-shirt he wore an apron that said MR. GOOD LOOKIN' IS COOKIN'. There was nothing but a box of cereal between them.

He plucked it quietly out of her hands. They both stood there in the middle of the aisle, staring at each other, his mouth slowly quirking upward, while Tessa's heart began to beat steadily in her ears. "You have time for a quick shower," he finally said, gently turning her around. "Dinner is going to be so much better than a bowl of Cheerios."

"Cinnamon Toast Crunch," she called over her shoulder.

"That, too."

There was no time to think, because he didn't take no for

an answer, physically steering her out of the tiny space. "Ten minutes. And don't be late. I hate it when my food gets cold."

It's only dinner, Tessa reminded herself. Like roommates. Still, the smell of the onions and garlic, the shock of the surprise invite, and the hard muscles of Mr. Good Lookin' somehow gave her a second wind.

She walked into the kitchen ten minutes later with her hair wet, wearing shorts and a black T-shirt that said *Everything Sounds Better in French*.

Leo was tossing delicious-smelling cheesy pasta in the most enormous aluminum cooking bowl she'd ever seen. He gestured for her to pick up the bottle of red wine and two glasses that were sitting on the counter, while he grabbed the bowl and headed out the sliding door to the tiny brick patio.

There were salad plates on the table holding fancy greens and oranges and pistachios. A couple of roses from their elderly next-door neighbor Mrs. Bender's everblooming rose bushes were stuck in a bell jar in the center.

Wait. Mr. Unromantic had cut *roses* for the table?

Apparently, he'd also strung a solitary string of lights across the patio and looped them around the trunk of a big oak tree, making the tiny backyard look like a romantic fairyland.

Leo held out a chair for her. Their outdoor dining set was cobbled together from both of them—an old yellow chair from her, a blue one from him. Different colors and not matching, yet somehow together, they did. Their only other piece of furniture was an old glider, painted a bright aqua blue, a gift from Tessa's mom, who was happy to get it out of her garage.

Tessa sat down. A warm breeze blew in from the hills, and in the distance, little downtown lights were twinkling. A perfect late spring evening. "Sit. Rest. Eat," he said.

She couldn't help smiling as he held out her chair for her. "You know you just proved that you're the perfect maître d'."

"Owner," he corrected. "The *boss*." He seemed to consider that. "I believe that dinner is—should be—an experience. One to be savored and enjoyed."

Just then Cosette appeared from her travels around the garden with something in her mouth. Which she gingerly placed at Tessa's feet.

Leo startled and stepped back. "Is that a...dead..."

She bent over to examine it. "I can confirm that it is, indeed, a deceased chipmunk." Looking up, she found Leo watching reluctantly. "Didn't you ever have a cat?"

He raised a hand. "Dog person here. But even that's a commitment."

She chuckled at his obvious discomfort, so unlike the rest of his easygoing nature. "It's an offering of love and affection, so if it offends you, don't look." She reached down, lifted up the cat, and kissed her head. "You are a brilliant mouser, and Mommy is so proud." As she lowered her back down, Cosette purred, rubbed against her leg, then disappeared into the garden.

"Don't tell her that wasn't a mouse," Leo said in a low whisper, quickly whisking the "offering" into the garden with a broom.

"Hey, I may be Type A, but I don't expect perfection from my children."

"You probably want a bunch of those."

"Kids? It's probably the reason I stayed with Sam so long.

Don't you…want kids?"

He looked a little uncomfortable. "I guess I always thought of that as being down the line. Like, way down the line."

"Why is that?"

He was silent for a while, taking his time opening the wine. "My mom got sick when I was ten. The whole cancer experience sort of cut my childhood short." He paused, as if he were deciding whether to continue. "I guess I have a hard time even thinking about what it would be like to have kids myself."

She didn't quite understand it, but she saw that the sorrow of his mom's death had impacted him greatly and still did.

In a flash, he was back to being charming Leo. "My dad told me to try this tonight." He prepared to pour the wine. "His supplier said it was aged in oak barrels. Did you know you can only get two barrels from an eighty-year-old oak tree?"

"No, but that makes me feel sorry for the tree."

He rolled his eyes. "You would. Does it help that this vintage is French, and French barrels cost twice as much as American ones?"

"Yes. That does help. Thank you."

When he smiled, she felt relieved, glad to avoid more serious talk. As the bottle hovered over her glass, she held out a hand to slow his pour. "I should go back to the bakery and work more tonight."

"We've both been working eighteen hours a day. A night off and some sleep might be good for us." He raised a brow in question as he continued to hold the bottle over her glass.

"Okay, fine." She removed her hand. "But one glass is my limit. The last time we drank, I agreed to a fake marriage."

Leo tossed his head back and let out a hearty laugh. Which somehow gave her a little thrill.

He lifted his glass to hers, then waved a hand over the food. "*Mangia*. Eat."

Then he dug right in while she plucked a noodle with her fork, because suddenly she felt a little overwhelmed. With the trouble he'd gone through, with the glimpse into his inner life. With…everything.

Meanwhile, Leo had a large amount of pasta twirled around his folk when he halted. "Is something wrong?"

She set down her fork. "Just…thank you for making dinner. I appreciate it." How to tell him that in all the time she was with Sam, he'd never done this? Oh, order takeout, sure, but…no. Nothing like preparing a meal when she was too tired to even think about making one herself.

He paused with his fork almost to his mouth. "Seems like you might need someone to cook for you a little more often."

She tried to keep the conversation light. "As the oldest, I've whipped up a lot of quick meals for my sisters. Totally not the same."

"Sam didn't cook?"

That startled her. His bringing up Sam. "Not at all."

"When two people are busy in a relationship, it's nice for both to toe the line." He swirled his wine. "Sorry. I didn't mean to judge."

"Actually, you judged correctly. And you're right. My next fiancé is *definitely* going to cook like this."

"Good one." He took a sip of wine. "There's nothing like a good meal at the end of a long day—that's what my dad always says." He dove into the pasta. "My mom used to make this dish a lot. It's just butter and garlic pasta with fresh veggies. Good in a pinch, filling, delicious."

"There's more in here than butter and garlic. Mussels, for one. And some green stuff. Basil, maybe?"

"It's a secret." He grinned widely. The sight of which made her stomach flip—not good when confronted by a full meal. "If I told you, I'd have to kill you."

"Then I'll stop asking questions." She smiled over her wineglass.

"Just…enjoy it." He stopped forking it in to examine her plate. "And please tell me you're going to eat more than four noodles."

"You probably never met a carb you didn't like. I never met a carb that didn't stick to my hips."

"You have amazing hips," he said. She stopped chewing and looked up. "I mean," he said, clearing his throat, "I mean…"

She held up a hand. "You don't have to be nice. I guess I got the curves in the family."

That made him set down his fork. "I'm not being nice. You couldn't possibly not know you're stunning, Tessa."

This was getting really…awkward. He was just trying to get along. Or whatever. She shook her head. "Thanks, but time to change the subject."

"Ha. Well, let me tell you about the food. Gia and I used to eat in the restaurant every night after school. We'd literally finish our homework and sit down at a table in the back, and our dad would say, 'What do you want me to make you to eat?'"

"That sounds like a dream," Tessa said. "Did you used to

eat what was on the menu?"

"Anything we wanted. A lot of times there would be a big vat of something—like spaghetti or some *frutti di mare* or maybe even homemade pizza. It was fabulous."

"Both our cultures appreciate food," Tessa said.

"Well, except you French put four nuts on a plate and call it a meal." He said it with a deliberate, mischievous twinkle in his eye.

She couldn't let that one go. "And you Italians overflow your plates and go in for seconds."

"We have pizza." He sat back with a try-and-top-*that* expression.

"Crepes," she countered.

"You French eat *snails* and call it food."

"And you Italians douse your dishes in enough cheese to give a heart attack a heart attack."

"Frog legs."

Okay, this was war.

"Perrier," she added.

"San Pellegrino," he bit back.

"Champagne!"

"Chianti."

"*Paris*."

"*Rome*."

She threw her hands in the air. "Okay, I give up. You are still *so* competitive," she said. "But you work really hard, so I can't be too mean."

"I think competitive is…interesting. And you work just as hard." He flashed a smile that made her stomach flip.

What was it about him? This back-and-forth, this going toe-to-toe. It was kind of…exhilarating. In a bizarre way.

Leo set down his wineglass with conviction. "I'm going to do whatever it takes to save our restaurant. Not just for my family. For me, too. I'm learning more from my dad than just running the business; I'm learning about the *food*. I know if he saw how successful my ideas could be, he'd change his mind and let me try some new things. I just have to find a way to convince him."

"So why don't you do that?"

"Do what?"

"Show him your ideas in action."

"Tessa, he won't let me do farm-to-table. Or create a delivery service. Or *anything*."

"Have you thought about a trial run?"

"I've thought of just about everything." He pinched his nose in frustration. "He keeps telling me no."

"Then set something up privately. Like, showcase everything you can do on a small scale—just for him. And I'll do the dessert. It will be like a proposal. Except not on paper but in person."

Leo rubbed his chin thoughtfully.

Tessa waved her hand over the table. "Leo, look what you've done here with this simple meal—you've taken all the details and created an experience. I can tell you've loved doing it. And I loved it, too. So we can give *your dad* an experience. Show him we're serious."

"Okay, you've got me thinking. I somehow have to get him to try something out of his comfort zone."

He seemed so passionate about his ideas. Frustrated but determined. "I get how you feel," she couldn't help saying. "I feel the same way about baking." She couldn't help that her voice cracked a little. "I know what I want, Leo. And it's more than baking bread. I'm going to do everything in my power to make that happen."

He held his glass up again. "I think we just figured out what we have in common," he said.

"What's that?"

"We'll both do what it takes to have our families succeed— despite themselves. So maybe we're not as different as you think."

Maybe not. In response, she lifted her glass. "Salute."

"Santé," he said.

Their glasses clinked.

"Thank you for dinner," she said, setting down her wine and sitting back. "It was certainly unexpected."

He shrugged. "It was easy. Glad you liked it."

"It's really hard for me to hate you when you do things like this."

"Well then, maybe you shouldn't. Because I'm pretty awesome."

"Humble, too," she said with a grin. She wished he didn't look so handsome when he joked around. Because she was feeling those tingles again…everywhere.

They stood and began to clean up their plates.

Suddenly, Tessa had an idea. "I just thought of something *both* our cultures have in common. Have you heard of *faire la bise*?"

"Fair la *what*?" Leo asked.

"Cheek kissing. There are a lot of dos and don'ts about it."

"I grew up greeting all our relatives like that. But I didn't think there were rules."

She stopped stacking plates. "Oh, yes. Strict rules. For example, you never put your lips on someone's cheek."

"Yep. Just touch cheeks."

"And you never say MWUAH. Just let your lips do the talking." She kissed the air to demonstrate, her lips making a little smack. "And sometimes you can put your hand on the other person's shoulder."

"What does that look like?" He frowned.

"Okay, just stand there," she said. "Ah! Hello, my friend," she said in a French accent, walking up to him. "How was your day?" She placed her hands on his shoulders and leaned in, intending to graze his cheek with hers. Except he turned at the last moment and their noses bumped.

"Okay," she said. "Let's agree that I'm going left first. So offer me your right cheek, okay?"

Except Tessa was slowly realizing that this little game was turning into a huge mistake. Because sitting across a table from Leo, admiring him and his nice lips from afar, was one thing, but actually touching him was another. Even if it had only been a nose bump.

Looked like just one glass of wine was one too many around him.

Although she was sober as a preacher and completely coherent.

"Okay, got it." His eyes were lit with amusement. Clearly he was just thinking of this as…well, whatever it had been before she'd overthought it.

The air between them buzzed with currents. Unwanted, complicated, but definitely there.

Leo just stood still with a little half smile. And she couldn't read him at all. Like, could it be possible her whole body was ready to burst into flames while he was completely unaffected?

There was nothing to do but finish this and back up. As quickly as she could. "Ah, hello, Renaldo, so lovely to see you again," she said in her best French accent. Then she air-kissed both cheeks, making a polite little smack with her lips. This time he offered his cheek the right way, and it was over in seconds.

Whew. Cheek-kissing lesson over. *Note to self: bad idea.*

Except when Tessa released a breath and started to pull away, he grabbed hold of her arms and tugged her closer. And kissed her cheek. For real.

Her pulse jumped. Every muscle froze. The short, brief contact of his lips left a burning sensation on her cheek, and the firm, encompassing grasp of his hands felt imprinted on her cool skin.

"That's cheating," she said, struggling for lightness, but her voice came out raspy and hoarse.

She flicked her gaze up to his beautiful brown eyes, the same exact color of how she loved her coffee. He was staring at her—intensely. And she could not tear her gaze away. "Oh, Countess," he said slowly, his mouth turning up in the slight-est smile. "I *never* cheat."

Countess? She couldn't help the flush that rose to her cheeks. Because it was kind of cute. And very flirty.

Before she could say anything, he bent his head and lowered his lips.

She wouldn't be able to remember later who initiated the contact, but somehow—for the first time ever—they actually met in the middle.

He kissed her tentatively, slowly—at first. He tasted like wine and smelled like soap, and the way their lips moved together was a long, slow dance that became more intense, more heated—like water on the stove coming to an inevitable boil.

His arms slid softly to her waist, and she leaned into his hard body. The contact was electric, making her head swim and her knees weaken and the quiet, now-starlit little patio spin out around them.

Leo's lips were soft and warm and oh yes, very knowledgeable about kissing, and suddenly she was lost in the feel of him, his lean hardness, the gentle fierceness of his touch.

The kisses continued, deeper and more thorough. Leo took his time, moving over her mouth slowly. He savored her like he might his delicious food, kissing her with gusto, with assurance, and without compunction. His noticeable enthusiasm made her forget all her panic, all her reservations, and she found herself wrapping her arms around him to hang on as she lost her balance and her common sense.

The loud creak of the rusty back gate made them jump apart.

Tessa, dazed, pressed her lips together and struggled to get her weakened legs to hold her upright as Leo broke away and faced the gate, standing protectively in front of her. Someone was struggling with the rusty latch and cursing… someone who was crying.

Juliet.

Leo got to her first, unhooked the creaky latch, and opened the gate, steadying her by the elbow as he steered her toward Tessa. Cosette, who had padded out of the pachysandra to greet her, sensed something was off and bolted back into the brush.

"I'm so sorry," Juliet said, taking in the set table and the romantic setting. "I'm interrupting. I—"

"We were just having dinner." Tessa glanced at Leo, who nodded. She ran a hand along her lips, which were still tingling from his kisses. *Yikes. What just happened?*

As soon as she reached Tessa, Juliet's face screwed up in pain. "Jax broke up with me," she blurted. "For good." She burst into tears again.

Thank goodness was Tessa's first thought as she took her sobbing sister in her arms. "I'm so sorry, honey," she said. Jax was a jerk, but she was still heartbroken for her. Tessa comforted her sister, but she couldn't seem to stop the breathless, disoriented feeling that made her feel like she'd just stepped off a spinning amusement park ride.

Which was unlike anything she'd ever felt before with Sam.

Juliet dabbed at her eyes. "I'm ruining your evening. I tried your phone, but you didn't answer, so I thought it would be okay—"

"It's always okay," Leo interrupted. He sent Tessa a look that said *You take it from here.* "There's plenty of pasta left if you're, um, hungry, and I… I'll just clean up." He gave Tessa a little nod. "I'll be in the kitchen."

She mouthed *thank you* as she ushered her sister onto the glider. "Are you hungry?" She got a head shake and a sob. At the back door, Leo handed over a box of Kleenex that Tessa offered to her sister. "What happened?"

Juliet sobbed and plucked out three tissues. "I should have known when he cancelled the hike he said we'd take. Instead we went to dinner at that new winery in River Bend, but I just sensed something was…off. He seemed distracted the whole time, constantly glancing at his phone, jumping when it went off. When he left for the restroom, his phone was still on the table, and I picked it up. He'd been looking at a photo of a brand-new tattoo of his name on a body part that doesn't ordinarily see the light of day. Oh Tessa, I can't believe I took him back this last time. And I can't believe this happened *again*."

Again? Tessa bit back saying something that would upset Juliet further. Like the fact that she was going to string Jax up by his balls.

"I'm so stupid," Juliet said tearfully. "I thought he was going to propose, but he'd planned to break up all along. Over a nice dinner. Who does that?"

Tessa rubbed Juliet's back, something she'd done often in the past for both her sisters. And she wondered, were there any good men left in the world?

Leo is a good man, a voice inside of her whispered. A *really* good man. Who cooks. And brings Kleenex at exactly the right time.

She shook that voice out of her head. "Juliet, you always think the best of everyone." That seemed a lot better than *why would you ever take this awful man back in the first place?*

"I knew in my heart it was wrong, Tessa, but I did it anyway. I was…hopeful. I *needed* this to work."

She could relate. Hadn't she'd stayed with Sam because he was better than nothing? Because she feared no one would ever come around again?

"You're worth more than Jax," Tessa said. "Don't settle."

Leo came out of the house with a bowl of steaming pasta and a big glass of ice water. Which gave Tessa a heart pang. Because he hadn't run for the hills at the sight of a crying woman as Sam had, who made himself scarce nearly every time one of her sisters was in crisis. Leo set the food down on the table. "My mom used to say a good meal cures all heartache."

Aw geez. The guy not only wasn't afraid of crying women—he fed them, too.

And he didn't even evict seniors.

And he'd spent an hour lending his muscle to help his mom clean out that storage room today.

And, and, and.

"Thank you, Leo," Juliet said, blowing her nose. "Maybe I will. It smells terrific."

"I'll be upstairs," he said, hitching a thumb toward the house. "Call me if you need anything."

Tessa gave a little wave of thanks while Juliet gulped down the water. She tried to calm the fluttery feeling in her stomach. And not be like Juliet, who *always* got swept away.

It was easy to tell yourself stories to believe what you wanted.

Leo might be a fantastic chef whose adorable dinner left stars in her eyes. And he might have a kind side she'd never seen before. And he certainly possessed that magic combination of qualities that fired up her hormones, but she had to be honest with herself.

He didn't do relationships—he'd said so himself—and that was something she could pretend might change, but did people ever really change? Was he so wounded from his mom's death that he'd never thought about having kids? He was another heartache waiting to happen, and she'd barely survived her last one in this town.

Also, she didn't want to get stuck here, as she had with Sam. A man had made her stay in this town a lot longer than she'd ever wanted. She couldn't let another one keep her from her dreams.

She and Leo were both hardworking and ambitious people. Together, they could combine their talents and succeed. She hoped she could trust him enough to achieve their goals.

Save the business, then save yourself.

She couldn't let a few kisses stand in the way of her dreams.

That was the goal—to get the bakery back on its feet so she could leave. And she couldn't ever forget that.

CHAPTER THIRTEEN

A knock on Leo's bedroom door sometime later made him look up from the book he was reading in bed. But he didn't even get a chance to say *come in* before the door opened and Tessa walked in, tossing a pillow with a bright floral case onto his slate gray bedding and shutting the door behind her.

He'd been trying to read his book, a bestselling thriller, the best he could. But she kept popping up in his thoughts, sweet-smelling and soft. And those kisses kept replaying in his mind, over and over—the taste of her lips, the little murmuring sounds of pleasure she made in her throat, the feel of her melting against him in the tiny fragrant garden. So seeing her in a robe and little PJ shorts with cupcakes on them and carrying a pillow into his bedroom...well, it was like his fantasies had just come true. He had to blink twice to make sure it was really her.

He lifted a brow. "Things aren't going well, I take it?"

"Juliet ate your delicious pasta, and I made her some tea. And then I put her to bed in my room. She's going to have to get her things out of Jax's apartment tomorrow."

"I get it." He set his book on the nightstand. "But why are you here?"

He already knew. But he prayed it wasn't true. Because if she had to spend the night in this room with him, he wasn't sure he could control the outcome.

She stared at him like he was a Neanderthal, thick-skulled and dense. Despite the formidable expression he thought he wore, she moved right around to the other side of his bed, kicking off her slippers and unfastening her robe. Making herself at home.

Turns out, underneath she had on a T-shirt that said KISS MY CUPCAKE.

He was doomed.

"I have to stay here tonight," she announced as she crawled into his bed.

That made him look above his reading glasses at her. "*Have to* is strong language, Countess."

"Juliet already suspects things," Tessa said in her don't-you-get-it voice. "She saw a bunch of my stuff in that bedroom downstairs, and I told her the house has no closet space so I commandeered that room for my clothes."

"Did she believe you?"

"I think so, but she'd never believe it if she caught me sleeping on the couch. And there's something else... She keeps asking me things. Like she knows something's not right. So I couldn't take a chance." He must've still looked incredulous because she said, slowly and patiently, "Married people *sleep together*."

"Oh, okay," he said, starting to turn down the sheets. He made sure to toss her a wolfish grin. "Well, in that case, I'm happy to oblige."

For that, he got a pillow tossed at him. It smelled like her shampoo.

"I said *sleep*," she groaned. But he thought he saw her mouth turn up a little. "Do you have a sleeping bag?"

"Nope."

"Extra blanket?"

"Nope."

"I don't suppose you're feeling chivalrous?"

"As in, 'No, no, please, let me take the floor'? Not at all. Chivalry is dead. I'm all about equality."

"Okay, fine. I'm exhausted, and I won't take up much space."

"Don't you think we need to talk about what happened in the garden?"

"No."

"No as in, *absolutely not*?"

"No as in, *never. Again.* We just got…carried away by that ridiculous competition."

"You mean the which-country-is-better competition? And here I thought Italy won."

She waved her hand in the air. "Things like that are bound to happen when two adults live closely together like this. And I don't do casual. We shouldn't let the pretending get to us, you know?"

"Says the woman before she climbs into the man's bed."

She looked like she wished she had something else to throw at him. "Leo, I don't know where else to go."

"Okay, I get it. And I get how we're both not seeing anyone else right now and we just…slipped." He sighed and picked up his book. The words were insensible ink blots, and his heart was pounding so loudly he felt like his whole body was vibrating. What the hell was he doing? This was like letting a grenade into his bed.

She was about to pull back the covers and launch into his bed when she stopped and looked at him. "You're wearing clothes, right?"

His grin spread despite himself. She was so much fun to tease.

"Leo. Be serious."

"It's really hot tonight," he said, using the book to fan his face. "Enter at your own risk, Countess."

She shook her head. "You know what? You can joke all you want. I'm so tired I don't even care as long as you stay on your side."

He flapped down the covers, revealing navy boxers. "Don't get all hot and bothered. I'm decent."

She slid into his bed, collapsing onto the pillow and lying with her back to him.

That gave him a great view of her excellent cupcakes.

It wasn't like she was wearing anything revealing. But the sight of her in his bed, even turned away from him, made every nerve jump.

Her dark hair was splayed all over the pillow, her legs were toned and tan and looked like they'd be soft as silk, and her sweet curves were visible under the sheet. So close. *Too* close. And why was he having these thoughts? Because he was a man; that was it. With a very sexy woman inches from him. *In his bed*.

Not to mention the fact that just a little while ago, they'd had their tongues down each other's throats.

Following her lead, he took off his reading glasses, set them on his book, and turned out the light. For a moment they both lay there, listening to the sounds of the summer night entering through the open windows—the crickets, a motorcycle revving in the distance, the intermittent squawk of an insomniac bird. The delicious smell of citrus—her soap or body wash or whatever it was—drifted up to him from across the bed.

She smelled good enough to eat.

He snuck a glance. Now she'd rolled over on her back, one hand draped across her forehead.

Suddenly, her eyes snapped open, and she turned to him. "Why are you looking at me?"

The motion made her hair spill over. A thick, silky mass. Enough for someone to get lost in.

"I don't know," he said, clearing his throat. "Maybe it's because I'm still a little thrown that you're *in my bed*."

The moon shone on her face and reflected off her shiny hair. "I'm sorry, Leo. My sister was so distressed. You don't mind that she's staying over, do you?"

"Nah," he said, pulling the sheet around him and turning to the other side. "We'll make her pancakes in the morning."

"Thanks. I—appreciate it. I've got to go into the bakery at six, then I'm meeting your sister for breakfast around ten. Juliet promised she'd be up and out pretty early."

"No problem." He paused a few beats. "Tessa, can I offer some advice?"

"That sounds a little scary, but sure."

"Your sisters depend on you a lot. Which is sort of good. But…maybe you should try not picking them up off the ground all the time. Maybe they've gotten a little too used to you always being there for them over the years."

She sat up, her anger flaring. "I couldn't turn them away when they're in trouble."

"No. I wouldn't expect you to. That's not my point. But…I don't know. Maybe treat them more like you're their sister rather than their mother. Like, I'm just looking on from the outside, but it seems like maybe they rely on you for a lot."

"Okay. I'll think about that. Sleep well." He heard her roll over.

Okay, so much for that.

After a minute, her breathing became steady and even. He could see the outline of her body under his blanket, with one lovely leg on top of the covers. He forced himself to turn toward the wall—the only way he could stop himself from touching her.

The plan was in motion, and he had to stick to the script.

Except having Tessa in his bed was *not* part of the script.

Any playing in the sheets would lead to disaster. And he would never want to hurt her. He didn't do serious, and she didn't *not* do serious.

And in the meantime, he was going to need a few things.

A cold shower. A bigger house. And a less-sexy fake wife.

• • •

Leo awakened right before dawn, the sky just starting to lighten. As he came to consciousness, he was very aware of that same citrusy, floral scent he could only describe as… Tessa.

Make that Tessa's *hair*. His nose was in it. He jerked back his head, only to find that things were far worse than he thought.

He was *spooning* his wife. Silky strands of hair tickled his cheek, his body curving gently around hers, his arm draped across her waist, her calf resting against his shin.

For a second, he froze. His body seemed to conform effortlessly to hers. Her breathing was calm and soothing, and her warmth and softness could make a man do out-of-control things.

He shook those thoughts away and extricated his foot.

As he quietly slid it back, he noticed something else. The cat was asleep at their feet.

And Leo was still breathing.

A miracle of modern medicine, brought on by antihistamines and the desensitization shots he'd just begun at the allergist's last week.

Painstakingly, inch by inch, he extracted himself from her warmth. Cosette, looking highly offended by his movement, jumped down and hit the wood floor with a soft thud.

Tessa didn't move. Thank goodness. Because if she woke up, he'd never live this down.

He'd gotten himself away from her warmth, her scent, her lovely curves, just in time.

"I made coffee," Juliet said as soon as his foot hit the bottom stair, pointing to the coffeemaker. She was wearing one of Tessa's T-shirts, judging by the big *Bonjour!* across it, and a pair of running shorts. "Thanks for letting me stay last night. Tessa doesn't think her old apartment is rented yet, so I'm going to go talk to her landlord right away."

"No worries if you need to stay longer." *Please don't stay longer*, he thought. It was only spooning this time, but who knew what another night with Tessa in his bed would bring?

He'd just taken his antihistamine and was shuddering at that thought when the cat somehow managed to whiz by his feet and claim her freedom out the sliding door.

"Oh, sorry," Juliet said. "I came in to get more coffee and I accidentally left the door open." She followed Leo out into the backyard.

"Cosette! Come back here!" He had a busy day ahead, and he needed to find this cat now. Plus, he wasn't going to be responsible for losing Tessa's number one creature.

"You do know Cosette is a cat, not a dog, right?" Juliet asked from the edge of the patio, where she was sipping her coffee.

All he knew was that if this animal ran away, Tessa was going to kill him. "Cosy! Cosette! Cosetta! Come here, girl!" He bent over and patted his thighs. The cat looked at him from atop the gnome's mushroom in the middle of the garden and gave him what he swore was an *eff-u* look before disappearing into the ground cover.

The desensitization therapy might be working, but he was a little nervous about touching the cat so soon. But what else could he do?

"Cosette is fine. But now that we're out here, I have something to say."

"Okaaay," he said, wondering if Vivienne was this bossy, too. Because there was a giant hole in the fence he hadn't gotten to fix yet, and if this cat bolted, Tessa would never forgive him.

And whatever Juliet was about to say was definitely going to affect whether or not he made those pancakes.

"Tessa's always taken care of us," Juliet said. "And she never asks us to take care of her. But that doesn't mean we don't have her back."

He straightened out from the middle of the pachysandra, a prickle at his neck. "What are you saying?"

She shook her head solemnly. "Tessa's had an awful year. I don't really understand what's going on here, but this little arrangement is tying her up and preventing her from meeting someone else. Someone *decent* who really cares about her. No offense, Leo—you make great pasta, but…my sister never would have married you so suddenly. Not for real."

He narrowed his eyes. Was she really onto them? And should he take offense that Juliet had told him he wasn't great marriage material?

"You have no idea what it's like to be a woman in a small town, do you? She lost a fiancé. Which might actually be a good thing, but if you two part ways, she's going to be marked forever."

He knew Juliet had a flare for drama. But *forever*? That seemed a bit much, even for her. "What are you talking about?"

"The gossip. The whispering. It will make her put up even more of a wall so that if a man even tries to get close, she'll shut him down. She's really good at that."

She *was* really good at that. But she seemed to have lost her edge with him, judging by those kisses last night.

Which were a *huge* mistake.

Tessa acted tough and strong on the outside, but she was like one of her own cream puffs on the inside—soft, melty.

Vulnerable.

"Tessa's spent her whole life taking care of us. It's time for her to finally do what she wants. I hope you appreciate that."

"I do." He was about a foot from the cat, who was now sitting on a rock in the middle of the pachysandra, licking her paw. One step forward and a quick swoop, and he'd have her.

"She deserves someone to respect her," Juliet continued. "To treat her right. She's capable of doing anything for people she loves." She paused a long time, as if debating saying more. "Like throwing that scholarship."

Leo's swipe at getting the cat missed, and she scurried off to the far corner of the garden, next to the wire fence—and the hole he hadn't yet fixed. He straightened up and narrowed his eyes at Juliet. "*What* scholarship?"

Juliet ignored his question. "I don't really know what's going on here, but I do know that you wouldn't be asking that question if you really knew her." Juliet walked past him and into the garden, where the cat was delicately sniffing some chives, and scooped her up with one hand. "Sorry, sweetie," she said, setting her coffee cup down on the table and rubbing the cat's head. As she moved to open the sliding door, Cosette almost wiggled out of her arms before Juliet could scoot her inside.

"This cat, I swear," Juliet said. "The only one she loves is Tessa."

As he stopped for a second to let Juliet's words sink in, the way his gut clenched told him everything. There was only one scholarship. The scholarship that had allowed him to leave this town and experience the world and get a great education and jumpstart his life and his dreams.

That scholarship.

"I'm not saying she did it for you," Juliet said. "She did it for me. For me and Viv, actually, but especially for *me*." Juliet was staring at him like he was clueless. Which, actually, he sort of was. "You really don't know what happened, do you?" she asked. "You'll have to ask Tessa. But Leo, if you treat her wrong, or if you let her *actually* fall in love with you, I swear, I will unleash all of the Montgomery wrath on you like a curse for the rest of your life. You may have everyone else fooled, but not me. And I *will* come after you if you hurt my sister. *Capisce*?"

"*Capisce*," he said quietly. He had no idea what Juliet knew or didn't know. But he respected fidelity. And sisterly love.

Of course he didn't tell her this, but he was *excellent* at maintaining boundaries. And he would never lead Tessa on. Well, at least he *thought* he knew his boundaries—until last night, anyway.

But now he'd be sure to make them more secure than ever. Which he could do, because Leo *always* maintained control. His heart was *never* in jeopardy.

That didn't scare him nearly as much as thinking about Tessa throwing that scholarship.

They'd *both* wanted that scholarship more than anything. They'd *both* believed anything was possible with hard work and grit. But *he'd* been the winner. He'd left town and hadn't looked back.

Yet, judging by how hard she was working on perfecting those desserts, she was still as driven and determined as she'd ever been. So why on earth would she have thrown the thing she'd wanted more than anything?

CHAPTER FOURTEEN

"I'm starving," Gia said as she sat down across from Tessa at the Pancake Express that morning. The cutest breakfast place in town used to be a train station that got moved from a mile down the road, and it was filled with sepia-toned photos and railroad memorabilia like old signs and a road pick and signal lights. "Thanks for inviting me to breakfast."

"I'm starving, too," Tessa said. Being outside on a sunny Saturday morning instead of inside the bakery working felt... freeing. Also, the fun outing didn't allow her to think of the shock of waking up this morning curled against Leo's warm muscled body...too much. Or those kisses. Those huge-mistake kisses.

Sleeping was unconscious, but she had no excuses for what had happened in the garden. She just knew that it couldn't—wouldn't—happen again.

"Is it too early for you?" Tessa asked Gia, who'd showed up with her hair in a ponytail, a Blossom Glen Track T-shirt, and yoga pants. She was fresh-faced and eager, and that made Tessa smile.

"I've already run five miles," Gia said, setting down the menu and rubbing her stomach. "And I'm ready to order."

It was definitely too early for Tessa, who was ready to mainline coffee after barely sleeping a wink last night. Viv was taking her shift today, but Leo was having his friends over tonight to play cards, and she wanted to surprise him by making them some food. Which was traditionally wife-y, but she just wanted to do it as a nice gesture. So she'd better wake up quick.

The waitress, Dee Williams, was an old friend of Tessa's mom's. As soon as Dee lifted her glass coffee carafe in question, Tessa turned over her mug.

"Fill 'er up?" Dee asked, already pouring. "You look like you could use a heaping cup today."

"Or two," Tessa said. "How are you, DeeDee?"

"Oh, nothing's new. But everyone's talking about you and that hottie Italian Stallion getting hitched. He keeping you up at night? If he is, I have no sympathy for you, girl."

"Thanks, Dee." She took a big gulp of coffee and smiled. "For the coffee, not the comments." Which she'd made in front of Leo's sister no less. "You know Gia, right?"

Dee waved a hand dismissively. "You're eighteen, aren't you, honey? She knows it all. Besides, the coffee costs money but the commentary is free. That includes any advice." She chuckled at her own joke. "Leo is so much better than that idiot you were dating." She put her fingers over her mouth. "Oopsie, shouldn't have said that. But I'm really happy for you." She gave Tessa a squeeze. "This one's a keeper!"

"What makes you say that?" Tessa couldn't help asking.

"Every time he comes in, he tips thirty percent. Plus he's nice."

Tessa took another gulp of coffee and dreamt of what it would be like to live somewhere where everyone did not know your business. "Remind me not to leave you a tip."

"Ha-ha," Dee said to Tessa. "Coffee for you, sugar?" she asked Gia sweetly.

Gia wrinkled up her nose. "Can you make hot chocolate when it's hot out?"

"Aren't you the cutest. Of course we can."

"That sounds really good," Tessa said on impulse. "Make that two, please." Life was too short, right? "So, I've seen you running past the bakery some mornings." Tessa closed her menu as Dee sped off. "You like it?"

Gia nodded as she looked over her own menu. "Sometimes I run with Leo. He runs every day."

"Is that right?" Oops. "I mean—yeah," she said, taking a big gulp. "I don't know how he does that, every single day without fail." She sped on to disguise her gaffe. "Speaking of exercise, my sisters signed me up for a yoga class. Actually, Vivienne is teaching it, so Juliet and I sort of have to go. Want to come too? It's tonight at seven in the community center basement. I'm strangely looking forward to it." It seemed her sisters had made it their mission to get her out of the bakery. And it was an opportunity for the three of them to do something together, so she'd said yes.

"Thanks," Gia said, "but I have to study tonight. And I promised Leo I'd ride out with him to the farmers market this afternoon. He's making contacts for his new menu."

"That sounds like fun." But—studying on a Saturday night?

"People sell other things there, too, besides vegetables," Gia said, clearly excited. "Antiques, banana bread, pottery. It's fun. Plus I get to pick Leo's brain."

"About what?"

"Anything. We have a contest going. Who knows the most about *Friends* trivia. He's always trying to one-up me."

Leo liked *Friends* that much? One of the million things she didn't know about him.

Except she knew that he liked to sleep on his stomach.

With his hand under his pillow. When he woke up, his thick mane of hair was adorably tousled. And watching him lift himself out of bed and walk to the bathroom shirtless with abs she could wash her clothes on had been more eye-opening than a cup of coffee.

"Do you like him being back?" Tessa asked. The answer was already clear from the way Gia's eyes lit up when she talked about her brother.

Gia gave an enthusiastic nod as Dee set steaming mugs of hot chocolate in front of them. "My dad's still afraid he's going to pick up and leave, though. But now that you're married, maybe you'll both stay."

Tessa didn't know what to say to that. Leo had bought a house. That told her he was determined to work things out with his dad. But as for her…she'd done her time in Blossom Glen. She had zero intention of staying.

Gia's words sent a stab of guilt through her. What would the lie of their fake marriage do to her relationship with Gia in a few months when it was all over?

Sylvia Ortega, one of her grandmother's friends, walked up to the table and put her arm around Tessa's shoulder. "Congratulations on your wedding, Tessa. Who'd have thought you'd have such a whirlwind romance?"

Tessa laughed but couldn't help thinking that Sylvia was probably voicing what a lot of people thought—that she was way too practical or sensible to do such an outlandish, out-of-character thing.

But on a positive note, it was *definitely* an improvement over people feeling bad for her.

"Thanks, Mrs. Ortega." She smiled brightly. "Leo is wonderful."

She'd said that to go along with her fake marriage, but did part of her really believe it?

"You deserve every happiness. Congratulations!"

As Mrs. Ortega returned to her table, Tessa said, "I'm sorry, Gia. I didn't mean for this to be an embarrassing brunch."

Gia laughed. "I don't mind that they're saying you two had a whirlwind relationship," Gia said. "True love is true love, right?"

Tessa dug her nails into her palms under the table. How could she possibly endorse a decision like that for a teenager? "Well, we *have* known each other a long time," she hedged.

"Some time you'll have to tell me how you fell in love with Leo. It's so Romeo and Juliet."

Tessa laughed. "I'd rather talk about you. Biomedical engineering, huh?"

"I love science," she said. "And I want to make a difference." Just then, Gia glanced up from her hot chocolate, noticing something beyond Tessa's shoulder, then immediately looked down, her face coloring.

"What is it?" Tessa asked. "Do I need to turn around? More town busybodies on the way over?"

The color spread furiously over Gia's face. "No. I mean, it's just a boy from my class."

Tessa leaned over and dropped her voice. "Is he cute?"

"No!" Gia looked up. "Maybe. A little." She blew on her hot chocolate, making sure not to look up again. "You went to IU but lived at home, right?"

"Yes, I did," Tessa said calmly, but her brain was going a mile a minute. She'd invited Gia to breakfast to get to know her better, but also because she couldn't help comparing Gia to herself at her age. Leo had told her his worries about her decision to stay local for college, and she wanted to find out more.

"Well then, you won't judge me."

Tessa tapped her fingers on the table. "I think that wherever you go and whatever you do, you'll be terrific at it because you work hard and have passion."

"See?" Gia gave the table a little smack and sat back. "I knew you'd be on my side."

"I *am* on your side," Tessa said. She thought about her temporary marriage. About the dangers of advice-giving. About how maybe she should mind her own business.

Then she tossed all that to the wind. Because what if she could help Gia in a way that she hadn't been able to help herself?

She reached across the table and took Gia's hand. "I'm always here to support you—except there's just one thing to consider as you make your decision."

"What's that?"

"Pushing yourself to try new experiences is important. What seems comfortable and safe might seem…stagnating down the line." She certainly knew that firsthand.

Gia crinkled up her nose. "What do you mean?" Dee delivered their pancakes, and Gia tucked right in to eating them.

Tessa suddenly heard Leo's voice in her head telling her to treat her own sisters like sisters. And that meant sharing her own experiences.

She took a deep breath and plunged in. "You know my dad died when I was your age. It changed my whole life."

Gia shook her head. "That's really tough. I'm sorry, Tessa."

"I took on a lot of responsibilities overnight."

Gia kept eating pancakes, and Tessa wasn't sure if she wanted to hear this or not, but she kept going. "I felt like I had so many *shoulds*. Do you know what I mean?"

"You stayed to help your mom, right?"

"At the beginning, she needed all hands on deck. I worked hard, took over what used to be my dad's duties at the bakery, and tried to be there for my sisters when my mom couldn't be."

"Are you saying you should've left your family to go away to school when they needed you?"

Tessa sighed deeply. She hated using her own mistakes as an example, but...maybe it could prevent Gia from repeating them. "They *did* need me—at first, anyway. But after a while, I got comfortable. I started dating someone in town, and things fell into a routine. I think I used the same excuses to keep myself here long after I really needed to stay."

She'd stopped growing.

It had been easy to blame that on her situation—even on Sam.

Seeing how Leo was unstoppable, how he reached for the stars with his out-there plans, and how he believed anything was possible, had made her understand that sometimes you had to do something desperate to get yourself unstuck.

"And then you met Leo?"

"Leo..." What could she say about this complicated situation? "A man isn't a solution to any problem, Gia. But Leo is a big thinker, and he doesn't understand the word *impossible*. All I'm trying to say is, don't take the weight of the world on your shoulders when you don't have to. Or use that as an excuse not to grow."

Which, she could see now, was exactly what *she'd* done.

Gia was moving blueberries under an uneaten pancake, which Tessa translated to mean she might be thinking about what Tessa had just said. "I worry about my dad being alone," Gia admitted. "And I worry about if I'd be able to handle my classes away from home. Leaving seems…scary."

"Every single decision we make in life is scary because we basically have to guess whether it's the right choice or not. There's no magic crystal ball."

"That sucks."

"Yeah. But that's the fun in life, I guess," she said. Gia rotated a little in her seat and caught a peek at the boy across the way, who looked quickly away. "And now I have a question for you." Tessa tipped her head to the left. "Who's that boy who's been staring at you the whole time? He *is* cute."

Gia looked up, turned red, and went back to pushing blueberries. "His name is Aaron."

"He's definitely checking you out."

"I don't want to make my life complicated before college."

"Honey, life has a way of getting complicated no matter how hard we try to keep it simple."

Like kissing Leo. And not being able to stop thinking about him.

"My two favorite women," she heard someone say. Turning, she saw Leo standing at their table, reaching over to kiss her on the cheek with a big "MWUAH," which made her chuckle at his silliness—and bring the memory of last night rushing back. She was relieved when he crossed the table to hug his sister. "You ready for farm adventures?"

"Can't wait," Gia said, eating the last bite of her breakfast.

"We're going to learn all about growing different kinds of tomatoes." He sat down next to Tessa, peeking into her almost-full coffee mug. "Do you mind?"

She pushed the coffee toward him, and he quickly downed it. Then started on her hot chocolate. Maybe someone else didn't sleep so well, either.

"Hey, Gia," someone said. Tessa looked up to see the boy from across the way, brave soul that he must be, standing at their table. He was tall and blond and tanned, and he had a nice smile. "Hi, Mr. and Mrs. Castorini. I'm Aaron."

Tessa nearly laughed aloud. Mr. and Mrs. Castorini?

But *geez*, that was actually who they were, wasn't it?

Leo sat there, his thick brows knit down, apparently trying to look as threatening as possible.

Aaron seemed undaunted. "Can I ask you a homework question?" he asked Gia.

"A homework question?" she repeated, her cheeks coloring.

"Gia, we really should get going," Leo said, impatiently checking his watch.

Tessa elbowed him under the table. But she was thinking of something else besides his bad manners.

At Gia's age, Tessa might have said something to cut a boy off. Anger had made her cutting and quick around men. Anger at being stuck. At losing her choices.

It had grown and ballooned and…taken over. She didn't want that to happen to Gia.

"Leo," Tessa said, "come with me and see how they've planted that beautiful flower bed." She pointed to the edge of the outdoor seating area. "I was thinking maybe we could do something like that on your new restaurant patio." She turned to Gia and hitched her thumb toward the flowers. "We'll be right back."

She literally dragged Leo to the flower bed, where some wilted petunias baked in the sun.

"Nice flowers," he said drily. "Why are you encouraging my sister to talk to a *boy*?"

She shook her head. "Because she's seventeen, and that's what normal seventeen-year-olds do."

"Not under my watch. No dating till she's…thirty. At least." He quirked a smile.

She hoped that meant he was kidding—but she wasn't really sure.

Tessa crossed her arms. "Leo. Do *not* pull that big-Italian-brother thing with her. Gia's shy and quiet, and she's, well, missing out. Push her a little to let her have a life."

"My sister has the top GPA in her class. She's headed for great things. Why let some guy derail that?"

"He's just a friend."

He shot her a skeptical look. "Also, she's the top contender for the candle factory scholarship," he said. "I know she wouldn't let anything get in the way of winning. I mean, no one would, right?"

She searched his eyes. Was he talking about her? Of course not. Because he couldn't know anything about that, could he? "Leo, your sister's a great kid."

"I know." He beamed a look of pride. "She's amazing,"

"Maybe a little *too* amazing." She chose her words carefully. "Also, she's not really a kid anymore. She's almost eighteen and ready for college."

That got his attention. "What do you mean by *too amazing*?"

"What I mean is, she's got things a little too figured out."

He shrugged. "I tried to talk to her about the college thing. But she's so assured; it's hard to change her mind. I think you're over-reading."

"No, Leo." She grabbed his arm, which got his attention. "I have a gut feeling about this. I think that she feels an obligation to take care of your father. Promise me you'll talk more with her about this."

He searched her eyes for a long time. "Okay. If you feel that strongly, I will." After a pause, he said, "Look, about last night. I want you to know it won't happen again."

Oh, the kisses. As if she could forget them for more than a minute. "Right," she said. "Absolutely in agreement. A huge mistake." Embarrassing, never to be repeated, but…so, so good. In all the wrong ways, of course.

"Okay, great." He put his hands in his jeans pockets. "No more to be said, then."

"Is it still guys' night tonight?" She was relieved to change the subject.

"They're coming around eight. You sure it's okay?"

"Sounds fun. Um, what exactly does card night entail?"

Leo shrugged. "Eating pizza. Drinking beer. Smoking cigars."

"Sounds fun. But the cigars *will* be smoked outside, right?"

"Definitely," he said with a little smile.

"Okay, great." There was an awkward pause. "Have you talked to your dad yet about us preparing a full meal for him?"

"Well, we're going to visit a farmers market and a handful of local farms today. I wanted to get a handle on what kind of produce is available so I can plan it."

"You haven't talked to your dad yet?"

"Well, the restaurant is always so busy, and—"

Tessa shook her head. "I can't believe it."

He rubbed his neck. Was he afraid? "What?"

"You're chickening out."

"I'm *not* chickening out."

"And this is the guy who plunged into a fake marriage to jumpstart a business."

"Okay, fine." He rocked back and forth with his hands in his pockets. "I guess I'm a little…nervous."

"About your dad?"

"Yeah. If he doesn't like my ideas… I don't know. I just don't have a Plan B."

That was strange. Because Leo *always* had a Plan B. "Okay, I'm going to do what you did to me."

"What was that?"

"Well, you pushed me to act. And I did, Leo—meaning now you have to also. So we can do what we planned and get our *real* lives back." Except real, fake…sometimes it felt all jumbled.

"Okay, you're right. I'll take care of it."

She started to walk back but remembered something and turned around, nearly bumping into him. Leo gripped her by the arm to catch his balance. "Oops, sorry," she said. "I was just going to ask, if you encounter any fresh strawberries in your travels, will you bring me some? It's for a dessert."

"Sure, Countess," he said, searching her eyes in a way that suddenly made her face heat, remembering waking up next to him. And other things she needed to shove out of her brain. "No problem."

Tessa was relieved to return to the table, where Gia was sitting, scrolling through her phone.

Tessa said, "I think it showed a lot of courage for Aaron to come and talk to you like that."

Gia giggled. "He thinks you're my parents."

Leo chuckled.

"That's terrible," Tessa said, also chuckling.

"Even worse," she said. "He asked me out!" She sounded half-panicked, half-excited.

"Where does he live?" Leo asked, which earned him a firm poke in the elbow. Still, Tessa caught him scanning the outdoor seating for the boy, who fortunately seemed to have left.

"That sounds fun," Tessa said. "What did you say?"

She shrugged. "I told him I'd text him later."

"If you decide to go on the date, let me know," she said. "Vivienne does magic with outfits. She picked this out for me." She nodded to her cute blue blouse and white jeans. No flour included.

"There's our Italian stud," Dee said, reappearing with the bill. "Lucky you, marrying our Tessa."

"I am lucky," Leo said. "Hi to you, too, DeeDee." He snagged the bill from her hand before she could give it to Tessa.

Leo's gaze swept Tessa quickly up and down, *noticing*. Maybe his words were lukewarm, but the look he just gave her was scorching.

"You two are gonna make beautiful babies," Dee said. "Don't forget to leave me a big tip, okay, sugar?"

Leo laughed and slid some money with the bill under the hot chocolate mug. And, Tessa noted, a generous tip.

"Thanks for breakfast," Tessa said to Leo as they got up. "You two have fun today." She gave Gia a big hug. "This was great. We'll do it again soon, okay?"

"Thanks, Tessa." Gia smiled at her brother. "Thanks, Leo."

Impeccable manners. Too obedient, not pushing any limits. With a brother and a father who were perhaps too content with her fake self-assuredness.

Tessa had been like that once, but not anymore. She was in this to achieve their goal, no matter what it took. And that meant staying as far away from Leo as she could.

CHAPTER FIFTEEN

Monthly card night was going on as it always had. Except tonight, the guys met at Leo's, and they were gathered around the little dining table eating, drinking, and hanging out.

"Hey," Jack called to Noah from his leaned-back position at the table, "while you're up, bring me another beer, will you?"

"I got you another beer the last time," Noah said from the kitchen.

"Yeah, well, I brought you more chips last time," Jack said.

"Really?" Leo interrupted. "It's Saturday night, and we're arguing about beer and chips?"

It was ten p.m., and he was experiencing a first. He was actually getting a little tired of his best friends' antics, which included Noah chugging his beer and burping and Jack putting his dirty boots up on the table. Neither of which was unusual. But this time, Leo was *noticing*. Not that he didn't consider his friends his brothers-from-another-mother, but he couldn't shake the feeling that something was…different.

Take Noah, for example. He'd just stuffed a large amount of pizza into his mouth as he laid down his cards, and it was *annoying*.

"For Pete's sake, dude, use a napkin," Leo said.

"Oh, sorry." Noah grabbed for one from the center of the table and swiped at his mouth.

Jack picked up a napkin from the pile and held it up.

"These are *cloth*. With little sunshines sewn all along the bottom."

Leo shrugged. "Tessa tries to be green."

"Oh." Jack seemed to ponder that while he took a stogie from the cigar box, stuck it in his mouth, and tipped back his chair. "Got a match?" he asked.

Leo rummaged through the items in the ceramic bowl Tessa had set in the middle of the table to collect their keys, sunglasses, and the extra garage remote, and he pulled out the box of matches he'd stashed there earlier.

"What's that?" Noah asked.

Leo looked around. "What's what?" Noah pointed to the bowl. "Um, a bowl?"

Jack chuckled. "Looks like it's a handmade *ceramic* bowl with *painted fruit* that holds stuff."

"I'm not really understanding your point," Leo said to his friends.

"I really like the sunshine napkins," Noah said. "They're happy."

Jack threw one at him.

"Look," Leo said. "It's different living with a woman." And frustrating. Not because of the sunshine napkins, either. Because Leo couldn't stop thinking about Tessa.

The kisses, her in his bed, *the scholarship*. The more he got to know her, the more complicated, infuriating, passionate, enthusiastic—did he say passionate?—she was.

His sister couldn't stop talking about her brunch with Tessa the rest of their afternoon together. And then Tessa herself had surprised him by dropping off homemade pizzas for his friends tonight. She'd made them—in between all her other work—because she knew the guys would like them.

How could he have *ever* thought she was an Ice Queen? Or unambitious?

And what about that *scholarship*?

Nothing about her could be taken at face value.

"Yeah," Noah said, looking around the house at the pillows Tessa had put on the couches, the rug she'd bought, and the pictures Leo had helped her hang. "Everything matches. And the flowers in those pots on the patio aren't even dead."

"Let's go out there and have some cigars," Leo said, hoping to change the subject.

He was a little agitated. Not just because he was low on sleep.

It was what Juliet had said.

That's what was bugging him. Once he and Tessa talked it out and he found out what really happened, he would be back to his normal self; he was certain. And he planned to do that as soon as he saw her. Even though he was afraid of what he might learn.

Jack trailed right behind him as he walked outside.

"Are you okay?" his friend asked. "You seem a little on edge."

Leo gave him a death frown. "I don't want to hear any more *married* jokes, okay?"

"You mean about sunshine napkins? Fruit bowls? A living room with matching pillows? And…whoa. What's *this*?" Jack walked over to the garden shed, which was dark green with gingerbread trim and double barn doors, and opened them.

"Is it a she-shed?" Noah asked, a little too excitedly.

"I'm using it as a workshop." He really didn't want to tell them about his kitchen-island project, which he'd just started this afternoon. That would just make him more of a punching bag for their jokes about married life. He quickly reached over to close one of the doors, but Jack put out his foot to stop him.

"What are you building?" Jack swung both doors fully open and flipped on the light. There, resting on two wooden sawhorses, was a freshly sanded door. The other door leaned against a wall, along with two other smaller panels. "Are those the doors we loaded into your dad's truck a few weeks ago? You brought them home?"

"This is beautiful," Noah said, running his hand along the sanded surface. "What are you making?"

"The kitchen can use an island," Leo said. "I thought it would be a fun piece of history to use the original bakery doors for Tessa. I bought some new wood for the end pieces; I just need to stain everything and get a countertop. Then I'm going to surprise her."

"Isn't Tessa going to see it?" Noah asked.

"She never goes in here because she hates spiders." He smiled. "Plus I keep the door locked, and I'm the only one with a key."

Jack put his hands on his hips. "Seems to me that you've been pretty busy trying to meet with farmers, plan menus, source food, try recipes… Why are you spending your time building an island?"

"Because this kitchen is really tiny and we need more work space." He shrugged. "That's it."

Noah's phone rang, and he excused himself to answer it.

"You built it for her, didn't you?" Jack said, not letting it go. "So she could *bake*."

"Well, she works downtown too late at night," Leo said.

"I know what's going on here," Jack said, not unsympathetically. "And it's not just about building a kitchen island."

Leo shook his head in warning. "I don't go analyzing your relationship with Shelby." Shelby ran a dance studio. And as of last week, Jack was dating her. In all likelihood that might have changed, though.

"Shelby and I don't have a relationship, Leo. We have sex. But spending all your spare time staining old doors to make a beautiful piece of furniture like this… Just be careful is all I'm saying."

"If you're saying don't let her fall in love with me, trust me, that's not going to happen. She doesn't hesitate to let me have it every time I say something she doesn't like. Which is, like, every other sentence." He shook his head. "Besides, the marriage is just until we get the businesses going again."

Jack shook his head. "Leo, you idiot. I'm not worried about Tessa falling in love with you. I'm worried that *you're* falling in love with *her*."

Leo caught himself before he showed any surprise. But then he shrugged the comment off. He didn't fall in love with anybody. He made sure of it. "I'm going to say this one time and only one time. I'm not interested in falling in love. I'm interested in saving my dad's restaurant. And her family's bakery. That's it, plain and simple." He walked over to the outdoor table. "Let's smoke some stogies."

On the patio, they sat drinking beers and blowing smoke rings into the air. The cigars tended to give Leo a headache, but it was a tradition they'd been carrying on together for years.

Cosette jumped up on Leo's lap, which shocked the heck out of him. And not only because he didn't immediately break out into hives.

As he stroked her back, she purred and settled in, gracing him with her presence, while Noah cut pieces of the dessert Tessa left for them.

"What is this thing?" Noah asked. "It's like blueberry pie."

"It's called a *galette*," Leo said, trying to pronounce it like Tessa had but failing.

"Is that Spanish?" Noah asked.

How could this man be in charge of an entire design department? "It's a French fruit thing with a crust. Just taste it."

"You know, Leo, there are benefits to being married," Jack said as he bit into his piece. "For some people. Not myself, of course. But this is phenomenal."

"That pizza was pretty awesome, too," Noah said. "I really like Tessa. You could do a lot worse."

"Who are you texting?" Jack asked Leo.

"Tessa. She's all alone in the bakery. It's getting late. Time for you losers to head home." They needed to leave, and he needed to get a few things off his chest.

• • •

When Tessa approached the backyard a little later that evening, she smelled the lingering scent of tobacco smoke, making her wonder if guys' night was still going on. She sort of hoped not, because she'd had a caramel sauce spill that made her feel sticky all over, and she couldn't wait to take a shower.

"Hey, Tessa," Noah said as she walked through the gate. He and Jack looked like they were saying their goodbyes.

"The food was fabulous. Especially the dessert." Noah gave Tessa a hug, fist-bumped Leo, and headed out.

"Thanks for making the food for us," Jack said. "See you tomorrow, buddy." He patted Leo on the back.

After they left, Leo held out the dessert plate. "One piece left," he said. "Want it?"

"No, thanks," she said, collecting dishes in a stack.

He took the plates out of her hand. "You've done enough for us. There's pizza left over. Want me to bring you some?"

"I think I'm going to go in and take a shower. It's been a long day." As if to demonstrate, she yawned, wanting to appear as tired as possible to avoid a repeat of last night.

She noticed some cigar ashes scattered under the table, and looked around for the broom, but he'd put it in the...

He ran ahead of her and blocked the door just as she got to the shed. "You should sit down. You've had a long day."

She frowned. "I can spend a few minutes helping clean up. It's no problem. Really." She moved to enter the shed, but again he blocked her entrance.

"I'll get the broom. Because, um, there are tons of spiders in there. *Nests* of them. Why don't you go look for Cosette?"

"She's right there." Tessa hitched her thumb over her shoulder. A huge meow confirmed that Cosette had hopped out of the garden and was headed over. Leo was acting so strangely. "Is everything okay?"

"Yeah. Great." He rubbed his neck, a sure tell that he was nervous and something was up. "Thanks for all you did. The food was terrific."

"I'm glad everyone liked it."

He placed a hand on her shoulder, as if he were trying to steer her around. "So now I think you should go in and take your shower and let me clean up. Okay?"

"Okay," she said reluctantly.

She turned to go into the house but spun back at the last second, catching him trying to wedge himself sideways through the shed door.

"Leo. What the hell are you doing?"

"Uh, getting the broom." He smiled a strange, uncomfortable smile.

Just then, the cat zipped past them and into the shed. Tessa used that as an opportunity to run after her, pushing the door open wider and flicking on the light.

Awash under the long fluorescent bulbs was a project... taking up nearly the whole length of the shed. A sanded door on sawhorses. Tessa gasped, her hands flying to her mouth.

"It—it's not a big deal," he said hurriedly from behind her. "It's just a little project I'm working on, okay?"

That's when it dawned on her exactly what she was looking at. "That's the door from the bakery."

"Yes." He walked up to the door and ran his hand over something near the top. "Come see. It's the year your family's shop opened."

"1922," she said, running her hand along the engraved numbers. Somehow, that made her eyes water. "What's this for?"

He heaved a sigh, like he had no choice but to tell her the truth. "It's an island—or, it's going to be. For the kitchen."

"For the kitchen?" He'd made them an island? From her family bakery's original doors?

"Yeah. I was thinking now you can bake here instead of by yourself downtown."

He'd used something symbolic and original. And he didn't want her to have to bake by herself.

She tried to say something normal like *it's beautiful*, but suddenly her throat closed up and her vision blurred.

Leo looked at her nervously, then focused intently on the door. "See the panels? I'm going to sand and stain them. And Jack knows someone who will give me a great price on a marble slab, if that's what you want. I mean, we needed this, right? It's a small kitchen without any work space, and we both like to cook and…"

She stared at him. He was fisting and unfisting his hands and transferring his weight from foot to foot.

She ran a hand along the smooth surface. Sawdust littered the ground and filled the air with the smell of wood.

She reached up and kissed him on the cheek. "Thank you."

"This isn't part of our business deal." He was still clearly uncomfortable. "And I didn't do it for any reason other than I see you work so hard and I hope this makes things a little easier for you. And…we need one."

"Leo, I don't know what to say. It's beautiful."

It wasn't even the island itself that made her emotional. It was the fact that he'd made it *for her*.

CHAPTER SIXTEEN

Leo waited patiently for Tessa to finish her shower. He sat at his grandfather's desk working on his computer, but trying to make the restaurant accounts balance was giving him a headache. Out of boredom, he popped open the secret drawer, only to be confronted by Tessa's mom's proposal, which he'd stashed there so Tessa wouldn't see it. He prayed that the lunch he'd finally scheduled would turn the tide with his dad. At last he heard Tessa's footsteps as she padded out to the living room in her robe and slippers.

He slammed the secret drawer shut.

He knew her routine. She liked to wind down in the evenings by working on a puzzle. Her puzzle boxes were all stacked under the coffee table, and they were all French-themed—Monet, the Eiffel Tower, a Parisian café scene, Provence.

She settled in to work, pulling a felt roll out of the closet and unrolling it on the coffee table.

"What puzzle are you working on?" He already knew. Her current challenge was a thousand-piecer, a Monet painting of irises in his garden at Giverny, loaded with purples and greens. And she was about thirty pieces away from being finished.

Except by five minutes in, she began looking under the felt. In the box. Dropping down to search behind the couch.

"What are you looking for?" Leo innocently looked up from his book.

"I must've lost some pieces in the move. I'm bummed, because I'm almost finished."

Slowly, Leo reached into his pocket and pulled out a handful of pieces.

She froze, on her knees, gripping the coffee table.

"Wait," she said slowly. "*You* have my puzzle pieces?"

"I might have taken just a few." Four, to be exact. And he was going to hold them for ransom.

"Um, okay. Why?"

"For every question you answer, you get one back."

"No, Leo. Come on. It's been a grueling day." Her hair was wet, and her shampoo filled the room with its fragrant scent. Her robe and slippers made her look sweet and vulnerable. But now she looked like she might kill him if he didn't give her back those pieces ASAP.

"Humor me," he said. "This will help us to get to know each other better. So we avoid those embarrassing gaffes in front of our family and friends."

She heaved an overly patient sigh and sat down next to him on the couch. "Fine. Go. Ask if you must."

Leo suppressed a twitch of nerves. He was going to tell her the truth. Because he wanted—no, *needed*—the truth from her.

And he was going to do what he'd never done before.

Get to know her. Understand her. Without getting carried away by physical attraction. A first for him.

"Let's try it. What's your favorite color?" he asked.

"Blue." She held out her hand for a piece and wiggled her fingers impatiently until he handed her one.

"Okay, that makes sense. Because the kitchen dishes are blue. And you wear a lot of blue tops. And your eyes. Very blue." He sounded like a fool. He also forced himself to stop staring into them.

"Next question. What's your favorite food?"

"That's easy. Pizza." Her hand stretched out again. "Fork over another one, buddy."

Okay, he was going to have to step it up or he was going to run out of pieces before he got her to tell him anything meaningful. "The questions are too easy."

"Not my problem," she said. "This is *your* game."

"Aw, come on. Don't you think games are fun?"

"I think *puzzles* are fun. By myself." She chuckled a little. "Maybe that's a big difference between you and me. You're always upbeat and cheerful. You seem like you'd be a huge game player."

"I'm not always cheerful. But I try." He paused. He really didn't want to get into talking about himself. But how else would she trust him if he didn't do what he was asking her to do?

That was part of getting to know someone. Give and take. He wasn't *that* much of a relationship newb.

"Before my mom died, she made me promise her something."

"Leo, I'm just going to stop you for a sec." She held out her hands. "Because this sounds a lot more serious than 'What's your favorite food?'"

"I want to tell you this, okay?" Game or no, he wanted her to hear it.

She rearranged the pieces she won back on the coffee table and studied the puzzle—longingly, he thought. Like she'd much rather be left alone to finish it. "Well, okay then. Tell away."

He plunged in before he chickened out. "When my mom first got sick. I didn't understand much about what was going on, but I knew it was serious. I remember crying a lot, not being able to sleep, not being able to do my schoolwork. So my dad took me to see her at the hospital. I was relieved she was alive."

"Oh, Leo." She put a hand on his arm. "You were so young."

"She knew I was upset. And how hard it was for me to see her sick. She said we might have to be separated but I would never be separated from her love." His voice cracked despite himself.

"Leo. No." She was getting choked up, too. This game night was not exactly going as he'd planned.

He forced himself to finish the story. "She reached out and touched my cheek and said, 'Leo, I want you to keep smiling.' She said it would break her heart if she looked down from heaven and saw me devastated by her death. I had to go on, and I should do that by looking up and seeing the brightest side. That life was beautiful and full of love, and I shouldn't let my sorrow prevent me from seeing the beauty in it."

Tessa swiped at her eyes. "Leo, that's—that's really sad. But also very beautiful."

He tapped a puzzle piece on his palm. "She believed that we'd be together again one day, and until then, she told me, she'd always be with me, watching me. So I had to live my life to the fullest and show her that I would keep my chin up and be happy."

Tessa shook her head. "I'm really sorry."

He realized in that moment that no matter what she had

to say about the scholarship, he already knew who she was. And he'd been wrong about her. So wrong.

"So you tend to smile and be as upbeat as possible because of a promise you made to your mom?"

He shrugged. "In reality, I'm a real grouch." Then he grinned.

She rolled her eyes. "You can't even say you're grouchy without smiling. That's sick." She tapped a finger against her lips. "Or maybe there's something else going on here."

"Nope. Nothing else."

"I mean, something you might not even be aware of."

Okay, this *definitely* wasn't turning out the way he'd planned.

"Maybe you keep things light for another reason. Because it hurts to go deeper."

"You lost me."

"Like, in a relationship. How many have you had?"

"I've dated *lots* of women."

She shook her head. "I'm not talking about that. I'm talking about more than dating."

"I've had relationships," he hedged.

"What's the longest you've dated someone?"

He shrugged. "Three months."

"Svana?" she asked.

"We only dated for a month." Why did he start this ridiculous game again? "Look, maybe things haven't worked out with women because I just haven't met the right one, okay? I have plenty of stable relationships in my life."

"Okay," she said, holding out her hands in defense. "No judgment." She paused. "Just a month with Svana, huh?"

Did she seem happy about that? He snapped a piece in

place. There were two pieces left in his hands. "Here comes another question. Why didn't you want to date me in high school?"

"That's easy. Because you didn't want to date *me* in high school. I was a nerd, and you weren't."

"I *did* want to date you, Tessa," he said, looking her directly in the eye. "Until I ran into you kissing Sam by your locker."

"That was a long time ago." She'd gotten quiet. And wasn't meeting his gaze anymore. But he wasn't going to let her off the hook.

"I want to know why you chose Sam over me."

He set the third piece down, and she pretended to study the puzzle. "You were the guy everyone loved. You had millions of friends. I was never in your league."

"I liked you, despite all our competing against each other. You must have known that. I even asked you out, and we had a great time. Remember?"

Ah yes, he'd remembered everything about that date for a long time. Tessa waved her hand dismissively. "You liked me for about ten seconds, and you would've moved on to the next girl. And with our families not talking—"

"Our families not getting along didn't end what was going on between us." He tapped the puzzle piece on his knee. "So, what's the *real* answer?"

"I never thought you were serious about me, okay?" She held out her hand. "Give it over, Leo. I answered your questions."

He felt that something was off, that she wasn't telling him everything. He should just end the game, because she was getting angry with him. But perversely, he turned his mouth up in a mischievous grin.

"Leo, I'm warning you. I did what you asked. Now give me the last piece, please."

"Here it is." He dangled it in front of her. "It's yours if you answer one last question."

"No more questions."

She lunged for it, but he lifted it out of reach, causing her to lean against him.

The force tipped them both backward on the couch. Tessa was on top of him, both of their hands firmly gripping the piece. "Give it up, you cheater," she said. "It's mine!"

Her blue eyes snapped with frustration as she refused to surrender. Her damp hair tickled his face, its sweet fragrance surrounding him. For a moment he contemplated giving up the piece and taking her soft, sweet-smelling body in his arms.

"I'm sorry, Countess," he said coolly, meeting her infuriated blue gaze. "I can't give you the last piece until you answer one last thing." His voice was quiet, his grasp unyielding. "I want to know what happened with the scholarship."

• • •

Tessa gasped. She was hovering over him, pillows askew, one hand on his shoulder and the other clamped around his as they fought for the last piece.

And she was trembling. From being near him and from the truth that hovered on her lips.

She'd been okay keeping all of this to herself for so many years. She'd lived with the consequences of her choices, even as they'd eaten her up on the inside.

"That's ancient history," she said as calmly as possible. It was in the past, over and done.

"I want to know the truth," he said quietly.

"There's nothing to tell." She forced herself to meet his gaze. "We were neck and neck, and you won."

"I don't think that's the whole story," he said.

She bit down on her lip to stop from tearing up. "Who told you?" But she already knew the answer.

Her suspicious, troublemaking sister who could never leave well enough alone. Well, both her sisters would qualify for that distinction, but she suspected the culprit was their very recent house guest.

"Juliet loves you," Leo said. "*She* wants to be the one to look out for *you*. I can't fault her for that. It's about time someone took care of you for once."

That made her tear up for real. She pushed up to get space, to sit upright on the couch, but Leo was right there next to her, waiting for the truth.

She wanted to look away. Away from his beautiful brown eyes. Away from his strong jaw and thick wavy hair and the knowing gaze that seemed to see right through her.

"Just tell me." His voice was practically a whisper. She wondered how many women that deep, gravelly voice had caused to spill all their secrets. "I was part of this, too. I need to know."

She looked at his handsome face. It was predatory. Waiting. But he wasn't really a predator, was he? He'd been aggressive about this fake-marriage scheme, but he hadn't ever forced her into anything; she'd agreed on her own. And he'd done it because he loved his family. He cared about his sister. He'd been kind to her mother and grandmother—and her sister. He was making her a gorgeous kitchen island, for goodness' sake, to get her out of that bakery.

At every turn, his actions broke down all her assumptions.

But telling him the truth, opening up to him, would make her vulnerable. And if she fell for him, she couldn't withstand another heartbreak in this town with a million eyes. Where everyone followed each little misstep with a high-powered microscope.

Don't you dare fall for him, Tessa, a voice that sounded a lot like Juliet's chided from inside.

Yet part of her wanted him to know the secret she'd kept hidden for all these years. And maybe he deserved to know. Because she'd hurt him because of it.

She took a deep breath. "Juliet took my dad's death very hard. I mean, we all did. But her especially. We were all mourning, and my mom was beside herself with the business, working overtime to keep it on its feet. We thought it was just the stress, you know? The grief. But it wasn't.

"Juliet wasn't getting out of bed. She stopped eating. Stopped seeing her friends. Her grades were falling. The doctors said her grief had turned into a major depression."

"That's terrible, Tessa."

She couldn't meet his gaze or she'd never get through this. "I would get up and work for a couple of hours and then drive her to Indianapolis for therapy or to the doctor, and my mom would sit with her in the afternoons. And during all this, Vivienne was just twelve. Her childhood got cut short by my dad's death, and then…then she needed someone to watch over her and protect her and make sure she could still be a kid, while we were all stretched so thin."

Tears spilled out of her eyes. The memories were still so painful.

Leo reached over and took her hand. She swallowed hard and continued. "I had to do everything in my power to help my family at a terrible time. That meant growing up fast. So—"

Unable to go on, she gave a little sob. Leo reached over and held her hand. And finished her sentence for her. "So you threw the final calc exam. You let me win." He looked a little bit stunned, but his firm grip didn't falter.

"I want you to know everything was my idea. If I'd gotten that scholarship, my mom would've driven me to NYU personally and shoved me out of the car. She *never* would have let me stay."

He took her other hand, too, holding tight. "Tessa, I'm so sorry. I had no clue."

Her pulse was thrumming, her heart pounding. "I did throw the exam." She took a big breath. "But that's not all. I had to make sure you wouldn't ask any questions."

"There's more?"

"I made sure you caught me kissing Sam. I wasn't dating him. I didn't even start dating him for years afterward. But I had to make sure you were hurt and angry so you wouldn't ask any questions." She swiped at her eyes. "But it turned out *I* was the one who got hurt."

Leo frowned. "What are you talking about?"

She shrugged. "I had a huge crush on you. It was hard enough to lie to you. But when you laughed at me, I figured you never really liked me to begin with."

He raked a hand through his hair. "Seeing you with Sam

shocked the hell out of me. I—I don't even remember what I said."

"You turned to your friends and said it was a miracle anyone would kiss me at all."

He winced. "I said that because I was hurt, not because I meant it."

"Sparring with you was the high point of my life at school. Deceiving you almost killed me, and I couldn't tell a soul." She shrugged. "I just couldn't think of another way out."

He smoothed his thumbs along her knuckles in a comforting gesture that should have been calming but had exactly the opposite effect. "You gave up everything for your family. Including your chance to get out. And I got it instead."

She shook her head adamantly. "Don't feel sorry for me, Leo. Everything worked out." Well, at least now she was determined to make sure it did. "I have no regrets." What choice did she have, really? Her sister's life versus her happiness. There was no question.

"You've got it all wrong, Countess." His voice was low and a little scratchy like sandpaper, and it sent a shiver up her spine. "I don't feel sorry for you at all. What you did at eighteen was selfless and…inspiring."

His eyes were warm with feeling. But not pity. He was looking at her like he respected her as his equal. And more.

"You still surprise me at every turn." He brushed her hair back and gazed at her tenderly. "I can't change the past." His voice was low, a whisper. "But I promise to do everything in my power to make sure you can lead the life you want to lead in the future."

She was stunned. She could barely breathe or swallow,

and she was still struggling to hold it together. "If we manage to make our businesses successful, I can finally do what I want. Your wild ideas just might make it happen. For that I'll always be grateful."

Relief rolled through her. From finally telling her story. To the man she'd least expected to ever tell.

For all these years, she'd believed he thought she was... plain. Unattractive. The sensible, practical sister. That he'd befriended her just to show everyone he was being decent with the competition.

But that hadn't been true.

And now he was looking at her, heat in his eyes. He met her gaze with a silent question as he leaned closer.

She answered by bringing her lips to his. It was a no-brainer, really. She could no sooner resist him than she could a puffy brioche fresh from the oven.

His lips were soft and warm, and he tasted like...well, like everything she'd longed for. Freed by the truth, their kisses took on a new, wild freedom, so different from those kisses in the garden. Each kiss, each heartbeat, seemed to veer into an exciting, unknown territory she'd never experienced before.

Somehow they ended up horizontal on the couch, their bodies flush. She felt the shock of being against his solid chest, their legs entwined, his hands dragging in her hair.

Leo had a way of moving his lips over hers, slowly exploring, taking his time, that made her melt in his arms. She angled her head and kissed him again, more fully and deeply, her mouth opening on a sigh.

Tessa had been kissed by the same man for years, but she'd never felt this dizzy sensation, this...falling into a place where the world fell away and there was just the two of them, tangled up together on an old purple couch. She met him stroke for stroke, unable to hold back, past all logic and sense. She was too lost in the feel of his hard strength, his simple clean scent, and the honest moment still reverberating between them.

Without even knowing what she was doing, she ran her hands over the hard hills and valleys of his chest, kissing him with all she had. He made a sound in his throat and whispered, "What are you doing to me?" He was looking at her with tenderness and maybe even the same awe that she was feeling. Which pleased her more than she could admit.

He was dangerous to her in ways Sam had never been. Leo was more defiant, more challenging, far more of a risk-taker. And a *far* better kisser. Yet in his arms she felt…safe. Free to be herself. And she hadn't felt like that with a man in, well, ever.

In the fog of kisses, a rap sounded, first far away, then more urgent. They broke apart, both of them breathing fast. For once, Leo wasn't smiling. He looked…dazed. Confused. As floored as she was.

Tessa's heart was still slamming into her chest, blood rushing in her ears. As their gazes locked, Tessa noticed Leo *the Legend* Castorini was…trembling.

Just a little. But definitely off his game.

As was she.

They both looked to the door, where Juliet stood, staring at them. Vivienne's head popped up right behind her.

Oh no.

"You have so many sisters," Leo whispered, the corner of his mouth tipping up.

"Only two," she said back.

"Seems like two thousand," he mumbled as they untangled themselves and sat upright.

Juliet cleared her throat. "I'm sorry," she said, scanning the scattered pillows and the puzzle pieces on the floor. "I…I was able to rent your old apartment. Isn't that great? But there's one tiny problem. I have to stay just one more night. If that's okay."

"And I came with her," Vivienne said, looking uncomfortable, "to see if you guys wanted to hang out…but maybe that's not such a good idea."

Tessa got up as gracefully as she could, her legs unsteady, her lips still tingling. Leo seemed unfazed, coming to stand next to her.

Juliet hitched a thumb toward the spare bedroom. "I'll just—I'll just be reading. My book. In my room." Juliet glanced from Tessa to Leo, whose perfect hair, Tessa noticed, was a little mussed.

"And I'll just take off and see you guys tomorrow," Viv said.

"Stay," Tessa said, trying to sound convincing. "We were just going to watch TV. Right, Leo?"

"Right," he said but not with much conviction.

"Oh. Okay," Juliet said. "Well, I'll go put my bag away, and maybe I'll join you."

"I'll help you," Viv said, wisely following her down the hall.

That left them facing each other in dead silence. Except for the tiniest little meow.

Cosette crawled out from under the couch and walked out to where they were standing.

"Oh, no. She was under the couch," Tessa said.

"Is that a problem?"

"Well, do you think she got a little squished under there? With us…on top?"

Cosette plopped herself down on the floor right in front of them, lifted her back leg into the air, and began to give herself a bath.

"She's basically telling us she couldn't care less what we do." He turned and took her hand. "And did your sister just refer to the spare room as *her room*?"

"You don't mind if they stay?"

"I'll pick a movie." He paused, deadpan. "But is it okay if I choose one with murder and mayhem?"

Tessa shook her head and chuckled. Every day, she seemed to like Leo more and more. And every day, the barriers she'd put up to protect her heart seemed to be tumbling down. This was getting even more twisted than his silly puzzle game.

• • •

Leo walked straight into the upstairs bathroom and turned on the shower. Standing under the pounding stream, he tried to beat thoughts of Tessa out of his mind.

He'd *never* thought she was ugly.

He'd always thought she was fricking *gorgeous*. All that thick wavy hair; those big wide eyes that could never quite hide what she was really feeling. She didn't have the ability to hide her emotions behind a smile like he did.

She wasn't hard-hearted, cold, or emotionless. She was melted chocolate.

And he wanted to lick every bite.

Okay, that was a little ridiculous. But he meant it.

He'd never been so…aroused. He'd definitely never felt this way for someone who also had the capacity to annoy him so much.

Honestly, he'd never felt this way for *anyone* before.

And he'd never worried about a few kisses before like he was worrying now. Not because they weren't amazing. But because he'd been filled with a feeling that he made certain to never mix with sex.

Tenderness.

He liked and admired her. And he absolutely did not want to be just friends with her.

He *wanted* her, plain and simple.

But she deserved someone who was dedicated, faithful, and capable of giving her 100 percent. Not someone who avoided love at all costs because it simply hurt too much.

Leo dried off, brushed his teeth, and collapsed onto his bed, trying to decide if he could really muster the ability to watch television. As he rolled on his side, a scent permeated his brain—lilies of the valley, ocean breezes, grassy hillsides… he had no idea what he was smelling, but he knew this: it was *hers*, left behind from when she'd slept in his bed last night.

She'd left her scent in his bed and her imprint on his soul.

And he was in big trouble. Because he'd gone and fallen for his wife.

CHAPTER SEVENTEEN

The following Saturday, Tessa got Vivienne to cover her in the bakery so she could go over to Leo's for the big lunch "presentation" that he'd arranged for his dad. They'd been so busy preparing the last few days, there hadn't been any time to think about the couch incident. She was brushing her hair and retying it in a ponytail when her grandmother came up behind her at the old mirror that hung in the supply room at the back of the bread shop.

"Is that lipstick?" her grandmother asked.

Tessa rolled her eyes.

"I saw that," her grandmother said.

"Well," Tessa said, finishing her hair tie, "I can't look like I've been up since four thirty this morning, can I?"

Her grandmother came up behind her and tugged at her ponytail, something she used to do when Tessa was a girl. "You're nervous for him."

"Yes." She met her grandmother's eyes in the mirror. "He's poured everything into this. Farm-to-table, organic, delivery options. And it's all much different from what his father is used to."

"And you're going to support him?"

"I'm in charge of dessert," she said proudly as she reached into the old fridge and pulled out an enormous cake lined with a row of strawberries, layered with airy patisserie cream, and topped with piped-icing flowers.

"You made *fraisier*," her grandmother said, clapping

her hands.

"It's summery and delicious, and it wows with its looks."

Juliet whistled from behind her.

"Hey, what are you doing here?" Tessa asked.

"Lunch hour," she said. "*That's* spectacular."

"Will you make me a gluten-free one?" Vivienne asked, walking in from the main shop. "Because that looks incredible." She looked a little sweaty, and her ponytail was askew, causing Tessa a little pang of guilt. Tessa hoped that if they got things off the ground, they might be able to afford to hire someone before the end of summer, freeing Vivienne to return to her life in Paris.

Tessa's mom motioned for Tessa to stand next to the cake and pulled out her phone. "Smile," she said. Then she made everyone gather around it and took another. And then Vivienne took over and got some artsy shots for Tessa to use on her channel.

All of which made Tessa feel really good, because her mom seemed proud of what she'd baked. And it wasn't even bread.

"Who have you made that for, exactly?" her mom asked.

"Leo's father, aunt, and uncle. I think that's all who are coming. He's just really worried about what his dad will think."

"Well, I admire him for what he's doing," her mom said. "An improvement in any business in town helps us, too."

"I wish Leo the best," her grandmother said as she bagged the piping hot loaf of bread fresh out of the oven that Tessa had baked especially for the lunch. "Even though your cake is going to be the star of the show. It looks professionally made."

"Thanks, Gram," Tessa said, hugging her. The compliment meant a lot. And also, it seemed that they were willing to be cordial, which was a good thing, right?

"Well, good luck," Vivienne said, wiping her hands on her apron and hugging Tessa.

"Break an egg!" Juliet said.

There were more hugs from everyone, then her grandmother tucked the bag of bread under Tessa's arm like a weapon while Vivienne held the door. "Thanks, family." Tessa was a little teary-eyed as she walked the few steps out the back of the bakery to Leo's new little patio next door. Her family was rooting for her. She was proud that her cake passed muster. Now she could cheer Leo on.

The first thing Tessa noticed was that strings of little white lights were on, even though it was noon. The area had been transformed into an adorable space filled with tables covered with traditional red-and-white-checkered tablecloths. There were even little planter boxes hanging off the iron fencing around the perimeter planted with red geraniums. For today, several tables were pushed together and covered with a large white tablecloth.

Tessa had just set the cake on the table when Leo appeared at the restaurant doorway wearing a plain white apron. She sucked in a breath. She wasn't sure exactly what got to her the most—his dark wavy hair against the white of the apron, his muscled arms, or the look in his eyes, which was hopeful, excited, and, she would also say, nervous. Judging by the way he walked out and began fussing with the glasses and silverware, making sure everything was perfectly aligned, *nervous* was correct. And noticeably different from his usual laid-back, easygoing self.

"Hey," Leo said, stopping his table rearranging to face her, his gaze sliding quickly up and down her in an appreciative way. That's all it took to bring thoughts of last week rushing back. Of being tangled up with him on that couch, his big arms surrounding her in a way that made her feel safe and yet very much in trouble at the same time.

"How—how are you doing?" she asked. Her stomach was in knots, the back of her neck was sweating, and her palms were clammy. She was a wreck but was making a big effort to be calm for his sake.

They had to get his father's blessing. Both of them were counting on it. If they didn't, this whole wild scheme would be in vain.

"You really want to know?" he asked.

"You look completely prepared." She waved a hand over the table. "And everything looks beautiful."

"To be honest, I'm a little anxious," he said, a smile spreading slowly. Because of course he *would* smile even now.

"You're going to do amazing."

"*We're* going to do amazing," he corrected.

"Okay," she said. "We. *Us*. However you want to say it." They were partners. Business partners. Who were becoming friends with an inconvenient attraction. And that was all.

That was all it could be, because after they succeeded in helping their families, she was leaving. For good.

He squeezed her hand quickly, briefly, and she squeezed back. "I'm really glad you're here."

That hand squeeze had been so brief, and it had been over in a few seconds. Yet the heat from his touch shot right up her arms and spread everywhere, including into her already-flaming cheeks. She turned away and began fussing with her cake to hide her reaction to his touch. "Can I put this in your fridge?"

He noticed the cake for the first time, examining it closely—the strawberry halves marching in a perfect line all around the perimeter of the cake, a light pastry filling between the layers. And all the fancy icing flowers on top.

He rubbed his neck. Now it was her turn to be nervous. Was it not what he'd expected? Was it too much? Not enough? "Tessa, I—" His steady brown gaze turned from the cake to her. "This is incredible."

She blew out a pent-up breath. "I even made sure all the strawberries were as close to the same size as possible." She had fussed way too much over every single detail. But she didn't regret it. She wanted this to be a success, she suddenly realized, more than she'd wanted anything.

"It's perfect." The intensity of his look made her light-headed. Which could probably turn out to be a little scary on top of all her nerves.

She nodded toward the bread bag. "This is still warm."

"You baked that special?"

She smiled. "No one can resist warm bread. Is there anything else I can do?"

"Pray," he said with a little chuckle. His gaze settled on her in a way that made it hard to look away. A warm, fuzzy feeling spread through her abdomen and into her limbs, which hung heavy and awkward on her body.

"I have to tell you something," he said, rubbing his neck. "I sort of didn't—"

"What is it?"

Just then, Gia burst out the back door carrying some cut

pink flowers in little vases. "Hey, Tessa," she called as she put them on the table. "Wow. Look at that!" She admired the beautiful cake from several angles. "I'm so glad you're here, because Leo's been a real crank this morning."

Tessa saw a warning look pass between brother and sister before Gia flew back into the restaurant, taking the bread and the cake with her. She was almost sure those flowers were peonies clipped from the bushes growing on the side of their house. Meaning: Leo had cut flowers?

Before Tessa could ask Leo what was going on, Aunt Loretta and Uncle Cosmo walked out onto the patio.

"This is quite a surprise, Leo," Uncle Cosmo said. "A fancy lunch, and none of us even knew."

As they *ooh*ed and *ahh*ed over the new patio and the beautifully set table, Tessa turned to Leo. "A *surprise*?" she asked. "As in, your dad has no *idea*?"

He turned very red. He dropped his voice. "That's what I wanted to let you know. I tried to tell him a couple of times, but I…I don't know. I didn't want to give him a chance to say no, so I told him this morning. Are you angry?"

"Leo, I'm so nervous, I'm not sure."

"Don't be nervous. It's going to be great. I hope. And… I'm sorry I didn't tell you sooner."

She saw how nervous he was. And stressed. So she shrugged. "It is going to be great. I believe in you."

She *did* believe in him. No matter what happened.

Loretta pinched Leo's cheek, then clutched her chest. "My heart is fluttering with excitement. What time did you get here this morning, anyway? Never mind; don't answer that. I can't wait to taste everything. Just remember, your father is a bear."

Leo hugged his aunt. "Bears kill people, Aunt Loretta."

"He's a big, cuddly teddy bear, underneath the big bad bear. Don't forget that, either."

Uncle Cosmo slapped him on the back. "Leo, you've worked hard. We're proud."

Leo placed his arm on Tessa's shoulder and guided her to a seat at the table, then went to get his dad.

Tessa's mouth was dry, and her palms were sweating. She could barely manage polite answers to Aunt Loretta's questions about her dessert. At last Leo guided his father outside onto the patio. Mr. Castorini walked over to the table, acknowledging Tessa with a brief nod as he took everything in. As he scraped his own seat back, he said, "The patio looks nice, Leo. But we've got a lot of work to do this afternoon, so let's get to this lunch, whatever it is."

"It's just lunch, Dad." Leo sent Tessa a confident nod.

All her thoughts were jumbling up inside as she forced a smile. Not just about Leo and how they'd finally cleared the air between them, but about herself and her own work. She might not be a professional baker, but she had no doubt her cake was beautiful. And no matter what happened at this lunch today, she felt…proud.

Mr. Castorini glanced up from his seat at the head of the table, his gaze resting on Tessa. She gave him a little wave and a smile.

"Hello, Tessa. You're part of the test group now, too?"

She tried to read if he was saying that in a nice-inclusive way or a bad-intrusive way. But she decided to hope for the best.

She tilted her head in Leo's direction. "Chef invited me." Then she did her best to smile widely, even though her face felt as stiff as cardboard. But smiling worked for Leo, so she could try it for his sake.

Her response got an unexpected wink from Leo. Which made her smile for real. And blush. *Again.*

Gia came back with a cutting board full of sliced bread.

Leo stood up at his place across from his father at the opposite end of the table. He rubbed his hands together and cleared his throat. "Thank you, everyone, for coming today for this special meal brought to you by Tessa and me." He gestured and smiled in her direction. Tessa felt touched but didn't want any credit. Leo deserved the spotlight today. But he didn't seem to feel the same way, because he said, "Tessa, would you like to tell them about the bread?"

"It's warm, and it smells good," Gia said.

Leo's father eyed the bread like it might possibly contain poison. "It's not French bread," Tessa rushed to say. "It's very crusty on the outside and soft on the inside, the way they make it in Italy. French bread typically doesn't contain oil, but Italian bread does—so for this loaf, I used imported Tuscan olive oil." She pushed the plate a little toward him. Aunt Loretta helped pass it down. Leo set a plate of dipping oil with herbs in the middle of the table.

Gia didn't hesitate to dive right in. "This is so good. What's in here?"

"It's Italian peasant bread. With oregano and rosemary." She rushed to add, "But I can make it without the herbs next time if you think it's too much." She hoped Leo's dad had heard the word *Italian*, which she'd enunciated loud and clear.

"This entire meal is all organic," Leo said. "Every vegetable came from local farmers. The seafood was flown in from the east coast, and it's so fresh it was literally swimming in the Atlantic yesterday. And it was all sustainably sourced."

His dad snorted a little. Aunt Loretta shushed him.

Mr. Castorini frowned at his sister before addressing Leo. "How much did you pay for seafood that was swimming yesterday?"

"More than the frozen stuff that you buy from the general restaurant suppliers," Leo said, cool and steady. "But Dad, the extra business this generates will make up for it."

"It's not going to taste any different," he said.

Tessa grabbed her stomach, wishing for antacids. *This* was what they were up against.

And she'd thought her *mom* was stubborn.

If Leo's dad wouldn't buy in to what Leo was trying to do, she could kiss her opportunity to make beautiful desserts goodbye. She knew in her heart that she was meant to create more than bread. She just knew it.

But there was more. She could tell from the care Leo had taken and the hard work he'd done that he was passionate about what he was doing. She could hear it in his voice. See it in his uncharacteristically guarded demeanor. She understood now more than ever that Leo wanted the restaurant to be a success, and not just for his father. He seemed filled with pride in his work.

"All this fuss and money," Mr. Castorini said, waving his hand over the table.

"Dad," Leo said with restraint, "will you please just give this a chance?"

Aunt Loretta and Uncle Cosmo glanced worriedly at each other. Gia seemed oblivious, still eating bread. But Mr. Castorini was cranky, and Leo seemed to finally hit his irritation point. If Leo, the usual tension-breaker, couldn't defuse the situation, who on earth would?

Leo left and returned with beautifully plated summery salads. "These are mesclun greens with pistachios, shallots, blood oranges, and a citrus dressing."

Mr. Castorini folded his arms. "Were the oranges still on the tree in Florida yesterday? And if they were, how much did it cost to get them here today?"

Tessa's eyes darted over to Leo, who looked a little strange. His color was high, and his lips were pressed tightly together. If he were a normal person who wasn't happy all the time, she'd think he was actually getting a little…angry.

"Actually, Mr. Castorini," Tessa surprised herself by saying. "because the climate is changing, there are orange trees in southern Indiana now." Did she actually say that? She did a mental head slap. Because that was an *awful* joke.

Loretta laughed. Cosmo frowned. And Leo…blinked.

Okay, that wasn't funny—at all. But it had possibly prevented Leo from saying something nasty to his dad.

"Actually, blood oranges come from Sicily," she continued. "They're known to have raspberry notes in addition to the usual citrusy ones. I know that because I've made *granita* before. That's—well, you know what that is. It's an Italian shaved ice. In fact, I'd love to make you some if you happen to have more of those oranges, Leo."

Now she was rambling and going overboard. But at least she'd said *something*. And that felt really good. And it was a little scary, but she was still alive. So…brava for her.

The side of Mr. Castorini's mouth quirked up a little. "Thank you very much, Tessa." He speared some salad on his fork and examined it carefully. Tessa wanted to tell him to *just eat it already*—because all this tension was killing her—when the gate clinked open.

Her mom stood on the new patio. Her apron was gone, and she was wearing a dress. And makeup. She looked really nice. And she was holding up a bottle of wine.

If she wasn't mistaken, it happened to be the really expensive vintage sent by Great Aunt Adele from Provence. French wine at this very Italian meal? *Oh no.*

"Hi, Leo," her mom said pleasantly. "Loretta, Cosmo, Marco." She said their names like she said hi to them every day instead of not for the past twenty years. Then she addressed Leo's dad directly. "I brought some wine in celebration of our children's accomplishments."

"They haven't accomplished anything yet," Marco said practically under his breath.

"Of course they have," Tessa's mom said with a big smile. Her mom looked really pretty when she smiled. Which she needed to do more often. "They've had the courage to marry despite us, and they've come up with these incredible plans." She waved her arms over the patio to demonstrate. "That's a reason to celebrate, isn't it? That we've raised children with minds of their own who have come together to help save our businesses."

Wow. Her mom blew her away. How had she not seen that before?

Her mom placed the wine in the middle of the table. "This is an excellent pairing with seafood. The grapes are from Giverny, which of course is where Monet painted." She looked at Leo. "In our tradition, a bottle of wine with a meal is good luck. We Montgomerys wish you every success with your new venture."

Her words and gracious gesture made Tessa a little teary.

This was such a weird day. First of all, her mom never dressed up during a workday. She also almost never drank, let alone at noontime. And third…how long had it been since Tessa had seen her without an apron on? Tessa vowed to give her more excuses to get out of the bakery.

Leo walked up to her mom and hugged her. "Thank you for the wine, Joanna." He guided her to the table. "Please join us."

"I didn't want to intrude," she said with a sweet smile. "But if you insist." Her gaze wandered to Marco, who looked at her a little grumpily and signaled for her to have a seat.

Leo grabbed a chair, and Gia ran in for another plate. Her mom sat down on the end, near Marco, who stared at her like she'd just landed in a spaceship in the parking lot.

"Our children are always innovating," her mom said as she proceeded to open the wine herself. "It's the way of a new generation, Marco." She poured the wine and passed him a glass, smiling. "Cheers."

He glanced from her to the glass. Tessa, holding her breath, caught Leo's eye. He was as focused on the moment as she was.

Slowly, Leo's dad took the glass and lifted it, first to Leo and then to Tessa. "Okay, fine. Cheers." Then everyone drank and dug into their food.

Leo approached Tessa's chair. "I'm glad your mom came," he whispered in her ear, which sent an unwelcome shiver running down her back. "Is your grandmother around?"

Tessa nodded toward the bakery. "She's working today."

"I'll be right back." He gave her shoulders a squeeze before running next door.

Aw geez. How could she not like this guy?

This was turning into a real family affair. For better or for worse. While her grandmother was nearly always Tessa's fiercest ally, she also had the Montgomery propensity to cut with a phrase.

"The bread is fantastic today, Tessa," her mom said. "The crust is perfect."

"I totally agree." Gia waved a torn piece in the air. "I can eat just this for lunch, it's so good."

Then Tessa's grandmother appeared on Leo's arm...with both her sisters in tow.

Holy cavatelli. They must have closed the bakery for lunch. The last time that happened was when her grandfather had died.

Tessa's already roiling stomach took another plunge. She needed to get off this roller-coaster ride before her lunch ended up coming right back up.

Leo appeared like magic with more chairs and more plates, and everyone had a seat.

"This looks so sweet," Vivienne said, snapping photos with her phone of everyone around the beautifully set table.

That was the thing with Viv. You'd better not chew with your mouth open because you just never knew when she was shooting a little video of you—sleeping, eating, or doing something else she could hold for ransom.

Tessa's mother poured more wine, a sure way to soften everyone's spirits...and taste buds.

"The wine is excellent," Uncle Cosmo said.

"It's good," Leo's dad said. "But Italian grapes are sweeter. Italian wine has been made for the past four thousand years. And Italy has the perfect climate for growing grapes."

"Funny, Marco," Tessa's mother said, "but I wonder why it is that thirty-eight of the top fifty most expensive wines are from France."

"Hi everyone," Juliet said from her place with a little wave. "I just wanted to say that I'm a certified marriage counselor, and I want everyone to be aware of *harsh lead-ins* and *defensive responses*, okay?"

"We don't know what you're talking about," Aunt Loretta said sweetly, "but it's so nice to see all you Montgomery girls. You've all grown up so lovely."

Just then, Noah and Jack appeared from around the corner of the building. "Vivienne told us about the big lunch," Noah said. "We came to support you."

Leo looked thrilled to see his friends. And Tessa knew that somehow there would always be enough pasta for all.

"We came for the free food," Jack said, slapping Leo on the back. "Just kidding. Mostly. And to wish you well. Knock 'em dead, buddy."

"Here, we brought you this," Noah said, handing him a gift bag.

"What is it?" Leo asked. Tessa could already tell by its shape that it was a candle.

"It's called *Calm Breezes*. Great for stress relief, like when this is all over."

"Thanks, Noah," Leo said. Juliet took the candle from the middle of the table and sniffed it as everyone dug into the fancy salads.

"How are you doing?" Leo whispered as he came around to clear the plates.

He was asking how *she* was doing? "I'm so nervous I can't even taste my food," she admitted.

"No, Tessa," he said in a low voice, only to her. "You need to enjoy every single bite, no matter what happens. Because we worked really hard and it turned out...awesome. *No matter what happens.*"

Before she could respond, he gave her hand a little squeeze and then disappeared back into the restaurant.

Aunt Loretta looked at her strangely. So much so that Tessa made sure she didn't have any food on her face. Leaning over, she said, "Leo must think a lot of you, Tessa, to give you his mother's ring."

Tessa's hand suddenly felt paralyzed on the table. The sun was shining, reflecting off the ring in prisms of sparkling light that must have caught Aunt Loretta's attention, making it look more beautiful than ever.

Leo had given her his mother's ring? Her thoughts whirled. Maybe he'd done it to make their marriage look authentic to his family. But it was sentimental. Valuable. Full of memories. Not to mention it had belonged to his beloved *mother*. She'd had no idea.

"I-I love it," she managed, twirling it a little, where it caught even more light and looked even more beautiful. "It's so unique."

The older woman quietly patted her hand. "Like you, sweetheart."

"Thank you, Aunt Loretta," she said, lifting her glass in return.

"Sapphires in a wedding band mean faithfulness and sincerity," Vivienne said. "I learned that when I was doing some wedding photography last year."

"They can also match a person's eyes," Leo's dad said.

"Did—did Leo's mom have blue eyes?" Tessa asked.

"Like the summer sky," his dad said, smiling a little.

"I'm honored to wear it," Tessa said. This was terrifying. The ring—this lunch—underscored that real people were involved with their scam. And feelings. And...her own were being messed with, too.

Fortunately, at that moment, Leo came through the door, carrying steaming bowls of linguine. He served his dad first, then everyone else.

Tessa recognized calamari and mussels, and judging by the fragrant scent, the pasta was covered in a garlic butter sauce.

Everyone waited for Leo to finish dishing out the pasta, except Noah, who immediately dug in until Jack knifed him in the ribs.

Leo took a seat next to Tessa, giving her a wink. "Dig in, everyone."

"Wait," Marco said, frowning after a few bites. "This is your mother's recipe."

"That's right, Dad," Leo said, stopping with a fork halfway to his mouth.

"I—I haven't served this recipe in the restaurant for...a long time."

Oh no. The seconds ticked. No one broke the silence. Tessa wracked her brain to think of a quip, but not even a bad one came to mind. Leo himself seemed to be struggling with what to say.

The table was so silent, you could hear the birds twittering in the trees behind the parking lot. Finally, Leo spoke. "I wanted to do something to honor Mom. Taste it, Dad." His strained voice seemed to include a silent *please*.

"Oh. I see," Marco said, examining the dish as carefully as if he'd been using a microscope. "And these are the fish that were alive yesterday?"

"Swimming in the Atlantic," Leo said with a grin.

Leo's dad carefully speared some linguine on his fork and brought it to his mouth. Tessa felt the vibrations from Leo's knee freaking out next to hers. On the opposite side of the table, her grandmother looked at her and smiled, a small comfort.

Marco set down his fork and chewed the bite slowly. When he finally swallowed, he said, "The seafood is very tender but not mushy. The pasta is al dente. The dish is perfectly warm."

"So then you like it?" Leo asked.

"It's just as your mother made it," he said, his voice cracking a little, "except for the recently swimming seafood." Marco lifted a glass to his son. Well, make that Tessa, too, because he looked at her as well. "You have my permission to work your magic together. And we'll see what happens." Then he drained his wine and set the glass down on the table with a definitive thud. "Eat, everybody. It's delicious."

"Marco," Tessa's mom said after tasting the dish herself, "our children have done an unbelievable job."

"I think, Joanna," Leo's dad said, "you're absolutely right."

"This was totally worth taking a break from my SAT flash cards," Gia said.

Tessa clapped her hands. Amid everyone's exclaiming, forks clinking, and everyone digging in, Leo reached over and kissed her. A short, quick, enthusiastic kiss—an impulsive, natural thing to do.

And then he grinned.

She high-fived him.

Which was weird and also something she hadn't done since she was twelve. But he laughed. And she did, too, because she suddenly felt giddy and shaky. Because their families were actually agreeing on something. And enjoying food together.

"You did it," she said, sincerely thrilled for him. "Congratulations."

"*We* did it, Countess."

The *fraisier* was the crown jewel of the meal. Everyone raved and exclaimed over that, too.

Strangely, Tessa hadn't been worried about it. She *knew* it would be delicious.

And she felt like this was Leo's time.

Her mother smiled. "I haven't seen a *fraisier* like that since I was at the baker's convention in Chicago a few years ago. I'm proud of you, Tessa." She looked at Leo. "And you too, Leo. The meal was superb."

"Thanks, Joanna," Leo said.

Tessa's mom turned to Marco. "Thank you for letting us in on the taste testing." She turned to Tessa. "I'm too full, and I drank two glasses of wine," her mother said. "I think I'm going to walk home."

"I'll walk with you," Marco said. "Leo's got it covered for now. I'll be back around four, okay?"

Tessa caught Leo's eye. He shrugged pointedly and took a sip of wine. If anyone else noticed the two notorious enemies walking off together, no one said a thing.

Leo had circled his arm around the back of Tessa's chair as they chatted and laughed with family and friends. Like it was the most natural thing to do. Like their families hadn't been mortal enemies for the past century. Tessa was overjoyed to be at Leo's side, celebrating their first accomplishment.

They'd passed the first test. They'd done it. *Together.*

CHAPTER EIGHTEEN

Tessa got home in time to make a salad for their dinner with a charcuterie board and some lemon iced tea they could enjoy outside on the patio. She took a glass of tea outside and sat in the little garden, enjoying the late-afternoon sun, the faraway sound of a lawnmower, and Cosette's little explorations.

She liked working normal hours. Having a life was…fun.

Something had changed between Leo and her. Something more than the high feeling of the successful day. She wasn't sure what it was, but she knew that it was getting harder and harder to keep her guard up around him.

The gate squeaked, and she looked up to find Jack walking into the yard, a manila envelope in his hand.

Tessa automatically poured him an iced tea, using the glass she'd brought out for Leo. "Have a seat, Mayor."

He sat down, lifting his sunglasses to the top of his head and looking around the tiny yard. "It's really peaceful back here."

"One of my favorite places," she said. "Thanks for coming to support Leo this afternoon. I think it meant a lot to him to have you guys there."

"It meant a lot for us to be there. Besides the free food, I mean." He gave a little laugh. "Although I personally think his dad caved because he has a soft spot for *you*."

"Whatever it was, I'm glad it worked."

He nudged the big envelope toward her on the yellow

table. "I brought your official marriage certificate."

"Thank you." She took it and set it on an extra seat, out of sight but unfortunately not out of mind.

He leaned back and put his feet up on one of the seats. "Leo's changed a lot since you two connected again."

"How so?" Her heart sped up a little despite herself.

"I just think he's looking at life a bit differently."

"In what way?"

"Well, he seems to be opening his mind to new things." He watched Cosette stalk a spider. "Like owning a cat."

"He *did* say that he was more of a dog person."

He studied her closely, which led her to believe that something was up. He seemed to choose his words carefully. "Well, I tend to believe his newfound love of cats might be because of the fact that he's no longer in danger of dropping dead after he comes into contact with one."

That was so bizarre. As if Cosette knew she was being talked about, she wound herself around Tessa's calves and meowed loudly. "I have no idea what you're talking about."

Jack leaned forward and met her gaze. "Leo's allergic to cats."

"Leo plays with Cosette all the time." Cosette sprung suddenly into her lap and took a minute to settle herself in a round heap with her tail curled about her body. "I've never once seen him sneeze." Allergic? No way.

"Leo isn't *just* allergic to cats, Tessa. Leo is puffy-eyed-wheezy-get-out-the-EpiPen allergic to cats. A few years ago, we had to take him to the ER after a college house party because he couldn't *breathe*."

She set down her glass, feeling shaky. "That...that's impossible."

"Come to think of it, I ran into him the night of your wedding buying antihistamines in the drug store."

Her head spun. She thought of how Leo seemed a lot more affectionate to Cosette lately, compared to that first night. She'd passed that off as him simply getting more used to her. And the night of their wedding…she'd thought he'd been trying to escape—to get away from her. But he'd snuck away to buy medicine?

"But Jack, Leo's fine now. Around Cosette, I mean. How can that be?"

"Yeah." He took a sip of tea. "Because he's been getting those shots."

Frowning, she tapped her glass. "What shots?" Then it dawned. "Oh my gosh. *Allergy* shots? Like, *millions* of allergy shots so he can live with my *cat*?"

Jack nodded, looking pleased that she finally put this all together. "That would be correct."

"Doesn't that kind of treatment go on for years?"

"That would also be correct."

"I don't know what to say."

Jack gave her a wink. "Leo's complicated. And I can't even tell you if he's capable of normal relationship behavior. But I don't think his dad is the only one who has a soft spot for you."

Tessa's head was reeling. "Thanks. For telling me that. I think."

"Hey, no problem," he said before he got up. "You and Leo can name your firstborn after me."

• • •

"What do you want to do now?" Leo asked after a quick dinner as they sat together that evening on the glider, watching the lights flicker on one by one in the valley below. "It's a beautiful evening."

"It is at that," Tessa responded a little formally.

What was wrong with him? Everything between them since he'd gotten home had been so…awkward. Trying to look at her during casual conversation and then eye-locking and completely forgetting what he was saying. Trying to say something normal but having it come out sounding like he was a nineteenth-century gentleman. (Had he actually said *Would you like to take a stroll?*) And starting a conversation only to have it fall flat. Like maybe he wasn't the only one feeling the awkwardness.

The million things he had to do to start planning his new menu offerings had kept his mind off of Tessa for most of the day. But as soon as he came home and found her waiting on the patio, sipping tea and reading a book, he knew he was in trouble.

He couldn't get her out of his mind. He was forgetting why he shouldn't get involved with her. Oh, yeah—so he wouldn't hurt her.

But all he wanted was Tessa.

"Maybe we should go for that stroll," she said.

Their eyes met, and he definitely got the feeling from what he saw in them that she was not really serious about the walk. "Maybe. Or we could do a puzzle."

Did he just suggest that? He hadn't put a puzzle together in about twenty years. And he could go another twenty not feeling bad about that.

"I just bought a new one," she said. "*Lavender fields of Provence.*"

"Oh, fun," he said without real enthusiasm. "Or we could go visit the neighbors."

"We could."

"Or we could just talk," he said.

"I was very proud of…us today," she said. Okay, good. Now they were getting somewhere.

"Same. We make a good team." He looked at their two hands, joined together. Somehow he'd started holding hers. It felt natural, holding her hand.

She squeezed his hand a little. "Leo, I'm going to ask you a question, and I want the truth."

"Okay, sure. What is it?" Her tone made him nervous. He usually thought so clearly about women, but she had him all jumbled up.

She sat up and stared straight at him. "Are you allergic to my cat?"

His first thought was that he was going to murder Jack. "Not anymore."

She let go of his hand and threw her hands up. "Why didn't you say something?"

He blew out a breath. And looked into her eyes, as blue as the summer sky. "Because you'd had all the stress of your breakup and the business folding and then this crazy marriage. I just couldn't make you give up something important to you, and I—"

The next thing he knew, his arms were full of soft, curvy woman. Kissing him. Wrapping herself around him, flooding his senses with her softness and her scent, with the touch of her lips on his.

Soon Leo was lost in her kisses, which were enthusiastic at first, and then deep and slow. He angled his mouth to kiss her more thoroughly, cradling her face in his hands.

His heart was pounding, steady and fast. And half of his head was pushing the panic button. He was feeling too much, allowing himself to cross a line that he never crossed. He pulled back a little. "Maybe we should talk about where this is going, because I want to be honest, I'm not sure—"

She interrupted him. "I'm okay with doing this just for fun," she said a little breathlessly. "Because when our agreement is done, I'm moving. Whether I get into pastry school or not. I want to experience a different place. And I want to learn to bake. So maybe I'll move to Chicago and get a job in a pastry shop."

"Oh." Just what he wanted to hear—which was also what he'd never expected to hear from her. But…she was moving? Definitely?

"I wanted to tell you something else," she continued. "I owe you a thank-you. You helped me get back something really important that I'd lost for a long time."

"What was that?" His mind was still stuck on *I'm moving*.

"Myself," she whispered. "I was…I was stuck. You showed me what was possible. I mean, it seemed impossible, but we actually have a shot at this. And did I tell you my mom's already gotten three new clients based on your dad's connections?"

He shook his head. "Tessa, you would've done everything anyway. Just on a slightly different time schedule." He believed that with all his heart. No one he knew worked harder or was more determined than she was.

"You gave me the courage to put my dreams front and center again," she said with feeling. "I can't even tell you the difference that's made."

He shook his head. "It wasn't one-sided. You took a chance on me, on this wild scheme. You believed it was actually possible." She'd believed in *him*.

She smiled. "Well, I really believe you can accomplish anything you set your mind to."

"Tessa, you're a force. Anyone who can move my father—"

"He just has a soft spot for me. Because of the cannoli."

He circled his hands around her waist. "So do I," he whispered.

He bent his head to kiss her. Her lips met his, the contact soft and lush and electric. She wrapped her arms around his neck, and he took in the feel of her in his arms, the taste of her, sweet and addictive.

The contact made him dizzy. Points of light danced behind his eyelids like the tiny lights that dotted the valley before them. *What is she doing to me?* He'd known a lot of women. He knew *a lot* about sex. But this…this felt…

Well. He didn't want to overthink it. Just that he couldn't get enough of her lips, her scent, her amazing curves. And her enthusiasm for kissing him back.

And he was filled with a desperate need to show her, not just tell her, how beautiful she was. So she would know beyond a doubt. He wanted to erase all memory of that loser who had hurt her and made her question herself. *Permanently.*

For the first time in his life, Leo was…lost. In her sweet scent. The softness of her skin. The kindness and generosity of her spirit.

Whatever this was, it was a whole lot different than anything he'd experienced before.

On impulse, he tugged her up from the glider.

"Where are we going?" she asked as she took his hand.

"Just trust me."

He led her around the house to the front door, where he suddenly scooped her up. She let out a little squeak.

"Clean slate," he said. "No faking this time."

"No faking," she whispered, her arms around his neck.

Then he carried his wife through the door and up the stairs to their bedroom, where they spent time showing each other the many ways that French and Italian culture can actually mingle together quite well.

· · ·

A long time later, they lay awake in the dark bedroom, Tessa's head tucked under Leo's chin, her hair spilling over his chest. A light breeze drifted in through the windows, as well as an occasional *whoo* from a resident owl in the old oak tree.

She felt a little stunned. A little blank.

But something niggled at her brain. "Since this is just for fun," she said, "I hope you don't mind if I ask you a question."

"Okay, sure," Leo said as he reclined against the headboard. "Anything."

She sat up on one elbow. "Sam told me I don't have a passionate nature."

"Sam needs to piss off."

She burst out laughing. "I'm serious about needing to know what you thought…about me."

He lifted a brow in surprise. "Are you serious? You want a critique?"

She nodded vehemently. "I need to know." She didn't want to guess like she did with Sam about their lovemaking. "When he cheated," she explained, "I was taken by surprise. So I want to know how you felt about…everything." She knew how *she* felt—that being with him was mind-*effing*-blowing. But she wasn't about to tell him that.

He touched one of her curls. Tentatively, like he was thinking very carefully about what to say. It made Tessa nervous, like he was struggling to find the words, trying to be nice. She held her breath, waiting for him to speak. "Tessa, if making love with you was a wine, you'd be DOCG."

Okaaay. "I have no idea what that is."

"It's an Italian wine classification that denotes the highest quality. It takes into account the grape ripeness, the wine-making process, and the barrel maturation."

"Oh. Thank you. I think." He was comparing her to Italian wine? Was that a good thing?

"Let me put it a French way. You're an MF."

"That doesn't sound very complimentary at all." Then she suddenly got it. Tessa stared at him, her eyes becoming watery. "Do you mean MOF?" She pronounced it *Moff*.

"Yes, that. Even I know about the most prestigious French culinary competition of all time." He lay back and smiled widely. "To me, you're Julia Child."

She laughed, but she really felt like crying. Because he'd just said the exact right thing. In the sweetest way. "Even the fabulous Julia didn't get the *Meilleur Ouvrier de France*. You just put me on a scale with the finest French chefs of all time."

He smiled slowly and broadly. "*Exactly*."

She met his gaze, and there he was, looking at her with a

secretive glint in those big, moony Italian eyes.

And just like that, something in her heart broke open. Leo was kind and funny. He got her more than any other person she'd ever met. He was invested in her success. And he wanted her to be exactly who she was. So for however long this lasted, she'd take it. With both her arms open wide.

• • •

Much later, they were about to fall asleep when she asked, "So how bad are those allergy shots?"

"Horrible," he said without hesitation. "I mean, I'm probably going to need *years* of you making this up to me."

She rolled on top of him, her hair falling on his chest. "I'd better start right now."

He looked up at the woman in his arms, who was beautiful inside and out, and smiled. "Well, if this is the payback for not telling you about my cat allergy, I'll take the shots for the rest of my life." As he rolled them over on the bed, she let out a little squeal. And then he kissed her again.

CHAPTER NINETEEN

On a sunny, golden late afternoon a few weeks later, Tessa set out walking down their street in her best heels, which she absolutely wasn't used to walking in. Especially along a sidewalk made even more crooked by tree roots that pushed up against the concrete like too-tight shoes. But she chalked that up to the charm of their old neighborhood. Lilac opened her front door as she passed and waved, wishing her good luck. Because tonight, Leo was making dinner not just for family but for a restaurant full of people.

It was showtime. All their planning and hard work were coming to a grand finale.

Lilac ran down her little gravel driveway to meet her. "Wow," she said, looking over Tessa's black dress and heels.

"Is it too much?" Tessa gave a nod to her lace-covered dress. "I'm going for nice, not hot."

"You can't help what you are, girl," Lilac said, grinning. "Tessa, you're just like the Very Hungry Caterpillar."

"I look like a caterpillar?" Figures Lilac would use something related to work to describe her. But...a caterpillar?

"No," she said, getting teary. "You look beautiful, like a caterpillar who discovered she's really a butterfly. And one look at you might just take Leo's mind off any nerves he's having over his grand-opening dinner. Things are going well with you two, I take it?"

Tessa frowned. "How do you know that? Was it in my horoscope?"

"No, honey. It's written all over your face. You look *happy*."

She *was* happy. Really happy.

Looking at her oldest friend, she said, "I feel like now is our chance to really help our families' businesses. We've worked so hard, you know?"

"And?"

"And what?"

"And what about you and Leo?"

She couldn't help smiling. "I don't even want to put a label on it. Just that it's...really good."

"Don't be afraid, Tessa," Lilac said, giving her a side hug. "You deserve *really good*. You deserve the *best*."

Tessa hugged Lilac back. For the first time, she felt that she did deserve happiness. She was filled with pride at their efforts—and respect and admiration for him and for herself. Tonight, they were going to show the world the fruits of their labor. And that was as far as she'd allow herself to think.

And you know what? She *knew* she looked hot—in a PG, family-restaurant kind of way.

"I'm excited about tonight. And nervous for Leo." She knew she looked good. She felt great, too. She was just worried for Leo's sake. She hoped everything went as planned.

Lilac smiled. "What's there to worry about? You've done all the hard work."

"My biggest fear is that no one is going to show."

"Um," Lilac said, tapping her chin, "somehow I don't think that's going to be a problem."

Frowning, Tessa asked, "What do you mean?"

"Well, I just got back from the grocery store, and...there's actually a little line forming."

Tessa checked her phone. It was only four o'clock. "What do you mean, a line?"

Lilac pointed down the street. "Oh, just one that snakes around the bakery and up that little side street is all."

A line. Like in the old days? "Maybe that advertising we bought paid off. I'm glad people still read the weekly neighborhood paper."

"Well, that must've been quite an ad." Lilac looked down at Tessa's feet. "Wait here for a second." She returned a minute later with a drawstring bag, looking something up on her phone.

Tessa found a pair of rainbow flip-flops in the bag. "Oh, that's sweet. Thank you. For this and…for supporting me. And believing in me."

"Gosh, Tessa, they're just flip flops," she said, hugging her back. "I love you, you know that. She pulled back and shook her phone. "Now for what's really important." She began to read, "Venus and Mars are conjugating in your ninth house of adventure, and Mars is in your sultry eighth house of intimacy—"

"Lilac! I have to go. What's the bottom line?"

"Knock 'em dead! The cosmos says you're ready for this!" She gave her a big hug. "And I do too!"

Tessa hugged her best friend. "What I'm really lucky about is having a great friend like you."

· · ·

The flip-flops did wonders for Tessa's feet but nothing for the gaggle of geese fluttering in her stomach. By the time she'd walked the three blocks downtown, she couldn't believe what she saw.

A line of people stretched from the restaurant, around the bakery, and clear up the "little" side street that Lilac mentioned, which wasn't little at all. And wait a minute… when Tessa examined the line closer, she realized that people were splitting off from the restaurant line to form a line to Bonjour! Breads as well.

People were checking out the bakery while they were in line for the restaurant.

The *bakery* was getting business, too. That brought tears of joy to her eyes.

Oh, *hurray*.

There was no way into the restaurant unless she walked through the crowd, so she plunged straight into the noisy tangle of people.

As she got closer, someone yelled and waved, "Contessa! Yoo-hoo! Hi!"

Contessa? Who in the world…

It was a red-haired, middle-aged woman she'd never seen around town before. "I'm Beverly," the woman said. "You know, Beverly Roseberry from your channel. You're even cuter in person! I came from South Bend to meet you."

"Beverly? From my YouTube channel? Hi!" Of course. BeverlyRoseB commented all the time. And had a yellow tabby cat named Charlie. "How's Charlie doing?"

"Oh, getting into mischief as always." She pointed to the two women on either side of her. "These are my best friends."

"I'm Charlotte," one said.

"And I'm Daisy."

Tessa immediately recognized them as people who followed her channel and commented often on her videos. It was amazing that her little channel with a few hundred subscribers could bring a handful of nice people out here to support her.

"We have a reservation," Beverly said. "Good thing, too, or we'd never have gotten in. It's going to be packed."

Tessa greeted them and gave them all hugs. "How did you find out about this?" Because she certainly didn't post about it. In fact, in the past few weeks, she'd barely posted any videos at all.

"Well," Beverly said, "the wedding videos you posted were so cute, and seeing you with Leo and how you both worked so hard to make this happen…"

Wedding videos? And they knew Leo's *name*?

She was always careful not to identify anyone in her life by full name. And she would never post a…

Vivienne.

"We were hoping to meet Cosette, too," Charlotte said.

"She's at home," Tessa said, "but you're welcome to stop by and see her." Did she just invite strangers to her house?

Well, they weren't really strangers. And they sure looked a lot more trustworthy than DrLongschlongMD.

Tessa thanked them for coming and was greeted by still more people who knew her name. She was a little dazed when she finally managed to break through the crowd and enter the back door of the restaurant.

It was shockingly quiet in the dining room compared to the noisy buzz in the street. Noah was setting out tea lights on all the tables. "You look nice, Tessa. I love the black lace. Very… *Pretty Woman* of you."

"Thanks, Noah. You look really nice, too." He was wearing a sweater with a bold geometric black-and-white pattern.

Under his black skinny pants, his socks matched the sweater.

She was just about to put her nice heels back on when there was a commotion from the kitchen, and Aunt Loretta, Uncle Cosmo, Leo's dad, and Leo himself burst out of the swinging door.

Aunt Loretta was wringing her hands. "So many people," she said. "We don't have room."

"Don't worry, Loretta," Cosmo said. "Leo will figure this out. Look at all the business!"

"Go tell all those people that this is not the Olive Garden, Leo," Marco said, pointing to the door. "Reservations only."

"We *did* take reservations," Leo said, "but a lot of local folks just showed up, like they usually do. I hate to turn them away."

"These are more than local people. Where are they all coming from?" His dad sounded a little panicked.

"I have no idea," Leo said. "We placed a couple of ads in different places. Our social media accounts are still really young."

"I just heard someone outside say that the food critic from the *Chicago Tribune* is in that line," Tessa said.

That's when Leo looked up and saw her. He smiled a slow smile that warmed her to her toes and, despite the chaos, filled her with a flood of calm assurance.

"Are you serious?"

"As serious as a Zagat rating," she answered with a shrug.

In that moment, she knew that whatever this chaos was, they would handle it. It was going to be okay.

Leo walked up and took her hand, steering her a little out of the way. "You look amazing," he said. "I really love the rainbow flip-flops."

"They're from Lilac. She never misses an opportunity to support a cause."

He kissed her, right there, in front of everyone, making her blush from head to toe.

She couldn't tell if anyone really noticed except for Vivienne, who was in their face, taking photos.

"Vivienne, what are you doing?" Tessa asked, breaking away from Leo's lips.

"Capturing how cute you two are."

"Wait a minute." Tessa pulled out her phone and called up her channel. "I have five thousand subscribers! I have ads on my channel!" She looked up incredulously. "Do you know what that means, when you have ads?

"Yep," Vivienne said. "It's so exciting. People want to see the nice young couple who are trying to save a restaurant and a bakery."

Tessa handed the phone to Leo. "Look."

"Well, I'll be," he said, passing it around to his aunt and uncle and dad. "Tessa, you've brought a hundred people here."

Tessa nodded to her sister. "Vivienne did."

"The power of social media," Aunt Loretta said.

"It was more than that," Vivienne said. "Tessa, you're great at communicating and being friendly and funny. I just provided some emotional content to bring them here."

By taking videos of her when she wasn't looking and sharing God only knew what, but hey, it worked, right?

"Well, what are we going to do about it?" Marco asked. "They're here to see the cute couple, so go give them the cute couple."

"I have an idea," Leo said.

Of course he did.

"Instead of turning people away empty-handed," Leo said, "let's all go out there and give them a taste of the restaurant."

"The health department doesn't allow us to serve people on the sidewalk," Uncle Cosmo said.

"How about vouchers for a free appetizer?" Leo asked. "I can hand them signed business cards for that. And then…we can hand them something delicious."

"Bruschetta," Loretta said. "We can make up as many carry-out containers as we can."

"Okay, everybody," Leo said, giving Tessa a wink. "All hands on deck."

. . .

"We ran out of business cards and bruschetta sometime after dark," Leo's dad said as he set an enormous bowl of *frutti del mar* on the table at ten thirty that night. Leo poured wine for his dad and Tessa's family as they sat and ate and talked over the bizarre evening.

"Yes, but we met tons of people," Tessa said.

Tessa's mother held out her glass. "You two charmed the crowd."

"And the food was excellent," Leo's dad said.

Tessa's grandmother nodded wisely. "Everyone had a great time. They'll all be back."

"The bakery stayed open late and made a ton of business," her mother said. "We had some croissant dough ready to go, so we made a bunch of chocolate croissants. And we sold a ton of coffee, too."

Leo couldn't believe the success. It was more than he'd

ever thought possible.

Tessa reached into her apron and pulled out a bunch of business cards, opening them like a fan. "Guess what these are, Mom and Gram?"

"Well, business cards, obviously," her mother said. "But whose?"

"Turns out that some restaurant owners and a specialty bread place caught an episode or two of my videos, and they went in and checked out the bakery. They're interested in buying our bread."

Turns out both businesses were profiting from them working together. *Bravo.*

Tessa's mom got a little teary-eyed. "Who knew that something you started for fun would create such a pot of riches?"

"Well, not riches yet," Tessa said, patting her hand. "But this is a very good start."

"It's the power of social media," Vivienne, who was leaning against the end of the booth, said.

"Vivienne," Leo said. "We owe you a lot. Thank you." He smiled at Tessa, who looked tired but happy. It made him think he'd like to see that relaxed and contented look on her face for an entirely different reason.

"Hey, no prob," Viv said, waving her hand dismissively. And smiling from ear to ear. "Turns out you two are a magnetic couple. You have great chemistry on film." She shook her camera a little.

Tessa frowned. "You still haven't told us what footage you uploaded."

"I swear I didn't upload any video that Juliet might have taken of you after you threw up in the bathroom on your wedding day." Then she chuckled.

"Dad," Leo said before Tessa had the opportunity to follow through on a death threat or at least snatch Viv's phone. "You look tired."

His dad chuckled. "I haven't been this tired since your mother was alive and business was booming. Thank you, Leo. Thank you, Tessa. Looks like all your fancy new ideas worked."

"Not so fancy," Leo said. "Just a little bit…updated. Same good food."

"Well, you were right," his dad said.

Whaaat?

"But maybe I was right, too," his dad added.

Okay, the world was back to normal again. "What do you mean?"

"People loved you both as a couple. They loved you as a married man in charge of a family restaurant. You've both worked really hard to make this happen."

Well. Full-blown praise from his dad, and a thank-you to boot. He'd take it and run with it.

"Our families have that in common, Marco," Joanna said. "Work ethic."

After the delicious meal, Tessa stood to help Leo clear the table. "Where did Juliet go?" Leo asked.

"She left early," Tessa said, her brows knitting with worry. "Jax showed up with a date."

Her mom and grandmother looked at each other. "Maybe we'll bring her some takeout."

"And dessert," Vivienne said.

As Tessa walked into the kitchen with Leo, she said, "Maybe I should go, too."

He gently grabbed her elbow. "Your mom is going. And your grandma. It's up to you, but I think they might be okay for tonight."

"Are you gently telling me not to mother my sisters?"

"Maybe I'm gently telling you that you don't have to be the *only* one to mother your sisters. And that your sisters are smart women. Maybe it can wait until tomorrow."

She shook her head and smiled. "You're full of ideas, Leo Castorini. But I have a feeling that this is a good one."

"I feel pretty good about things," Leo said. "Tonight was a success, the bakery's got a few leads, but most importantly…" His voice trailed off as he looked at her—a little tired, a little disheveled, but her eyes dancing with the same excitement he was feeling.

"Most importantly?"

"I get to go home with the woman in the rainbow flip-flops and the beautiful smile."

He took her hand and tugged her close.

And his heart was fuller than it had ever been.

• • •

"I'm so proud of you," Tessa said to Leo as he opened the door to their house at the end of the evening.

"Of me?" Leo asked, flicking the light switch and entering the kitchen. Cosette, who was curled up on Tessa's favorite chair, lifted her head and blinked at the insult of being awakened by bright lights. "We had at least a dozen YouTubers there, thanks to you. And the Chicago food critic's going to write us up. None of that was my doing."

"It was Viv," Tessa said. "She did something. I'm not quite

sure what the magic was, but it made hundreds of people appear. I still think you should have let me grab her phone. I bet she did post some kind of embarrassing footage."

"I'm sure we can find out if we watch what she uploaded."

"Never mind that," Tessa said. "Let's check tomorrow. I'd rather stay oblivious tonight. Knowing Viv, it's probably videos of me asleep with my mouth open and drooling."

He gave a little chortle. Then he got serious. "We did it. We made it work. Well, at least…we're off to a great start at saving both our businesses. We make a great team, Tessa."

She walked up to him and wrapped her arms around him. "Leo, I feel so hopeful about everything. For the first time in a long time."

He looked into her eyes and smiled. "Me too." Except he wasn't sure how much of what he was feeling had to do with their success tonight—a lot, obviously—and how much was due to simply being with her. But he couldn't put that into words. Instead, he kissed her in the warm lights of their kitchen, the new island gleaming with its brand-new top. The place looked like…home.

"Want some wine?" he asked.

"Sure." She left him to get the glasses.

Leo reached into the cabinet for a bottle. While he was waiting for her, he flipped through the mail pile.

And spied something that made his heart skip a beat.

A business envelope. With a Chicago address.

His heart nearly stopped. Closer inspection confirmed what he already knew.

The pastry school.

A million emotions flooded him. The sense of celebration that had pervaded the evening seemed to hold its breath.

What if she didn't get in?

What if she *did*?

"Tessa," Leo called, "I—I think you might want to come over here."

He thought about waiting until tomorrow to tell her. Of ignoring it just for a few more hours. But that really wasn't his decision, was it?

Tessa kicked off her flip-flops and walked over to where he'd been about to pour their wine. Cosette hopped up on a barstool and purred softly until Tessa scooped her in her arms and kissed her head, saying, "Hi, Cosey. We've had quite a day!"

She finally noticed the envelope in his hands. "I'm sorry about the mail pile," she said as she released the cat, who, judging by the way she sprung out of Tessa's arms, had had enough love for now. "I know you like things tidy. I was just so busy—"

"Tessa, darling, I didn't call you over here to chide you about not sorting the mail."

She gave him a funny look. "You're acting weird. What is it?"

He dropped his eyes to the mail. "See for yourself."

She looked at the envelope, her eyes widening when she saw the return address. She gasped, clasping her hands over her mouth.

He poured them both a glass, feeling that he for sure needed some wine right about now. But he kept his tone optimistic. "To the future," he said, handing her one. "Go for it."

She looked at him solemnly. "What if it's a rejection? This might be my only chance."

He seemed to consider that. "Come on. Just raise your glass." He waved his wineglass toward hers to encourage her to pick it up.

She lifted it with shaking hands and clinked glasses, then took a big gulp. "Leo, I—" She closed her eyes. "I guess I'm a little afraid." She paused. "Make that a *lot* afraid."

"Afraid is good." She looked like she was trying to believe him but wasn't quite getting there.

"And what if I got in? Everything will change."

Yes. That was *exactly* what he was worried about. "Change is good," he said with his best smile. "Open it."

At least, he hoped it was.

• • •

Tessa shook the envelope. Then she walked over to Leo's desk and held it up to the little lamp on top.

"What are you doing?" Leo walked up beside her and squinted into the light. "Wow, you've got quite the tremor there."

She shot him a dagger-laden look. "I was thinking that maybe a rejection is lighter than an acceptance. A rejection is *sorry, goodbye*, and an acceptance is *we need your money, your forms, and here's all the info about the classes…*"

"So, which do you think it is?" he asked, looking over her shoulder.

She set the envelope on the desk. "I can't tell." She wanted in so badly. She wanted to learn how to make pastries the right way. From real French chefs.

But she also wanted this safe, sweet haven they'd built here. The sparks between them that were just beginning to…

become something—both for their business ventures and for each other.

They were a great team. And maybe something more.

Leo rubbed his hands up and down her arms. Looking from her to the envelope, he said, "Sweetheart, no matter what's in there, we're going to handle it." She let that *Sweetheart* sink straight into her bones. "No matter what happens, you're a very talented baker. And I, for one, couldn't be prouder."

"You just said *we*," she whispered.

He turned her around and held her hands. "We'll get through this together, just like we've done everything else so far."

That made her tear up. She took strength from his firm, warm grip. From his positive words. "Thank you, Leo. For all your support. It means a lot."

He picked up the envelope and held it out to her, lifting a brow.

She shook her head and pushed his hand back. "You do it. I'm too nervous."

"Okay. Here goes." He ripped the top open and pulled out a single sheet of paper. As she held her breath, he squinted at the print. "I need my glasses."

"Leo, *please*."

"Okay, okay. *Dear Ms. Montgomery*," he read. "*As you know, the Chicago School of French Pastry is a renowned institution and the only school in the United States devoted exclusively to the techniques of baking French pastry.*"

"Leo!"

He was enjoying this way too much, as evidenced by the little twinkle in his eye.

After a quick wink, he started reading a *third* time. And she knew from the way his hand shook a little that this time was for real. "*Dear Ms. Montgomery, The Chicago School of French Pastry is pleased to welcome you into our July class*." Tessa grabbed Leo's arm. A giant grin spread across his face. "*Our faculty of world-class bakers is excited to lead you on your journey in becoming a professional pastry chef.*"

Tears blurred her vision. She hadn't really comprehended anything except for *professional pastry chef*. And the fact that Leo set down the letter and took her in his arms.

"You did it," he whispered against her hair. "Congratulations."

She'd done it. She'd gotten in.

The tears were boundless. She sniffled and clutched handfuls of his shirt. She was not a calm or beautiful crier, but that didn't seem to scare Leo away.

Finally he held her at arm's length. "Tessa. I get happy tears, but—is something wrong?"

"What will we do about your restaurant? The desserts? My family's bakery?" She almost added "us" but stopped herself. Was there an *us*? It sort of felt like there was.

"Your program lasts for five months, not five years. We'll manage."

He was so calm. So positive. Trying to channel that, she took a big breath.

"This is your dream," he said. "This is what you want, right?"

"Very badly," she said without hesitation. She couldn't help but think of how Sam used to think her wanting to go to pastry school was ridiculous. That it would be foolish to leave her job and him when she was already a baker. She'd listened to that line of reasoning for *way* too long.

Leo smoothed back her hair and handed her paper towels from the kitchen to blot her eyes and blow her nose. "Now's your time. Your time to shine."

"Oh, Leo." He got what she was trying to do. He got *her*. She threw her arms around his neck and kissed him. "Thank you for being you."

"I'm so grateful I'm me right now," he said.

She pulled back and assessed him. "Why is that?"

"Because right now you're all teary and you're looking at me like you *really* like me."

"Funny," she said, "I was thinking that you really like me, too. Because you've called me *darling* and *sweetheart*, all in the past five minutes."

"I think we're both really grateful people." His lips met hers for kisses that left her dizzy and breathless, the little room spinning around her. "Congratulations, Tessa," he whispered. "You deserve it. You deserve everything." His eyes held a sentimental look as he rubbed his thumb gently over her cheek.

"What is it?"

"I should have been saying that to you fourteen years ago."

"Well," she said, "I think that this time, we *both* won." And went back to kissing him.

CHAPTER TWENTY

The next morning, Tessa had a spring in her step and was humming a happy tune as she went about baking the loaves from yesterday that had risen and began making the fresh dough for tomorrow, as she'd done every day since she was eighteen.

Everything was the same, but in reality, *everything* was different.

She was different.

She was headed off to make her dream come true, one that for years didn't seem possible.

Even setting up the bread wasn't so bad. The difference was *freedom*. For the first time, she could choose her course. And that was absolutely thrilling.

And Leo was more than okay with it—he encouraged and supported her. He was proud of her.

She tried to just be happy in the moment. Which she was, even if it seemed too good to be true. For once, everything felt…right.

The bell over the door tinkled, as it had been doing all morning. The big commotion over her YouTube channel and the new things going on at the restaurant had brought people flocking in. This time it was Max Hammond, her mom's longtime accountant, strolling in, wearing a suit and tie. "Good morning, Tessa," he said pleasantly, setting his briefcase on a tabletop. "Can I get a half dozen of those melt-in-your-mouth croissants? I love those things."

"Hey, Max," Tessa greeted him as always. "How are you?" Inside, she did a mental fist pump. For the first time in years, his mere presence didn't give her heart palpitations from having to discuss bad news about the business.

"Great," he said. "I heard about the huge crowds last night. And the potential new baking contracts. Congratulations."

"Business is picking up." Tessa gave a thumbs-up. With all the ideas she and Leo had planned, she felt that this was only the beginning.

"Glad to hear it," Max said. "Maybe your mom will reconsider selling to the Castorinis now?"

Tessa halted, her tongs suspended over the croissants. She couldn't have just heard that. "Well, things are really looking up. We're going to be doing much better now." She had no doubt that her mom would rather cut off her right arm than sell her beloved bakery to the Castorinis, regardless of the fact that there'd been some recent fence-mending.

She decided that she did hear that wrong and was just about to ask what Max was talking about when he said, "Well then, she should probably destroy that paperwork I drew up."

Tessa's heart began a slow, hard pound. Okay, this was not a misunderstanding after all. She hadn't misheard. She flicked up her gaze to address him directly. "Max, are you saying my mom was actually preparing to sell the business to the Castorinis?" Had the lowest point actually been that low? Did her mom start some kind of sale proceedings out of desperation?

He suddenly turned bright red. And cleared his throat.

"Clearly I've overstepped. I thought you must have discussed this with Leo. I'm just so thrilled business is booming."

"With Leo?" Discuss *what exactly* with Leo?

"I'm sorry, Tessa. You'll have to take this up with him or your mom." He left a bill on the glass bakery case, grabbed his bag of croissants, and hurriedly left.

Vivienne appeared from the back just as Tessa was gripping the counter in disbelief. "What was that all about?" she asked.

Tessa's heart sank into her stomach as she realized her sister had heard everything. "Do you know anything about this?"

Viv shook her head. "Maybe Mom was considering selling months ago, when sales were really awful. That has to be it."

Tessa tried to talk herself down. She wasn't worried about the sale. Things were so much better now. There was no *reason* to sell. And surely Leo wouldn't have known about something so catastrophic and not said anything.

Would he?

. . .

In the early afternoon, Tessa left the bakery, unable to concentrate. The little house was quiet, Leo hard at work at the restaurant. After feeding Cosette, she walked over to the nook where Leo's grandfather's desk sat. She sat in the sturdy oak chair and ran her hand along the smooth, cool grain of the wood as she looked out the window into the tiny backyard.

There was the wind chime that Leo had hung on a low-hanging branch for Cosette, who liked to sit on a rock and bat at it.

And the flowers she'd planted in two old barrels, now spilling over the edges.

She turned her gaze to the inside. The main sitting room was orderly and neat, the bright pillows she'd picked out lined up on both couches—the purple one and the leather one—and her plants arranged on the floor in front of the bay window. The mail sat tidily in a basket, the electronics lined up on a charging pad. And in the middle of the tiny kitchen...the now-finished door-turned-island that had stopped her late-evening forays downtown.

It was a *home*. Something both of them had made.

It didn't look like two people forced by desperation into a fake marriage lived here. It looked like two people lived here who had given the best parts of themselves to merge their lives with compromise and care.

They'd both made it clear that their arrangement was strictly business, but somehow everything had gotten tangled up.

But it was...wonderful.

It had been so simple to fall for Leo. With his easygoing, charming personality. With his kindness. With his brilliant scheme to save both their businesses.

Neither of them had uttered the L word. But they'd begun to use words like *we* and *future*. Words that she'd taken for granted meant that he'd be sticking around.

Surely there had to be some explanation.

Leo was *honest*. He'd seen her for who she really was. He'd seen past the walls she'd put up. And he'd somehow done what no other man had done—actually broken through them.

Tessa put her elbows on the desk and dropped her head into her hands. She shuddered, a sinking sense of dread passing through her. What if Leo had gone behind her back to secure the bakery for *his* family? He certainly had the same competitive streak as always. What if Leo had *used* her? Or had intended to at some point?

What if he'd somehow pressured her mother into selling? Would he do that? He'd certainly held the unpaid dues over her head to get her to agree to his scheme.

Tessa hated herself for thinking those things. She ran through various other scenarios in which he would've known about the sale of the bakery and not said anything, and none of them were good, either.

Her elbow accidentally—okay, maybe not so accidentally—hit the little knob on the top right drawer: the secret drawer that Leo's grandfather had added long ago.

It popped open just a hair. She went to close it—because she definitely shouldn't snoop—but she saw a flash of something in there. A piece of paper. Cosette hopped up on the desk and sat right in front of her, staring at her with big green eyes.

"It's private, Cosette. Not my business. I've never read anyone's diary or scrolled through anyone's phone. Nope. Not me."

She got a big, warning *meow* for that.

Was that a mind-your-own-business meow? A turn-back-before-it's-too-late meow?

If Leo had done this behind her back, she wanted to know. Her loyalty was to her family. She had to protect the bakery, first and foremost.

But the truth was, she was really aiming to protect something far more personal.

Her heart.

. . .

"Hey, Dad," Leo said early that evening as he stood at the old printer in the back office, waiting for it to crank out a document. His dad, who'd been running around the kitchen with his apron on, had popped his head in. "Everything okay?" Leo asked.

Dinner hour had kicked in, and the dining room was already packed. The murmur of conversations, the sounds of clinking utensils, and occasional laughter spilled out pleasantly into the cramped little room.

His dad smiled. "The patio and dining room are both full. I never thought I'd see the day when this place was…happy again. Full of people talking and eating and having a good time. Young people, old people, kids… Maybe that fancy degree of yours did us all some good."

"Well, Tessa and I might have brought in some business, but they keep coming for our family's signature dishes."

"People like the organic," his dad said in a conciliatory tone. "They like that we're buying local. They like the takeout. And they like trying some old things new ways." He placed a hand on Leo's shoulder. "And I like having you for a partner. I learn new things." His dad embraced him and slapped him heartily on the back. "That wife of yours is good for you. And she can bake. Make sure you treat her nice."

Leo chuckled and held up the paper he'd pulled off the

printer. "I'm surprising her for her birthday with a trip to Chicago to see the Monet exhibit. Just printed the tickets. It's still okay to take off that weekend we talked about?"

"We've got you covered." Leo's dad looked at his watch. "It's a beautiful evening, and you've been working day and night. Why don't you head out of here early? I'll close up."

Leo looked around at the bustling waitstaff and the customers lined up at the door.

"Go on." Marco made a sweeping motion. "Take off while you can. Go home to Tessa."

Leo never left when there was work to be done. But his dad was right—it was a warm, clear summer evening. And he'd just been given a rare opportunity to enjoy it.

So he thanked his dad and walked out of the restaurant, checking his watch as he went. 7 p.m. The earliest time he'd left work since he came back to town. On the way home, he noticed that the florist, Cara Rayburn, was closing up. He waved to her from the street, then, on impulse, rapped on the glass door.

"Why hello, Leo," she said, pushing her horn-rimmed glasses up and smiling as he came through the door. "I just can't get over how much more foot traffic we've had lately. Whatever magic you Castorinis are making over there across the street has helped all our businesses. What can I do for you?"

"I know you're about done for the day. But you wouldn't by chance have any flowers that I can bring home to my wife, would you?"

"Tessa's favorite color is blue, isn't it? Just like those pretty eyes of hers."

"I can confirm that." Yes. He knew that now. And a bunch

of other things, too. Like how to make her laugh. And how much she loved flowers.

"I have just the thing. Give me a second."

Cara went to her refrigerator and pulled out some pretty blue flowers on long stems. He had no idea what they were, but since Tessa knew the names of every flower from here to Texas, he'd be okay.

He was going to keep the Monet tickets a surprise for now. And the special hotel room overlooking Lake Michigan. It would be fun to explore Chicago in preparation for her move there.

His dad was right. They'd both been working nonstop for weeks. Tonight would be a great break. A fun surprise.

As Cara handed him over a pretty bouquet of beautiful blue and white flowers, he thanked her and placed some money on the counter.

"Leo, you've overpaid me," she said, holding up a bill.

"Thanks for going out of your way, Cara." He waved as he headed for the door.

Tessa was going to love this. He couldn't wait to see the happy expression on her face. She'd probably clap her hands and do a little dance, then jump into his arms.

He loved her enthusiasm about simple things. The way she saw beauty in everything and made him notice it, too. Maybe she'd even teach him the names of these flowers.

"That's so sweet and considerate," Cara said. "You must really love her, to surprise her for no reason."

That caught him a little off guard. He was doing something a real husband would do for his real wife. A wife he loved.

He pushed all that out of his head. He could bring Tessa

flowers *just because*, without overthinking, and just live in the moment.

. . .

Leo found Tessa inside the living room, sitting on the couch, the room dim as the sun began setting. Which should have been his first red flag, because any other warm summer evening would find her digging in the garden or sitting outside with Cosette, not indoors staring at a piece of paper in her lap.

"Hey." He left the flowers and the tickets on the counter and walked into the living room. "You okay?"

As she looked up, Leo's heart dropped into his stomach. Her eyes were red and a little puffy. "What is it, Tessa? What's wrong?"

"Leo, we have to talk." With trembling fingers, she held out the paper.

Puzzled, he tugged it from her hand, then let out a curse. *The proposal.* The stupid, horrible proposal. Why hadn't he destroyed it? He'd buried it in his desk and forgotten all about it. Releasing it like it was on fire, he watched it sail onto the coffee table.

He was about to say *I can explain* when she said, "Max Hammond came into the bakery today and let it slip that my family's bakery might be up for sale."

My family's bakery. The way she worded it sounded... formal. *Ominous.*

Leo frowned as he realized what had happened. "Wait. You went looking for this instead of coming to me?"

"I hit the drawer of your desk with my elbow, and it

popped open." He must have given her an incredulous look, because she said, "Okay, the truth is, I was upset. I did pop it open a little. And there it was." She glanced at the paper. "A proposal for you and your dad to buy our business and retain my mother temporarily as an employee. Dated *after* we were married. How could you, Leo? How could you do this behind my back?"

The hairs on the back of his neck prickled. He'd made a promise to Joanna not to tell Tessa anything. That's what had gotten him in this hot water to begin with. So what was he going to say to her now?

Before he could say anything, Tessa continued, "How could you coerce my mother into signing something like this?"

He held out a hand in defense. "Wait a minute—what? That's not what happened. I—"

She snorted. A skeptical snort that proved she didn't believe him at all. Or want to hear him out.

That made his anger flare. "You still don't trust me, do you?" Leo prided himself on being a protector of those he loved. On being *trustworthy*. He'd never given her any reason to think otherwise.

"This is not about what I think of you," she snapped. "It's about a bill of sale for my mother's business." She picked up the paper and waved it in the air. "That she *signed*!"

"I thought we were way past fake marriages and over-the-top business arrangements. I thought we trusted each other, Tessa. I thought you knew me by now." *And know that I would never hurt you*, he finished to himself. If he'd sounded hurt, it was because he was.

She shook her head. "I don't know what to think."

"Your mother came to *me* with this." He tapped the paper with his finger. "I hid it, thinking you'd turn the bakery around so much that my dad wouldn't be able to afford to buy it, even if he wanted to. Or that your mother would change her mind because business had improved. That's it. The whole truth." He tossed his hands up in a gesture of surrender.

He'd laid all the cards on the table.

"But why didn't you tell *me*?"

"You'll have to ask your mother about that."

"I don't like secrets, Leo." She shook her head sadly. "Secrets always come out."

Oh geez. That ass Sam. "I was *protecting* you."

"I don't want your protection." She stabbed the air. "I want your *honesty*."

She didn't want his *protection*? He'd hid this from his dad. And held off her mom, too, for that matter. He'd shouldered the burden of keeping it quiet, thinking the deal would never come to fruition. "I kept this from you so you could be free to create without worrying. Without feeling so responsible that you'd stay here and sacrifice yourself for *another* fifteen years." None of which, apparently, she seemed to appreciate.

She shook her head solemnly. "I can't abide someone hiding the truth from me again. It makes me wonder if you'd planned this all along—to take over our business without my knowing."

"Are you serious?" His usual calm was cracking.

"What am I supposed to think?"

She might as well have punched him in the gut. She'd accused him of hiding something. Of not telling her the truth.

Of coercing her mother. Of *using* her. "You want honesty?" he said, his voice sounding an octave higher than normal. "Then fine. Good thing this has just been for fun. We've accomplished our goals, and now we can both leave with no attachments."

He saw his words hit the mark. She blinked, and her face colored.

"For the record," he continued, "I'm not the one going around snooping in people's desks. And also for the record, I've always believed in *you*. I'm not Sam, Tessa."

She sat rigidly straight on the couch. "I'll work on finding someone to supply the desserts before I leave for Chicago. I—I wouldn't leave you high and dry."

"I'm sure I can find someone to replace you."

She shot him a *what a jerk* look. Which made his heart give a lurch. Because he knew he'd just crossed an imaginary line—one that couldn't be uncrossed. Even now, in the heat of things, he knew, deep in his soul, that she was irreplaceable.

He opened his mouth, which still had his big foolish foot in it, but it was too late. She'd turned and started down the hall to her old room, leaving him to wonder what the hell had just happened.

CHAPTER TWENTY-ONE

It was 3 a.m. when Tessa, fully packed up, stood outside the top stair of her old garage apartment in the steady rain. Tessa knocked as softly as she could to avoid waking her old landlord, Mrs. O'Hannigan, but Cosette was meowing loudly in her carrier, protesting the jarring departure from her warm bed and the raindrops that were way too close. "Shhh, Cosette," Tessa said. "I'm sorry."

Yes, she was. For a lot of things. But mainly for letting down her guard. Why did all men suck?

Vivienne finally opened the door, rubbing her eyes sleepily. "Tessa!" She was wearing a T-shirt that said *Joie de Vivre* and sleep shorts, and her long hair was sticking up on one side. She grabbed Tessa's suitcase and let her in, closing the door just as Mrs. O'Hannigan's light flicked on.

Juliet walked out of the bedroom, wearing a terry robe and matching slippers, pulling her hair up into a quick bun. "What's wrong? Are you all right?" She looked from Tessa to the suitcase to the cat carrier. "Oh no."

Vivienne was already freeing Cosette, talking softly to her, and finding her a bowl of water. Juliet gave Tessa a questioning look, but all Tessa could do was bite down on her lip so she wouldn't cry. "Can I stay here tonight?" She tried to ask in a level, calm tone but her voice cracked anyway.

Juliet grabbed her by the arm and steered her to the couch, which was clearly Vivienne's bed, judging by the jumbled blankets and pillow. In one swoop, Juliet balled the bedding up and tossed it over the back.

"You and Leo had a fight? About the Max thing?" Vivienne asked. Juliet speared her with a look and shook her head in a way that clearly meant *not now*. "I—I'll make us some tea."

"We didn't *just* have a fight," Tessa whispered. "It's over."

"Oh, Tessa." Juliet put a hand on her arm. "I'm so sorry."

Just then, there was a knock on the door.

Juliet approached the window and peeked behind the curtain. She called over her shoulder to Vivienne, who was in the little kitchenette filling up the teapot. "Viv! You *didn't* call Mom and Gram, did you?"

Vivienne held up her hands. "Why does everyone always blame me? Not me this time."

"*I* called them," Tessa said. "I have to talk to Mom. I have to talk to *all* of you." She was going to do what she hadn't done in a very long time: confide in her family.

Juliet let in their mother and grandmother, who were both dressed in their robes and nightgowns.

"What is this about?" her mother asked, looking around at her three daughters.

"It's three in the morning," Gram said, tying a knot in her blue silk robe. "All of you are alive and breathing, so who's pregnant?"

"Tessa and Leo had a *giant* fight," Vivienne said.

"No one's pregnant," Tessa said as everyone sat down and Vivienne passed around mugs of tea. "Max Hammond came into the bakery today and let it slip that Mom was considering selling the bakery to the Castorinis."

Someone let out a gasp. It might have been Juliet. Her mother sat bone straight, her teacup in her lap, unflinching.

The woman should play poker, because she had no tell.

"When it was clear I had no idea what he was talking about," Tessa said, "Max got embarrassed and apologized and said I'd have to ask Leo. Turns out, I found a proposal drawn up for the sale of the bakery. In Leo's desk."

"Oh no," Juliet said. "Leo was planning to buy our bakery?"

"He said Mom came to him, and he didn't tell me because he believed that with all our plans, I'd make the bakery worth too much for his dad to buy. And he said I needed to talk to you, Mom."

"Leo would tell the truth," Vivienne said, nodding her head.

"Leo never told me about any of this," Tessa said. "I had to find it out for myself." She turned to her mother and pulled the paper from her shorts pocket. "Did the Castorinis force you to sign this?"

"Oh, Tessa, no," her mom said, looking distressed. "I'm the one who told Mark to draw up a proposal for the Castorinis. I *did* go to Leo with it and asked him to not say anything. More than that—I swore him to secrecy. I'm so sorry."

"You approached Leo with this?" And asked him to keep quiet? She struggled to let that sink in. Misery and panic flowed through her, freezing every muscle.

You'll have to ask your mother about that.

Her mom had initiated this. Leo had kept her mother's confidence because she'd asked him. And in return, Tessa had accused him of terrible things. Of coercing. Of wanting to take over the bakery. Of using her.

She'd ruined everything. *But why hadn't he told her?*

"Mom, why?" Tessa managed. "We got married to *save*

the bakery and the restaurant."

"You did *what*?" her grandmother asked.

Tessa tried to hold back her panic. She'd kept so many secrets. But she had nothing to lose now. She was going to tell her family everything.

She exchanged a glance with Juliet. "I haven't told any of you the truth. But Juliet guessed it. Leo's dad wasn't giving him any control and thought he should be married, and of course Mom wasn't budging about selling any pastries, so we…we came up with a plan to jumpstart both places. It was just a business agreement, but…but things got muddled. He was kind and fun and full of wild ideas and…" All of a sudden, she started crying.

Cosette carefully wove her way around Juliet and Viv and finally settled in Tessa's lap, the one good thing about this crappy day.

"You did this for us?" her grandmother asked.

Her mother sat down next to her and took her hands. "Tessa, you sacrificed your dreams to help our family. I—I've felt terrible about that for a long time."

Tessa shook her head. "That's all in the past." None of that mattered anymore. Only Leo mattered. Except he'd hidden this from her. She was so confused.

Juliet piped in. "Tessa, tell Mom the whole truth."

Tessa blinked at her sister in confusion.

"Tell everyone about the scholarship," Juliet prodded. "Come clean. It's time." Juliet, not one to wait for permission, plowed ahead. "Tessa threw the scholarship. To stay and help me. To help all of us. She did it for us."

"Oh, Tessa," Viv said, starting to cry, too.

"*Mon Dieu*," her grandmother exclaimed. "You stayed

here instead of going to New York?"

"I knew how badly you wanted to go away to school," her mom said, squeezing her hand, "but I never imagined you'd give up something so important. I never would have kept you in town."

"Mom, I know that. That's why I threw a test and let Leo win. I couldn't have left everyone. To be honest…I could never have succeeded anywhere when we were all hurting so much." She understood that now. She could never have left, even if she would have had more of a choice.

"Oh, Tessa," her mom said. "I can't believe I didn't see what you were doing. I'm so sorry."

"Mom, you don't need to apologize," Tessa shook her head. "It was my choice."

"To be honest, I don't know what I would have done without you at that terrible time. And then I guess we fell into a routine, and I took it for granted that you stayed. When you were with Sam, I convinced myself that maybe you'd be okay with working in the bakery, staying in town. I guess I selfishly wanted to keep you here."

"I think I had myself talked into that plan, too, Mom. Somewhere along the line, I stopped believing I could achieve my dream. It seemed too…uphill." She'd settled for Sam. She'd settled for everything because she'd lost confidence in herself. Who would ever dream that his cheating would be the best thing that had ever happened to her?

Her mom shook her head sadly. "After you and Sam broke up, I saw how miserable you were. I knew then that there was nothing for you here. That you weren't meant to work in the bakery your whole life. That's why I told you no pastries in the shop. I wanted you to go and get more from your life than just a shelf of pastries against a boulangerie wall. I was so thrilled when you applied to pastry school. Tessa, I want to sell the bakery so you can have tuition money."

Tessa jerked up her head. "Tuition money?"

"Yes. For your school. For your dream."

"We know you're going to get into pastry school sooner or later," Gram said.

"Mom's right, Tessa," Vivienne said. "You've done every-thing to help us."

"It's your turn now," Juliet said softly. "We want to help you."

Tessa was bawling even worse. Actually, so was everyone else. She looked at her mom. "I would never let you sell our bakery."

"Leo and his father would keep us on as employees for a few more years," she said. "Until we could make another plan. I thought that plan might work. You'd go off and create something wonderful, and maybe we'd find opportunity with your success." She shrugged. "It seemed worth the gamble."

Tessa squeezed her mom's hands. "Mom, I can't tell you how much it means to me that you would sell our business for me," Tessa said. "But it's not necessary. My YouTube channel is making some money, and the bakery is doing better, and I can apply for loans.

"And…and we can all stop talking about my wasted life, because I have to tell you that one really great thing happened… I got into pastry school. I just found out. I was waiting to tell you until we were all together." She thought about how encouraging and positive Leo was as she'd stared at that letter. How he'd held her hand and made her laugh and calmed her nerves.

"Oh, honey." Her mom hugged her. "I'm so thrilled for you." Everyone got up from their seats to join in. Except Cosette, who jumped off her lap before the sister avalanche hit and fled to the familiarity of Juliet's bedroom for some peace and quiet.

"So Leo was just doing what Mom asked him to do," Vivienne said after they'd all sat down again. "So go make up with him."

"I wish it was that simple." Tessa smiled sadly. She'd hurt him badly. Broken their trust. But he had too.

"I put Leo in the middle," her mom said. "I thought telling you was a huge mistake, that you'd never hear of me selling off the bakery. I didn't mean to drive a wedge between you and Leo."

Yes, Leo had been put in the middle. But when Tessa had discovered the secret, she'd jumped to logical conclusions. "Leo should have told me," Tessa said, crossing her arms. "Husbands don't keep secrets."

That had slipped out. Tessa reminded herself that Leo wasn't her real husband. But she'd thought at the very least that he was her friend. She'd trusted him. But he'd chosen to keep things from her. Just like Sam.

Unlike Sam, Leo hadn't done selfish things. He hadn't used her to get the bakery for his family. Or coerced her mother. He'd shoved the proposal into a drawer and kept it there.

But then he'd said goodbye. No strings. *Just for fun*. *Replaceable*. Each phrase hit her like a blow.

They'd both said terrible things.

But the bottom line was, Leo didn't want a relationship.

He didn't do relationships. And if she'd thought what they'd had was special, she was wrong.

"But you two are in love," Juliet said. "Everyone could see it. I just can't believe—"

Tessa saw everything now for what it was. "Leo made it clear from the beginning that our arrangement was business-only."

"Lovers have differences," Gram said. "But if it's true love, they aren't unsolvable."

"He doesn't love me, Gram. He kept something really important from me. Even if he meant to make things better, it was wrong."

"Tessa," Gram said, "it seems that you were very fast to accuse him of the worst, too."

Yes, she had. She totally had. But he'd played his hand. He'd told her what they had was nothing special.

"I think we might need something stronger than tea," Juliet said, jumping up and running to the tiny kitchenette. She returned with wineglasses and a bottle of red.

"I bought this to celebrate Jax's and my engagement. Which was pretty naive, because I actually counted that we broke up six times. Don't know why it took me number seven to get a clue."

As Juliet poured, Tessa said, "I'm sorry, Juliet."

Juliet sat there staring at her glass. "The truth is, I'm more relieved than sad. I think part of me knew all along that Jax wasn't right for me. I just *wanted* him to be right."

"I have a confession, too," Viv said. "Mikhail and I have been broken up for a year. And I never had a job at the D'Orsay. Well, I did, but it involved taking people's tickets at the entrance."

Tessa couldn't believe what she was hearing. Taking people's tickets?

Viv continued. "For the past year, I've worked as a tour guide, a ticket taker, a cashier at a macaron shop, and a crepe maker. Oh, I also took photos of couples in front of the Eiffel Tower."

"Viv…why?" Tessa asked. How many times had she wished she was Vivienne, strolling the streets of Paris? For all Tessa sacrificed, she'd at least felt that Viv was getting the opportunity of a lifetime. But to find out it wasn't was heartbreaking.

Vivienne fidgeted her fingers in her lap. "I'm so sorry, Tessa. Turns out I'm not really very good at art. I dropped out of the art program, and I wanted to keep doing photography, so I did all these odd jobs, thinking I could get a business started. But I ran out of money. So I came home. I didn't want you to know what a failure I was."

"Oh, honey," Tessa said. Viv looked so miserable, Tessa got up and sat next to her and hugged her. "It's okay for things not to work out. What's not okay is that you thought you had to hide it."

"You did so much for me. All of you did. I hope you can forgive me."

"We do things for one another," Juliet said. "That's what families do."

"That's right," Gram said. "Whatever made either of you feel you had to be perfect?"

"No one is perfect," her mom said. "That's how we learn in life. Through making mistakes."

"Somewhere along the line, I stopped sharing my own problems," Tessa admitted. "And if that's made me look like

I somehow don't have any, I'm sorry." She wiped her puffy eyes again.

"It's reassuring to see you've got problems, too, Tessa," Vivienne said. "But yours actually might be solvable."

"Not in the way I expected. But I'm going to take my chance to go to pastry school even without Leo in my life. And maybe one day I'll have my own little pastry shop."

"That's a wonderful plan," her mother said. "I'm going to put a call out for someone to take your place in the bakery. That will free you up, Vivienne."

"I can't thank you enough for helping out, Viv." Tessa hugged her sister again.

"I was happy to be able to finally give something back to you." Viv wrung her hands. "It ate me up inside, being in Paris without you. You must have hated all those photos I sent."

"I *will* make it to Paris one day," she told her sister. "And that photo of the little café with the pink chandelier—that's what I want one day in my own shop. A pink chandelier."

"Mom," Juliet said, "I thought you didn't want anyone who wasn't family to work in our bakery."

"It's time for that to change, too," her mom said. "I don't want any of you to feel chained to our family business. I'm sorry if I let that happen."

"I'm grateful to have you all, and I love all of you," Tessa said. "Very much."

There was a lot more hugging and crying. Cosette suddenly appeared at the distant edge of the couch, perched on top of a sofa cushion. She gave a wide yawn and set about licking a paw, still mortally offended at being displaced in the middle of the night and put off by the handful of sobbing women who were interrupting her beauty rest.

Finally, they all sat down to collect themselves. After a little while, Juliet asked Vivienne, "Did you say you can make crepes? All of this crying is making me hungry."

"I can make us some crepes," Gram said, standing up.

"Do crepes go with wine?" Juliet asked.

"Wine goes with everything," Gram said, giving Tessa a squeeze on the way to the little kitchen. "And crepes may not mend broken hearts, but family can."

CHAPTER TWENTY-TWO

When Leo woke up the next morning, he threw an arm around Tessa. Or rather, where Tessa *used* to be. His arm dropped, his hand hitting the cold sheet with a thump, bringing him fully awake.

For an instant he thought she'd left for work like usual.

But then a cold, hard knot took up residence in his stomach. A feeling of dread seeped through him as the memory of last night hit him hard.

He was alone. In the kitchen, even the low hum of the refrigerator seemed loud as he took out a can of cat food for Cosette and looked around. What he saw confirmed his worst fears.

Cosette's cat palace was gone. The kitchen was spotless, not a single cup or plate in sight, and near the door, no flip-flops were strewn. The stacks of romance novels that cluttered up the coffee table were gone, and there were no signs of Tessa's current puzzle.

The spare bed was tidily made.

And all her stuff was gone.

He had to sit down on the couch for balance. Just like that, their sham marriage had ended as quickly as it had begun. So quickly it took his breath away.

He was free to live out his dream the way he'd intended. Free of any woman tying him down. Free from his dad's expectations that he marry in order to fulfill his ideas for the business. Finally, he could lead his life on his own terms.

His plan had totally worked in every way.

He was footloose and fancy free again.

Except he wasn't.

On the kitchen island, his blue bouquet of flowers lay limp and lifeless. He promptly swept them and the printed tickets into the trash.

Tessa was gone. Yet he didn't feel normal or relieved or even excited to be on his own.

• • •

Leo usually drank one cup of coffee in the morning before work and he was good for the day. But today he'd had three. Which made him jittery but also feeling just as sludgy as the dregs of coffee left in the pot at the restaurant. It seemed like nothing was capable of snapping him out of his brain fog.

He'd almost ordered five hundred heads of lettuce instead of fifty. The breaking point came when he discovered he'd been adding numbers into an Excel file the entire morning only to find he'd screwed up every. Single. Column.

"What's the matter with you?" his father finally asked point-blank as Leo sat in the back room, trying to fix all the numbers.

He propped his elbows on the desk and ran his hands through his already-sticking-up hair. "I just ruined everything I've been working on because I made a really bad mistake."

A really bad mistake. Yes, he'd made a lot of those. And not just on this spreadsheet.

His father took a big sniff. "Did you take a shower this morning?"

"Yes!" He raked his hands through his hair again. "No. I don't remember."

His dad sat down across from him and closed his laptop.

"Hey! What are you doing, Dad?"

"How much coffee have you had today?"

"Not enough." Not nearly enough to function. And definitely not enough to forget about Tessa.

"Well, don't have any more, okay? You're going to scare your Aunt Loretta."

Leo sat back and folded his arms. He was tired. He was jittery. And a little sweaty. But feeling his forehead with the back of his hand didn't reveal a fever.

"Where's Tessa?" his dad asked.

"I don't know," Leo said honestly. "When I woke up, she was gone. And she took all her stuff. Even the cat."

"What did you do?"

Thanks, Dad. "Why don't you ever take my side, huh?"

His father waggled a finger in front of Leo's face. "Because you've got that guilty look. And Tessa is a sweetheart. So if you made her mad enough to leave, you probably did something wrong. Plus, you already *said* you screwed up."

Leo sighed. "She found a proposal for the sale of the bakery that Joanna gave me a long time ago. I hid it from Tessa because Joanna asked me to. And I hid it from you because…because I knew buying the bakery was the wrong thing to do. Joanna wants Tessa to have enough money to go to pastry school."

"That's very noble of her," his dad said.

Leo lifted a brow in question. "You don't sound surprised."

His dad shrugged. "Joanna already told me she felt she

had no choice. That time has passed. How much does pastry school cost?"

His dad knew? So Leo had hidden the truth for…nothing? "Twenty-five thousand dollars for five months of school in Chicago. Not including rent."

Leo's dad let out a low whistle. "Did you apologize for keeping a secret?"

"I did it to protect her. But she said she didn't need my protection."

"Did you tell her that you love her and you're sorry? Because that's what you do when you screw up. You know that, right?" He looked like he was thinking about that for a while. "Also, husbands and wives don't keep secrets from each other."

Ugh. The truth was everything; Leo knew that. Especially to someone who'd had it hidden from her in a relationship before.

Also, he couldn't bring himself to tell his father the rest.

He'd told Tessa he didn't want attachments. He'd told her that she was *replaceable*.

That made him wince. Seems that he had a very bad habit of saying hurtful things when he was angry.

"I think I'm coming down with something." *Fool's disease*, for sure.

"What's wrong?"

"I'm hot and cold. And shaky. And my chest hurts."

His dad muttered something under his breath that he recognized as an Italian saying: *Che cavolo*. Which literally meant *What cabbage!*

Yeah. That about said it all.

His dad played with a napkin on the table. "You took

your mother too literally, Leo."

"What are you talking about?"

"You were fifteen when we found out her cancer had come back. And you were so upset. You weren't eating or sleeping, and your grades were falling. We felt helpless with the cancer, with everything. Your mother couldn't bear to see you that way. I think she felt desperate to give you some advice to carry through your life that would help you to deal with her death. So she told you to be upbeat, to look on the bright side."

Always smile, Leo, she'd said, touching his cheek. *Promise me. When you give a smile to another person, when you make them laugh, it's like giving them a present. And it lifts you up when you're feeling sad.*

"It was good advice for a teenager," Leo said. "I get why she said it."

"My point is that life isn't all smiles, though. Sometimes we *need* to feel the pain. You might think you can escape it, but if you're human, you *must* feel the pain. That's how we know we love someone. We feel their pain as well as their happiness." He smiled. "And sometimes they cause us pain. Ha. Like when we disagree. But the pain helps us realize how much we need the other person. Plus, you get to make up afterwards."

"I get it, Dad." He forced himself to look at his father. "But this wasn't a little argument. I told her it was a good thing we weren't serious. That the marriage was just a business contract."

"A business contract? What are you talking about?"

Leo sighed. "We got married to save the restaurant and the bakery. I thought it would get you to listen to my ideas.

And get our families to work together for the common good."

"A business contract," he mumbled. "That's pretty desperate."

Leo shrugged. "I knew I could turn things around, but I couldn't get you to listen. I—I love you, Dad. And I'm sorry for the deception. But the joke's on me now."

His dad folded his big arms. "Leo, I was stubborn. And I'm sorry that you felt you had to make such a last-resort move. But I learned. And you can, too. You're an Ivy League graduate. You can figure this out."

"What's that supposed to mean?"

His dad sat back and stared at him and gave him a look like *you poor clueless sap*.

Yeah, he was feeling things, all right. In his head, stomach, legs, and chest.

He put his hand up and rubbed his sternum, which felt like the worst indigestion of his life.

So this was what heartache felt like. "I love her, Dad."

"Finally," his dad said with relief. "And by the way." He clapped his hand on Leo's back. "I love you, too. So stop wasting your time talking to me and go do something about it."

• • •

The next morning, Tessa had just tossed her third oven full of baguettes into the trash. If this kept up, all the headway the bakery was making with new business leads was going to go straight to hell.

She checked her watch. Hopefully not many people would visit in the next two hours. Then her sisters were taking her somewhere. Out of this bakery, out of town. *Away*. She'd said fine. Anything was better than thinking about Leo every second of the day. And night.

She walked out into the shop and found Sam bending over, looking at the bakery case. Which wasn't very nice-looking right now because she seemed to have forgotten how to use the oven. As she approached, he straightened out, smiling his same clueless smile as if they'd been friends every day of their lives. "Hey, Tessa," he said. "How about a chocolate croissant and a coffee?"

"I'm sorry, Sam, all I've got are bread loaves and a few plain croissants. And I'm closing early today."

"Oh. Well, I didn't really come to eat, anyway." He rummaged through his pockets. "Can I get your opinion on something?"

Her first impulse was to just answer his question and get him out of here as soon as possible, like she always did. He probably wanted advice about his tie or what to buy Marcy for her birthday. Or some other silly question she could answer in thirty seconds and send him on his way.

But then Tessa suddenly saw before her eyes a vision of her future, plain as day. A version without Leo. Where Sam still came in every single day asking for guidance about his wife, his kids, and his dog. Where she was still keeping her real thoughts and opinions to herself and pretending everything was just fine.

It was time to change that vision of herself.

She might be single, but she was not going to be a sad, lonely cat lady.

Well, she'd always have at least one cat. But the other stuff…no. She wasn't going to be *poor Tessa* ever again.

And she should have spoken her mind to Sam a long time ago.

Suddenly she was aware that Sam was holding an open jewelry box in front of her. With a diamond ring inside. Sparkly and perfect.

At first glance, she thought it was the ring she'd given back to him. But she was relieved for Marcy's sake that it was different. Oval, not round. Some pretty baguettes on the side. He'd done a decent job.

At one time, she'd wanted his ring more than anything.

Or at least she'd thought she did.

But now…her only thought was *poor Marcy*.

"Sam, I have to ask *you* a question," she said carefully. Something she'd avoided for way too long.

Maybe because of her fear of not wanting to alienate anyone ever. Because growing up not being able to talk to your next-door neighbors sucked. And going through the rest of your life in the same town as the guy who cheated on you also really sucked. She'd wanted to show everyone she was resilient and mature, that she could handle interacting with him in a civilized way.

But those weren't really excuses she could use anymore to avoid the truth. Which was that she hadn't been brave enough to confront him. Or hear the truth herself.

"Okay, sure," Sam said. "But I bet I know what you're going to ask. It's one carat, with a white gold band."

"The ring is nice, but that's not what I was going to ask you about."

She walked to the door and turned the sign from OPEN to CLOSED. Some people on the sidewalk gave her funny looks.

She'd never done that before. But she needed a few minutes.

She sat down at a table and waited until he came and sat, too. Then she took a big breath. "Why did you cheat on me?"

He colored, which she took as a semi-good sign. But she didn't expect or need him to apologize. She just wanted an answer. "Tessa, that was a dark time," he said, fidgeting his fingers. "I don't think we should get into it now, do you? Because of our friendship."

Tessa sat up in the chair. If she was going to do this, she was going to go all the way. "Sam, we don't *have* a friendship. You come in here and ask for advice, and I give it. Plus—you cheated on me. But I need to know—what made you do that?"

Tessa held her breath. She'd guessed his answer to that question a million times. A little overweight. A little plain. A little stuck.

Except there was one difference now. She wasn't afraid of the answer. She didn't feel plain and chunky anymore. And she wasn't stuck. Only…heartbroken. And not heartbroken over him. She'd gotten over Sam a long time ago. It was Leo she couldn't push out of her head.

Sam grew quiet. Another flush creeped into his cheeks. "Truthfully, Tessa, I felt like you…checked out."

From the door, there was a series of quick raps. Startled, she stood up, seeing the group of people out on the sidewalk press their faces up against the glass, trying to see in.

"Are you closed for the rest of the day?" a lady with a giant bag from the candle factory gift shop asked through the door.

"I'm sorry. Ten more minutes, and I'll be right with you."

She flashed ten fingers just to make sure everybody got it.

Her mother would kill her if she knew what she'd just done. But for right now, she needed to put herself first. For once.

She sat down again. Her heart was pounding in her ears. "What do you mean...checked out?"

He fiddled with his ring box. "Of our relationship. I think...I think you weren't really there for a long time."

"Of course I was there! And how dare you blame me; you're the one who cheated." She'd been *so* there. After all, she'd stayed in this town for him.

He shrugged. "All I'm saying is that maybe we were headed a certain way for a long time, and everyone we knew saw that, and there was no good way out. So, I found a way out. I'm not saying it was right."

"Couldn't you have just asked to break up?" But something was occurring to Tessa. That for years, she'd felt that she would never meet anyone else in this town.

Hadn't it been easier to accept that she was going to marry Sam and at least have a chance at a life with someone other than Cosette? She could have broken up with him... but she'd stayed.

She'd loved Sam but not the way...not the way she loved Leo.

I love Leo.

And she'd *settled* for Sam.

"I was always more invested than you were," Sam said, sounding more honest than he had in a long time. "I had a crush on you since high school. Remember how many years I spent begging you to go out with me?"

Yes, he had. He'd worn her down with asking. That's why

she'd finally gone out with him.

What a *terrible* way to start a relationship.

But she wasn't going to let him off the hook. "Sam, you made me feel like I wasn't good enough. Like…like I didn't deserve something better. You said I didn't have a passionate nature!"

He sighed. "I was angry. And…things weren't exciting between us like they were at the beginning."

Tessa found herself fisting her hands under the table. She saw it all now—and she saw how she let it continue.

"I'm sorry, Tessa. I should have talked to you, not tried to get out of our relationship by cheating on you."

Tessa looked at Sam. He looked the most sincere she'd seen in ages. And then she smiled. "You just said *I'm sorry*."

He rubbed his neck. "Yeah, well, I should have said that a long time ago."

"I'm glad you said it now. I'm sorry, too. We weren't right for each other. And…I'm glad you found someone."

She meant that. She was genuinely happy for him. Besides, Sam hadn't made her feel bad about herself.

She'd done that all by herself.

And she loved Leo with a certainty she'd never felt with Sam.

Leo challenged her. Shook her up. Saw through her like no one ever had. Let her be who she was.

And she'd ruined things. Driven him away. Though thinking back on the horrible things he'd said…maybe she'd never had him to begin with. Not really.

She stood up and gave Sam a hug. "That was a lot closer to being friends than we've been in a long time," she said. "And…the ring *is* pretty. I hope Marcy likes it."

"Thanks, Tessa."

As he opened the door to leave, she called after him. "Hey, Sam? One more thing."

He turned around. "Sure. What's that?"

"After you're engaged, you have to ask Marcy for advice. Not me."

He laughed. "Maybe I just wanted your blessing. And… your forgiveness."

Well, all right then. "See you around."

The group of tourists was still standing against the building, waiting patiently. Tessa put on a smile and got them their bread with some extra goodies thrown in for making them wait. By the time she saw them out, it was ten thirty. She had two more hours to go before their usual Saturday closing time.

She wandered back over to the door. No, she didn't think so. Not today. Then, before any more customers showed up, she flipped the sign to CLOSED.

• • •

That night, Leo hit Tessa's number for the hundredth time that day. "Hello?" said a too-sugary voice that Leo immediately knew was not Tessa.

"Juliet? Can I please talk with Tessa?" He was yelling over some loud sound in the background. A lawnmower? No, it was a clattering. Like *clack-clack-clack*. Followed by the squeal of brakes. What in the world?

"I'm sorry, Leo." Juliet spoke in a low voice. He heard a door shut, like she was moving away somewhere to talk privately. "Tessa doesn't want to talk with you. She feels like it would just be more rejection. And she deserves better, frankly. And she's asked that you please stop calling every five minutes."

"Please put her on the phone," he said. "Please," he added. Make that *begged*. He wasn't past doing that.

There was a long pause. "I can't. She's…taking a nap."

Leo paced the now-dark house. "At least tell me where you three are. I've looked everywhere—your apartment, your mom's house, the bakery." Leo did some deep breathing. Juliet was a wall, and she wouldn't hesitate to protect Tessa at all costs.

Juliet dropped her voice to a whisper, like maybe she didn't want Tessa to hear what she was about to say. "Maybe she needs a break from you." There was a long pause, where he heard someone in the background on a loudspeaker say, *This is the Brown Line to the Loop*. "Because you did the same exact thing to her that Sam did."

His anger flared, hot and desperate. "I'm not Sam," he found himself saying for the second time in twenty-four hours. "I kept a secret because your mother—"

"I'm not talking about keeping a secret, Leo," she snapped. "Although that was awful, too."

"Look, if you'd just let me—"

"I've got to go. The message from her is to please stop calling."

"Juliet, throw me a bone, okay? Just tell me where—"

The line went dead.

Leo sat on the purple couch and put his head in his hands.

For a second, part of him expected Cosette to hop up and start nuzzling against him.

But of course there was no Cosette in sight. And no Tessa.

What had Juliet been talking about, comparing him to Sam?

How could *anyone* compare him to that idiot? Sam cheated. Snuck around. Sam didn't care…

Sam. Didn't. Care.

Isn't that exactly what Leo had implied when he'd told Tessa it was a good thing they weren't serious? That what they'd had was just for fun? That she was *replaceable*?

Callous things to say. And yes, big fat lies.

Because every single ache he felt clear through his bones told him that *nothing* was light about this relationship. Nothing was funny.

Because he hurt *everywhere*.

Tessa deserved someone who thought she was a queen. A goddess. An amazing woman. Kind and beautiful and talented.

Because she was all those things and more.

She deserved better than a man who told her that what they had didn't mean anything.

It had meant *everything*.

He missed her laughter. The flour on her cheek. How she always kissed her cat on the head. The wonderful way her hair smelled.

Leo hadn't told Tessa the truth. Because he had never told *anybody* that truth.

Like everything else he'd ever done, Leo had taken his mom's challenge to the max. He'd let it permeate every aspect of his life.

Don't be sad. Be upbeat, be friendly, and make people laugh.

And don't get too attached.

But that hadn't helped him to avoid this pain.

No, he definitely wasn't laughing now. Because it hurt like hell.

• • •

A rap on the door later that evening startled Leo, who'd fallen asleep on the couch. Between the sudden flicking on of lights and blinking from the sudden brightness, the shadowed figure of his sister came into view. She invaded his space, making him sit up, and waved a tinfoil-covered plate under his nose. "From Dad," she said. "Everybody's worried about you."

"No need. I'm fine."

Gia, seemingly unconvinced, walked past him, flicking on more lights as she went, inspecting his house. And what was suddenly illuminated was not looking great. Dishes were heaped up in the kitchen. A day-old pizza box and a few meals' worth of dirty dishes graced the countertop. Clothes and shoes were scattered on the furniture and floor. Empty beer bottles peppered the island.

That might explain his splitting headache.

Gia turned to him, a concerned look on her face. "Who are you, and where did you hide my neatnik brother?"

"What time is it?" He moved the couch pillows around, searching for his phone.

"Ten p.m. There's lasagna in there." She nodded to the plate. "It's still warm if you want to eat it."

"Okay, thanks," he managed. But he'd rather eat sawdust.

"I'll put it in the fridge." Gia was frowning and not making eye contact. If his head wasn't hurting so badly, he would want to hear her launch in with her usual exuberance on details about the thousands of activities she was involved in, and how some things sucked but others didn't. But she wasn't saying much of anything.

"Dad told me everything was fake," she said in a deadpan voice that froze his heart cold. "Like, you lied. To all of us."

"Gia, it wasn't like that." But the sinking feeling in the pit of his stomach told him otherwise. He *had* lied. To the people he loved the most.

"I was excited about having a sister. Tessa took me to breakfast. I was getting to know her sisters. And I wasn't excited about it just for me—it was like suddenly the feud was over and we had…family."

He was an ass. And the fallout from his fake marriage had impacted…well, *everyone*. But Gia most of all. "I didn't mean for this to hurt you—or anybody." Leo took the plate from her and set it on the counter. As he approached his sister, she backed up a step.

She crossed her arms and kept talking. "I was excited about you coming home because I thought we were close. I thought you'd finally start seeing me more like an adult than just a baby sister."

"You're right about the lie. It was wrong, and I'm sorry."

How could he have ever thought that marriage would be *simple*? How could he make an arrangement as serious as a marriage and believe his feelings wouldn't get tangled up?

And how could he have believed that his entire family wouldn't be impacted?

Leo grasped his sister by the arms. "I love you so much, Gia. I hope one day you can forgive me. I looked on it as just business. It was a calculated decision I thought would be easy. Because—"

"Because you're a Neanderthal as far as women are concerned?"

He rubbed his neck. "Yeah. Exactly."

As his sister headed for the door, Leo let out a curse. He'd screwed this whole situation up so badly, and it was like a bunch of dominos. They just kept smacking into one another and hitting the ground.

"Gia, don't leave. Please. Come sit down, okay?"

She looked dubious.

"We have ice cream. Chocolate campfire flavor. Want some?"

Leo did something he hadn't done for a while: said a prayer. Because he needed his sister to know he loved her. That he was on her side. That he was older and wiser and he did have some wisdom to guide her.

Although not about relationships; that was for sure.

Two minutes later, they were both sitting at the little kitchen table. Turned out that Chocolate campfire was a huge hit. With Gia, anyway.

After a few minutes, he pushed his untouched bowl away. "I want to tell you a story about when you were a baby."

She glanced up at him over the ice cream, her expression still dubious. "Why?"

"Hear me out, okay? When you were, like, eleven months old, you kept trying to walk. You'd hold on to the seat of one of the kitchen chairs, and you'd take a step, then fall right on your butt. Then you'd do it again and again. Until one time... you finally did it. And not just a step or two. Like, a dozen. You were an amazing baby." He looked at his nearly grown-up sister and smiled. Because he still saw that little toddler in there. "You put all that determination and energy into everything you do, and I couldn't be more proud to have you as a sister."

"That's nice, Leo," she said in a flat voice. "But I'm not a baby anymore."

"My point is, you're determined, and sometimes you think you have to take everything onto your own shoulders. But everything's not all on you, Gia. I'm back in town now, and I'm here to stay. Dad's going to be fine. You've been here for him, and now, so am I."

She was listening but not exactly responding. So he kept going so he could say what he really wanted to say.

"Also, I'm glad you have a plan for your future. You have it more together than any teenager I've ever known."

Her eating slowed.

"I have a million pictures of your first steps. Did you know that? I think they're all in a shoebox somewhere. I'll find them."

He looked his almost-grown-up baby sister in the eye. "There's only one problem, Gia—maybe your plan is too easy. Because life is better when you take risks. When you're just a little bit scared. When you don't have everything all figured out. Don't let fear stop you from doing things that seem a little scary."

Like what *he'd* done. For years, he avoided feelings. And with Tessa, he'd been too afraid to face them. And too afraid to tell her how he really felt.

"I know you're going to make the decisions that are best for you. But I want to encourage you to push yourself a little. To get out there in the world and do all the things and have all the experiences. But whatever you decide, I want you to know that I'm going to be here supporting you. I just want you to know that now—now it's your turn to fly."

Gia picked the polish off a nail. "Leo, I have to tell you something."

"Sure. Anything. What is it?"

"After I talked to Tessa a few weeks ago, I decided to apply for housing at IU. I think I'll try it. Could be fun, you know?"

"That's terrific." He tried to play it cool. Act unsurprised. And did his best to hide his big exhale of relief.

"I love you, Leo." She gave him a smile that reminded him a lot of their mom's. "You're an okay brother. I know you care about me. Even if your love life is really messed up."

Ouch. He managed a half smile. "I love you back. And you're an okay sister." He sat back from the table and sighed. "I screwed up pretty badly with Tessa."

"Yes. But it wasn't all fake, was it?"

"No."

"Since we're being honest, I wanted to tell you something too. You remember Aaron? The boy at the Pancake Express? He's going to IU, too."

He *definitely* wasn't telling his dad that. "Okay, Gigi," he said, pulling out the pet name he hadn't used since she was a toddler. "Looks like you're going to college. And whatever you do, you're going to be great." He reached over and gave her a side hug. Then he rolled up his napkin and tossed a walnut at her just to make sure she didn't forget he was still her annoying brother.

"So, where's Tessa?" she asked.

"She's with her sisters somewhere." Suddenly, the noisy background from the phone call came back to him. The *clack-clack-clack*ing.

This is the Brown Line to the Loop.

He'd been so upset he hadn't been thinking straight.

They had to be on the L, the elevated train. In Chicago. Her sisters had probably gone with her to look for a place to live.

She didn't want to take his calls.

But maybe she'd see him in person.

"Tell Dad thanks for the food," he said, looking for his keys. "I'm going to Chicago."

CHAPTER TWENTY-THREE

The next morning, Tessa heard the doorbell ring from inside the house. They'd just gotten back from Chicago, and she'd stopped by because she'd forgotten a case of Cosette's cat food. Making sure first, of course, that Leo's car was nowhere in sight. She'd just grabbed the food and was staring at the dishes, beer bottles, and pizza boxes and wondering what kind of bomb went off while she was gone when the front door opened.

"Leo. You look terrible," she heard Juliet say from the living room.

"Really terrible," Vivienne added.

Leo. At the front door.

She ran to the room, where her sisters sort of had Leo cornered in the foyer.

"He's not smiling, is he?" Vivienne said, shaking her head.

"Definitely not smiling," Juliet said as Tessa walked up behind her.

"Well, Viv and Juliet," Leo said in his most patient voice, "for one, I live here, so I'm not sure why you're guarding the entrance to my house. And two, maybe I'd be in better spirits if you both would've told me you all had already left Chicago."

"Oopsie," Viv said, covering her mouth with her hand. "So sorry," she added. But she didn't seem sorry at all.

"In our defense," Juliet said, "we did tell you where we were staying. Right before we left."

Tessa pushed her way through the barricade of sisters to see Leo standing there. He was rumpled looking, his hair sticking up, his eyes a little wild. Which for some reason made her heart lurch wildly in her chest.

He caught her eye.

And that made her heart squeeze with hope.

But she tamped that down. Because…she'd ruined things. And because…because he didn't love her. He'd *said* that.

Happy, sunny, good-natured Leo had been so attractive to her. He'd made her laugh and taught her not to take herself so seriously.

But she needed more.

She needed someone to love her. To need her. And to not be able to live without her.

And Leo was not that guy. Because Leo didn't need anybody.

He looked at Tessa. "Could we talk?"

"It's okay," she said to her sisters. "I can take it from here."

"We'll be right inside if you need us," Juliet said.

"Thanks," Tessa called over her shoulder. Then she examined Leo further. He was bedraggled, his eyes rimmed with dark circles. One pocket of his shorts was inside out. And his T-shirt was on backward.

All of which, she thought, were very good signs. Because who wants a man to look terrific after a giant argument?

"I know you don't exactly trust me," he said, "but I—I was wondering if you'd come for a little drive with me. I want to show you something."

Come for a drive? That was the first thing he'd said? "Bite me, Leo. I'm not going for a little ride with you." She crossed her arms. He could talk to her right here or nowhere.

"Please. It's important. I...I think it might change your mind."

She assessed him for a minute, her heart beating a million miles an hour. "Okay, fine. But only because I want another ride in your car."

She got into the 'vette, and he drove them straight to the bakery. Except something was going on in the parking lot. There was a backhoe between the buildings. And construction tape. And a giant pile of dirt. He walked around and opened her door and gestured for her to follow him to see the site up close.

"Wh-what's going on here?" she asked. "Another patio?" Another money-making scheme?

"I'll get to that. But I have to tell you a few things." He stood in front of her, grasped her arms, and looked her in the eye.

"I'm sorry I kept the secret. We're equal partners, and by trying to handle this on my own, I was wrong."

Her skin broke out in goose bumps, and for the first time, she started to feel real, true hope. He was sorry for that. Okay. It was a start. But not enough. "You called me replaceable. You said that everything we had was just for fun, with no attachments. How could you say those things?"

"I was lashing out because you accused me of deceiving you. You said you didn't want my protection. I live to protect the people I love."

"I was wrong to accuse you of those terrible things," she admitted. "But I couldn't understand what I was seeing. And I deserved to know what was going on."

He took a step closer to her. "I should have known better than to hide something from you. And if you give me another chance, I swear I'll never do it again."

Then he pulled out all the stops.

"Tessa, food is sawdust. And I can't sleep in our bed without you next to me." He cleared his throat. "When I wake up in the morning, I miss seeing that little imprint of your body denting the sheets. But most of all, I miss your sweet smile. Your giving nature. I miss…you." He cleared his throat. "I miss you, Tessa." He raked a hand through his stuck-up hair. "Like, all the time."

Her heart was ready to pound out of her chest. But first, she had to say something to him. "I learned something about myself these past few days. I learned that I need someone to be my equal. But I also learned I deserve someone who can love me and who believes I'm irreplaceable."

He sighed. "I've been thinking about that, too. I think…I think I've avoided feelings for a long time. Because they're painful. Because I've learned to make light of everything. That worked for a long time to protect me from getting hurt. But you broke through my wall, Tessa." He grabbed her hands. "I couldn't help but love you. I love you so much. And I'm sorry for being an ass."

Okay, that got to her. And made her cry.

"Which brings me to the second part."

"The second part?"

He walked over to his car, opened the trunk, and came back with a large object, about three feet long, wrapped in white paper with a Christmas bow on top.

He set it at her feet. It stood taller than her knees.

"Sorry for the bad wrap job. Please open it."

Ripping open the paper revealed the huge trophy with the winged woman. From his dad's restaurant.

"Y-You're giving me your prized trophy?"

"It's not my prized trophy. It always meant more to my dad than me. Take a closer look."

She held it up and read the engraved plaque at the base. Instead of saying *Leonides Leonardo Castorini, Valedictorian*, it said, *Tessa Montgomery Castorini, Number One in My Heart.*

That ridiculous trophy made her cry. And not because she'd been desperate to win it so long ago. "You had it *engraved*?"

Leo shrugged. "Tony at the jewelry store did it really fast for me."

"Okay, there's more." He pulled a piece of paper out of his pocket and started to read. "We've always competed with each other, but that's because we're equals. Family is always the most important thing—to both of us. We've agreed to help each other achieve our dreams. And…and somewhere along the way, we fell in love with each other."

Now she was full-out bawling. "I was going to say that's the most beautiful thing I've ever heard, but…those words sound really familiar."

"It's what you told our families at our wedding. It sounded like the perfect vows."

He took her in his arms. "I love you, Tessa," he said. "I always will. I screwed up because I didn't tell you that. Actually, I've never told anyone that besides my family. But now, I swear, I'll tell you every single day if you will just forgive me and give me a chance to show you I can do better."

"I did a terrible thing by not trusting you." She clutched his hands tightly. "I know you always believed in me.

Because you've done nothing but support my dreams and make me think anything is possible. That's been a great gift, because…I've come to believe it. And I love you, too."

"I think that together we can accomplish just about anything." He bent to kiss her, looking tenderly into her eyes. She wrapped her arms around his neck and kissed him back, getting lost in the feel of his lips on hers, his big arms surrounding her tightly.

And that kiss…it was right. It was everything a kiss should be. Just like Leo was the right man for her.

"I forgot the most important thing," he said a minute later.

"What's that?"

"The space for your new patisserie." He waved to the pile of dirt. "If you want it. I mean, after you go and become a famous pastry chef."

"That's the space for your restaurant expansion. I don't want to take your—"

"No, Tessa. Listen—my dad was right. I don't want the restaurant to be huge. I want to keep it friendly, quaint, and…and I'm going to be doing more delivery things, so I really don't want the hassle of a bigger space. Plus we have the patio for tourist season. So—I like it just as it is."

He pulled a menu out of his pocket.

"It's a blank page."

"Yeah. Well, I thought we could showcase your pastries."

"In your menu?"

"Why not? Our customers can eat dessert and then go next door to get some more to take home."

"You're…" She was going to say ridiculous. Sweet. "Thank you, Leo."

He looked a little hesitant. "Maybe you don't see yourself

ever coming back to Blossom Glen after your program is done…"

"Leo, I was stuck here, but it wasn't because I was *here*. I was stuck in my mind. Stuck doing something that wasn't my dream and not having any choice. But I love our town. And I love you. There's nothing I want more than to come back and open my own pastry shop." She clutched her heart. "Thank you. For—knowing me. For letting me be me. I—love you."

"I love you too, Countess."

Then right there in the parking lot, right alongside the backhoe, their lips met.

Leo picked up the giant trophy and raised it high, tossing her one of his magnificent smiles that couldn't help but make her heart race and her knees go weak. "We'll both be here waiting."

EPILOGUE

It was nearly dark when Leo finally pulled off the express-way with the small rental van he'd used to help move Tessa's stuff back from Chicago. She must've been exhausted from her week of finals, graduation, and the move, because she'd been sleeping most of the way home. He figured she needed it, so he let her snooze while he drove.

He was ecstatic that she'd graduated. She'd loved every single minute of pastry school. And he'd loved every minute of all those long Saturday-night drives after closing the restaurant that he'd driven to be with her, plus the other weekends that she managed to drive back to see him. One positive from all that time on the road: he'd taught her how to drive a stick shift. It was fine with him that she loved his 'vette—as long as she loved him more.

The restaurant was getting quite a reputation with its expanded, farm-fresh menu and carry-out dinner experiences. He guessed he'd learned a few things himself.

But finally, he was thrilled to be bringing Tessa back home so that their life together could finally begin.

And he had a few surprises in store for her.

She woke up when he turned off the highway onto the road that led them into town, yawning and glancing out the window. "We haven't put our tree up yet, and it's already December twenty-first," she said as she rubbed her eyes. The flat Indiana fields were darkening, and farmhouses set off from the highway were dotted with Christmas lights. A fine sprinkling of snow covered the ground to make the holiday scenery even more perfect.

Leo looked over at her and smiled. "It's not too late to get a tree."

She smiled back. "It feels great to be almost home," she said, suppressing another yawn.

He held Tessa's hand across the seat as she watched the fields and soft hills roll by. "It feels great to have you home for good, sweetheart." He stole a glance at her. She looked tired and, now that he was thinking about it, a little pale. "You okay?"

"Fantastic, now that I'm with you."

That about summed it up for Leo, too, who continued to hold her hand as he drove. "I've been looking at the empty side of the bed for five months, and it's been…lonely."

"I really loved my time in Chicago," she said, "but whenever I saw something or did something, I was always missing you being there to see or do it with me."

"Our weekends together were pretty great." He made a turn. They were close to town now, which made his pulse accelerate a little. "And we had some really good Sunday-morning goodbye sessions."

She rubbed her hand over his arm. "And now we're going to have really good hello sessions."

He grinned. "And every-day sessions."

"Blossom Glen has been my home forever, but it's not home without you, Leo. So I feel like we're starting a brand-new phase of our lives. And that's why I want to tell you—wait." She glanced out the window, a puzzled expression on her face. "Why are we headed downtown?"

He'd made a right turn, in the opposite direction of home. "Oh, I just thought you might like to see how downtown is decorated." Which sounded lame, because she was obviously tired. "What were you going to say?"

"Oh, um, nothing important," she said as they approached the restaurant. The neon spaghetti sign in front of Castorini's Family Restaurant was lit, and the little blue meatball that suddenly appeared atop the noodles before the entire sign flashed. The roofline of the restaurant was strung with festive multicolored lights for the holiday.

"I see you kept the flashing meatball," Tessa said. "I especially love the Christmas lights you strung around it."

"Thanks." He gave her a little smile. "My dad kind of got used to it."

"It's a town landmark," she said. "Tradition is important."

"Yes, but so is innovation. And taking the business in new directions." He pulled up in front of the restaurant and held his breath. And waited for her to see the surprise.

• • •

Yep, Tessa thought, she and Leo were about to take life in a whole new direction, too, but she didn't have time to tell him about that now, because apparently he was planning some kind of surprise. In front of their parking spot, Bonjour! Breads stood as it had for a hundred years, awash in white icicle lights. In the window, her mom had placed a big lit-up angel with a halo of stars and sparkling fiber-optic wings, her favorite Christmas decoration. But the parking lot between the buildings was gone, and in its place was...

A little shop with a big plate-glass window, built on to the side of the building in between the restaurant and the bakery.

Tessa's mind went blank. "Leo." The word came out as a hoarse, mangled whisper, her throat choked with emotion. She stared at her husband, then the building, mouth agape. Leo was sitting back in his usual relaxed posture, but his eyes were waiting. For her reaction. And they were filled with love.

That's when she started to cry.

Leo parked the van at the curb and turned to her. "Come on in, sweetheart."

"Leo, I—" She tried again to speak.

He ran around and opened the van door for her, then led her to the new front door of the shop. The door opened to a little tinkle, a detail that didn't go unnoticed. She looked at Leo, who was grinning from ear to ear. "Your mom's idea," he confessed.

Suddenly, all the lights flooded on, and there, in front of her, standing on the black-and-white-tile floor, was everyone she loved—her mom, her grandmother, her sisters. Lilac. Leo's dad and Gia. And Noah and Jack.

The first things she noticed were the big squares of black and white tile that made it feel like she was stepping into an old patisserie in *Le Marais*.

The space inside was empty—except for all the people—*her* people—and except for a sparkling pink chandelier hanging down from the ceiling.

"Just like the one in Paris," Vivienne said with a little clap. "We found one online!"

Her mom was the first to approach her. She took her

hand and said, "There aren't any display cases yet, and we wanted you to have the final say about how you wanted your kitchen, so there are plenty more decisions to be made." Her mother was right there to hug her. "Welcome to your pastry shop, Tessa."

"Welcome home," Gram said.

That's when the waterworks really started up and she felt like she was going to lose it. Leo grabbed onto her with a firm hand.

She looked at her husband's smiling face. Then she walked into his arms, where he enveloped her in a welcoming embrace.

Home. She was home—right where she belonged.

Home with a twist. The same place, but she was different.

"I told you I hated giving you a shelf in the boulangerie," her mother said. "Because you deserve your *own* shop. We're all so proud of you."

"It's your time, babe," Juliet said, handing her a bouquet of blue irises and giving her a hug.

"We love you, " Viv said, taking her photo, of course.

"Look up." Lilac pointed to the ceiling while hugging her. "I painted the sparkly stars up there."

"What a romantic touch," Tessa said. "Thanks, Lilac."

And just as she got used to the shock of having everyone there, Leo dropped to one knee.

You could've heard a pastry drop.

"Leo, what are you doing?" she whispered. "We're married already."

"We are married, but we were never engaged." Her husband flashed that beautiful Castorini smile that made her knees go weak. "And this time, I want to ask you properly.

Tessa Marie Montgomery, will you be my wife—for real, forever?"

He was holding something in his hand. A box.

"Leo." This was over the top. But, she had to admit, so much fun.

"Just open it."

She did, to find an engagement ring. A beautiful solitaire, surrounded by a band of tiny diamonds and sapphires.

"It matches the wedding band," he said.

"It's too beautiful." She had no words. Actually, she couldn't see it very well because of all the tears. But she didn't much care. Because she had everything—make that every*one*—she loved the most in the world, right here in this room.

Leo beamed. "Nothing's too beautiful for you."

She kissed her husband. "I love you," was all she got to say before their family crowded in.

"Welcome back, Tessa." Leo's dad kissed her on the cheek. "Merry Christmas and a happy New Year."

"We're proud of you, Tessa," Noah said.

"Hear, hear." Jack lifted a bottle of champagne and handed it to Leo's dad. "You do the honors, Mr. C."

"Leo's been really mopey without you," Gia said, hugging her. "I can't wait for more cannoli." She rubbed her hands together. "And whatever other wonderful creations you make us."

Leo's dad opened the champagne and poured some for everyone.

"Can I say something?" Tessa set down her glass without drinking any. "I'm so glad that we can start our life together in the place we love, with the family and friends we love."

Then, as everyone else drank, she pulled Leo over to the side. "And now I have a little surprise for *you*." She took his drink out of his hand and set it on a pop-up table, making sure they moved far enough away so no one could hear.

"Tessa, what is it?" he asked. "Are you unhappy about something? Because you can literally change anything you want—"

She took both his hands in hers and looked into his worried brown eyes. "I couldn't be happier. But I have to tell you something." She stood in front of him, making sure she looked him straight in the eyes. "There's another project underway. It will be ready next summer."

He frowned. "What are you talking about?"

"It will end our families' feud forever, because it's actually a collaborative effort."

"You're making me nervous. Also, I have no idea what you're—" Suddenly, his eyes widened. She saw the exact moment the truth finally dawned.

"You're not—you're just tired from exams, right?" he asked. "Because that would be—"

She took one of his hands and placed it on her abdomen. "Our little collaborative project will be ready in about seven months."

"How—when—"

She grinned widely. "I can explain it to you later if you need me to."

"Oh wow," Leo said, stunned. "I'm—" He appeared to lack words, which was the best thing ever.

"Speechless?" she asked.

He laughed and rubbed his neck. "I'm—oh wow, he repeated. "Yeah, speechless is right." He shot her a look of concern. "Are you all right? You're exhausted. Why don't you sit—"

It had only been two minutes and already his protective instincts were kicking in. Which actually wasn't a bad thing at all. "Couldn't be better."

"I—I love you. I love you." The words were back, and they were beautiful ones. Leo took her in his arms and kissed her soundly.

"I love you, Leo," she said from inside his embrace, surrounded by his warmth and strength. And her heart was spilling over with happiness.

"Hey, what's going on over there, you two?" Jack called. "Come on out and have a toast with us."

"I can't drink," Tessa said. "But I'd love for you all to."

"You can't drink?" Her mother's hands flew to her mouth. "Oh my goodness!" she exclaimed, running over to Tessa.

"You know what this means, don't you?" Marco asked.

"It means we're all family," Gram said with a solemn nod.

"No more feud!" Gia announced.

Amid a lot of hugging and kissing, everyone cheered. "They all seem relieved that the feud is over for good," Tessa said to Leo. "This is a new beginning."

"For everyone," he said. "But especially us."

As Leo kissed her again, Marco turned to Joanna. "By the way, Joanna," he said, "there's a Michelin three-star restaurant in Indy. I'd like to invite you to check it out with me. As a research trip, of course. We could leave early on a Saturday and visit a museum or two, have dinner, and then drive back. Just to show we're friendly with each other."

"Well, we're going to share a grandchild," Tessa's mother said. "And we do business together. We can keep things friendly and businesslike, right, Marco?"

"I've heard that one before," Tessa whispered to Leo.

"Hey, lovebirds," Gia said. "I hate to say goodbye, but I have to go."

"Don't tell me you're going to study now," Leo said.

"Actually," she said with a smile, "I have a date."

"Oh no you don't," Marco said.

Joanna came up beside them and gently touched his arm. "We French have a saying. *Peigner la girafe.* 'Don't clip the little bird's wings.'"

"Mom," Juliet said in a warning voice.

Tessa's grandmother chuckled.

"What did you really just say?" Marco asked, glancing at everyone's smiles. "Somehow I get the feeling that that had nothing to do with a bird's wings."

Joanna's mouth turned up. "It means to comb the giraffe." In response to his puzzled look, she explained, "Think about it, Marco. Why on earth would anyone do that? It's useless."

Marco turned to his daughter. "Be home by ten."

"Eleven," she said, kissing her father quickly on the cheek. She hugged Tessa. "I'm going to be such a great aunt."

"Yes, you are," Tessa said.

As Gia hugged Leo, she said, "I gotta go. After my date, I've got some studying to do. Because Aaron's actually competing for the candle factory scholarship, too, and I want to win."

Oh no. "Scholarship or no, you're smart enough to make anything you want work," he said. "I love you, Gigi."

"Love you, too."

"Merry Christmas, everybody," someone said.

"Happy new year," Juliet said.

"Look at that full moon!" her grandmother said, glancing out the big window. "The moon brings miracles."

"I thought you said the moon brings a man," Juliet said, frowning.

"Does she say that every month?" Leo asked Tessa.

"This month it's in the House of Castorini," Lilac said with a chuckle. "That's a *very* good sign."

"Sometimes the moon brings a man; sometimes it brings a woman; sometimes it brings a whole new life," Gram said. "If you embrace the challenge."

"I'd rather embrace you," Leo whispered in Tessa's ear. "Like, for always. Happy graduation."

She turned and walked into his warm embrace. "Happy life."

AUTHOR'S NOTE

I hope you enjoyed this story about two competitive people humbled by love when they least expected it. And I hope it's given you a laugh or two. Like Tessa, life throws difficult decisions our way, and we can sometimes get stuck. Like Leo, we can avoid love because it can be dangerous to the heart. And we often dearly love and are loyal to our families even though they can drive us a little…well, let's just leave it at love.

Love can heal hearts and mend fences. And with all the challenges of these past few years, we need it more than ever.

I'd like to thank Liz Pelletier for taking me on the Amara team and giving me the once-in-a-lifetime opportunity to work with her and amazing editors Lydia Sharp and Stacy Abrams. Many thanks to the entire hardworking Entangled team, including Relationship Manager Heather Riccio, Associate Publisher Jessica Turner, Publicity Manager Riki Cleveland, publicist Debbie Suzuki, copyeditor Hannah Lindsey, Production Editor Curtis Svehlak, formatter Toni Kerr, and talented cover artist Elizabeth Turner Stokes.

And thanks, dear readers, for coming on this journey with me. I hope you leave with a smile on your face and a warm spot in your heart, because that's what I get from you. I couldn't do this job without you. Never hesitate to drop me a line. I love to hear from you!

Miranda Liasson
https://mirandaliasson.com

The Sweetheart Deal is a sweet, heartwarming, and humorous romance ending in a satisfying happily ever after. However, the story includes elements that might not be suitable for some. Death of family members, a longstanding feud between two families, mild sibling rivalry between sisters, and a brief mention of a major depressive episode in a grieving teenager are included in the novel. Readers who may be sensitive to these elements, please take note.

AMARA
an imprint of Entangled Publishing LLC